"In truth, I know so little about you, Mr. West."

"I haven't done you any harm."

"I think, perhaps... that you do not plan to."

His fingers came away from the ax handle, then tightened again as he drew a deep breath. His face was expressionless.

"I don't," he said finally, and planted the ax blade in the chopping stump. "Your virtue is safe."

"I wasn't thinking that way at all, Mr. West." She glanced away. She *had* thought about him that way. She had wondered about him in a hundred ways, much to her chagrin. "You've given me no cause to—"

"That's right. I brought a pile of skin and bones to my cabin rather than leave her to die."

"You've given me more than shelter."

"I've done what was necessary to keep you alive. I don't prey on sick women. And even if I did—" He turned from her. "You don't have anything to worry about, Mrs. Fairfield. Your bones are safe with me."

Dear Reader,

Once again we stand prepared to transport you to other places, other times. Let the summer heat, the hustle and bustle of everyday life, disappear from your mind as you journey into the past.

Kathleen Eagle has been one of your favorite authors since her first appearance, and in *Heaven and Earth* she will once again touch your heart. Young missionary Katherine Fairfield must deal not only with being widowed but with her forbidden attraction to rugged Jed West. Jed is rough-hewn and strong, a perfect match for the Oregon wilderness where he makes his living as a trapper. But he is also tender when he needs to be, and more loving than any man Katherine has ever known. Somehow these two must move heaven and earth to spend their lives together.

Caryn Cameron returns with *Freedom Flame*, a sequel to her earlier *Liberty's Lady*. This book is just as exciting as its predecessor, so don't let yourself miss it. In months to come look for new favorites like DeLoras Scott and perennial crowd pleasers like Kristin James. There's always something special going on at Harlequin Historicals.

Leslie J. Wainger
Senior Editor and Editorial Coordinator

Heaven and Earth

Kathleen Eagle

Harlequin Books

TORONTO • NEW YORK • LONDON
AMSTERDAM • PARIS • SYDNEY • HAMBURG
STOCKHOLM • ATHENS • TOKYO • MILAN

Harlequin Historical first edition July 1990

ISBN 0-373-028650-3

KATHLEEN EAGLE

is a transplant from Massachusetts to her favorite regional setting, the Dakota prairie. As educator, wife, mother and writer, she believes that a woman's place is wherever she's needed—and anywhere she needs to be.

To honor the rich blend of heritages
within the Eagle clan;
Mitakuye oyasin
All my relatives

Chapter One

⧼⧼⧼⧼⧼⧼⧼⧼⧼⧼⧼⧼⧼⧼⧼⧼⧼⧼⧼⧼

Oregon Country (now southern Idaho)
September, 1846

It was past the shady hours of morning. Katherinc's six-mule hitch pulled the lumbering prairie schooner under the blazing sun. She missed her bonnet, but she couldn't spare the effort it would cost her to search for it. With her elbows braced against her thighs she hunched over an aching belly and squinted against the relentless glare. Through force of habit she gave the mules another chuck of the reins. Six gray rumps lumbered along, six pairs of ears flicking at the buzzing deer flies. Her goading was ineffective; the mules had settled upon a rhythm, and they stuck to their pace. Katherine knew her fate rested precariously on the backs of six of God's most obstinate animals. The traces rattled, and the big wheels groaned, but the mules plodded steadily over rocks and wheel ruts, headed not for the end of the world, as their driver was, but for the end of the day.

Every jolt of the wagon aggravated the awful cramping in Katherine's stomach. It was only dysentery; on this journey she'd seen enough, *suffered* enough of it to know it for what it was. There was no need to panic. She told herself that the pain was only the Lord's way of jabbing her in the side to keep her alert. Each jerk of the wagon meant one more miserable rock left behind the wheels. Every mile she put behind her was littered with obstacles she would not have to face again. The Lord was beside her, and her mission lay west, somewhere beneath the blinding yellow sun.

Another jolt, another gut-twisting pain. The call to serve gave her the privilege to make sacrifices, she reminded herself, and she tried desperately to believe that it was true. She wanted to welcome the joyful burden, just as Thomas had so often admonished. She recalled the sincerity in her young husband's voice, the saintly sparkle in his eyes, and she rode out the cramp on the strength of his memory. Surely memories were God-given as well....

"It's the surest sign of God's calling that any man could hope to receive, Katherine." The light in Thomas's eyes was mystical, but his news was far from what she'd hoped to hear. He joined her on the stiff-backed deacon's bench in her mother's parlor. "The Missionary Board was willing to overlook my youth and my lack of experience and approve my request. It must be more than just a vainglorious dream on my part. I'm certain that God truly wants me in Oregon Country." He reached for her hand. "Wants *us*," he amended.

"But it's so far away," Katherine protested. She had convinced herself that the Missionary Board, for the very reasons Thomas had just mentioned, would refuse his application. Her dreams of a New England saltbox parsonage nestled in a stand of tall oaks with a small white church close by were fading ominously. She couldn't imagine what to put in their place. "The journey would be long and dangerous, and once we got there, who knows what—"

"God knows, Katherine. And He has chosen us. Don't you see? Perhaps our youth is the very reason." He squeezed her hand, which action only seemed to brighten the light in his eyes. "I have read Marcus Whitman's letters to the Board, and I tell you, Katherine, the work is there for us, waiting for our hearts and hands. The Whitmans have paved the way."

"But they won't be traveling with us. Marcus Whitman is a doctor, and he has made the journey more than once. He knows the safest route. I would feel so much better if—"

"Trust in the Lord, my love. There was a first time for Dr. Whitman, too. And for his wife. Narcissa has proved that the journey is possible for women. You're strong-willed, Katherine. When other girls would do nothing but needlework, you were always willing to hike the hills, take your turn at the oars when we fished, even bait your own fishhooks." He laughed, and then his voice became lower, as if he were sharing a secret. "We won't be alone, you know. We are never alone."

"I know, Thomas. I've read, I've heard, I've prayed—I *know* it's true." She lowered her gaze to their clasped hands. She knew she was weak. What she believed in most was Thomas. "I wish my faith were as strong as yours," she said quietly.

"You haven't changed your mind about us, have you?"

She shook her head as she turned her hand within his, putting them palm to palm. She had grown up believing that marriage to Thomas was her destiny. She had loved him from the time they were eight years old and he had pressed a fistful of bright blue lupines in her hand and disappeared around the corner of the schoolhouse. She couldn't remember a time when they hadn't known that Thomas would become a minister and Katherine the minister's wife. His dreams had always been hers.

"It's just that the prospect of traveling all the way to Oregon Country—"

"Is a bit frightening for a woman as gentle as the one you have become." His blue eyes reminded her of that first gift of flowers, but they glistened softly with his love for her. "I promise to take good care of you and mind how we go. Our mission begins the day of our marriage."

Katherine smiled. "Which can't come soon enough."

But it had come, and the memory was still vivid. The sun had warmed their late-November wedding day, and the glare off the snow that had covered the meadow adjacent to the small, leaf-strewn churchyard had been almost as brilliant as the reflection off the bright water of the Snake River. The winding river would take her where she wanted to go. Somewhere along its banks stood Fort Boise, along the way to the Whitman Mission.

A thin, spiritless groan quickened Katherine's well honed sense of guilt. She glanced back into the wagon box; the child was still with her, if barely. If Katherine had turned back to Fort Hall after the little caravan of white-bonneted prairie schooners had deserted her, she would not have had to travel quite so far on her own. But Nancy was weak, emaciated from the fever, and if she were going to die, it would happen before they reached either destination. Katherine was headed West, and she was not about to retrace any hard-won steps. With a fever-riddled wagon, she might be turned away from either outpost. In that case, she would stay on the road, she told herself. It was a straight and narrow path that led to Thomas's vision.

The terrible pain screwed itself another quarter turn into the core of her stomach. Lord, it had never been like this before. There must have been some blessing in all this somewhere, but she needed Thomas to tell her what it was. He had seen God's hand in everything. He had been her intercessor, her interpreter and prophet, and he would continue to be. She would not let him go. His memory was the single bright spot in a journey more arduous than anything she could have imagined so many months ago....

"Cheer up, Mrs. Fairfield. You have just been spared the tedious job of washing our clothes." Beneath the broad-brimmed black hat Thomas's smile was infectious.

"Thomas, I am covered with dirt, right down to my—" she lowered her voice a whole octave "—drawers. The thought of washing our clothes did seem like the promise of heaven this morning."

The wagon rolled beneath them, its springless undercarriage bouncing the wooden seat against their backsides as they watched the last of a huge herd of buffalo ford the stream ahead of them. By twos and threes the shaggy animals leaped to the far bank. The buffalo had gotten there first, and the party of wagons had to wait its turn, eating the herd's dust and watching it render the water unusable. There would be no clean clothes that day.

"Think of the feast of buffalo steak we shall have tonight, Katherine." Thomas chucked her playfully beneath her drooping chin. "How many blessings can you expect in one day? It isn't raining, is it?"

"No, it's finally stopped raining," she admitted.

"No wheels to coax out of the mud. Look at us." Thomas's wide gesture was worthy of the pulpit. "Glory be, our clothes are dry."

"But I feel dirty, Thomas. I've felt dirty for weeks, and what's worse, I *smell* dirty."

"Do you?" He made a show of sniffing her shoulder, and she could no longer suppress a giggle as she leaned away. "I cannot smell a thing."

"Your nose doesn't work properly anymore." Katherine swatted her husband's knee. "It's poised above the odor of your own body, which is outranked only by the smell of the mules."

"Such talk, coming from the minister's wife." The merriment in his eyes drew a smile that splintered the ring of grit around Katherine's mouth. He laughed. "Think of this, Mrs. Fairfield. We shall have no trouble gathering these pilgrims at the river when we find a potable one."

Katherine welcomed her pain when she remembered Thomas's death. It seemed to bring him closer to her as she relived those last moments of his life. She longed to bring back that time so that she could say the things she should have said. Perhaps if she had done some small thing differently, he might have lived even a moment longer. She knew it to be a blasphemous thought, like conjuring the dead, but it came to her anyway. He had died for a vision, and she had wanted him to live just to be with her. Breathless from the grip of another cramp, she remembered....

The light in Thomas's eyes had taken on a strange glow, and Katherine told herself it was the fever. It was a strain for him to keep her face in focus, but he was trying, and she wanted to believe his efforts were a sign of renewed strength.

To her horror he whispered, "I'm dying, Katherine." She shook her head and uttered a raspy objection, but he insisted, "I am...yes, I am...about to die." He drew his unruly eyebrows down slightly as he measured each syllable and its meaning. "I am finished now, and with so little...accomplished."

"That is not true, Thomas." Katherine daubed moisture over his dry lips with a soft cloth. What wasn't true? That he was dying, or that he had accomplished little? Who was she to contradict him when she could not entertain either absurd possibility, while he struggled with the knowledge that there was no longer a possibility? Possibilities were for the living.

"I don't understand why." His eyes were like two bits of glass, each shining out from the middle of a dark sinkhole. He searched her face. "Did He find me unworthy, Katherine? Am I lacking something that my...my resolve cannot possibly make up for?"

"You're ill, Thomas. It has nothing to do with—"

"But I was so close," he whispered. "All this time... preparing. I was so certain...of my..."

"You must fight this thing," Katherine pleaded. "You must not leave me alone here, Thomas. We're going to Oregon Country, you and I. You said it would be—"

"Yes. Do it for me, Katherine. Please." Blinded by her tears, Katherine felt a pitifully feeble squeeze on her hand, while a more powerful one wrenched her heart. "Promise me you'll build our church."

"Oh, Thomas, you can't—"

"Pray with me." He closed his eyes in preparation. "Let me hear...sweet, gentle sound...."

Katherine had promised in her heart, even though she had not brought herself to utter a pronouncement that would have given him permission to leave her. She had prayed, just as she prayed for Nancy now. Let her live. Let her survive this. But Katherine cherished little hope for the child, and with that realization she entered into the vicious circle of berating herself for her lack of faith, mentally shoring herself up, then renewing her commitment to the child on whose behalf she had chosen to be left behind by the rest of the wagon train.

At the sound of riders Katherine straightened her back and tamped down the pain, down into a deeper pocket inside her belly. Across the flat she could see five short-backed, stocky ponies loping abreast, each cutting its own swath through hock-high grass. Five bronze-skinned riders approached the wagon cautiously. The sunlight glossed their long black hair.

Katherine watched and waited as her mules kept to their dogged pace. In a race her heartbeat would have overtaken every hoofbeat, but she held tight to the reins and admonished herself to stay calm. These were not the first savages she had encountered along the way. Had Thomas been sitting beside her, he would have looked forward to another blessing. Within moments he would have been smoking their pipe, and within the hour he would have offered the Bible.

Katherine fought the urge to vomit. The pain was very nearly overwhelming. If she had been able to think of a way, short of wailing as she longed to do, she would have asked these men for help. They were armed with bows and arrow-filled quivers, but their faces were not painted like those of the Sioux she had seen on the banks of the Platte. She tugged at the reins to halt the mules, and she faced the men, who slowed their mounts within a few yards of the wagon. It would be a mistake to show any sign of weakness, she told herself as two of the horsemen circled the wagon slowly and approached from the rear. Katherine felt their eyes on her back just as Nancy offered a pathetic moan.

Casting a defiant look at the three men who stood quietly beside the mules, Katherine wrapped the reins around the brake and climbed over the driver's seat. She glared at the two who peered through the back opening in the canvas.

"Mama?" Nancy's voice, like the whisper of dry leaves, was death's harbinger. "Water..."

The two men exchanged words as Katherine reached for a spoon and a canteen. In the periphery of her vision the men behind the wagon were there, then gone. She heard more discussion as she spooned drops of water between the child's parched lips. "Here, little one," she whispered. "Try to keep this much down."

Outside the wagon's canvas walls, five horses trotted away. Clearly, the men saw what Katherine refused to give full credence. This time might be different, she told herself. This one was so innocent. She might be small enough to slip past death's notice.

Pale thin eyelids fluttered open. "Katherine?" The little girl tried to swallow, and Katherine, watching her expend the effort, longed to be able to make the child's throat work for her. "Can you put me with my daddy?"

"Oh, Nancy, your daddy—"

"In a deep hole," Nancy said. "Not like Mama."

"Don't worry about that, child. I won't... let anything—" Another promise. Why must the dying extract these promises? Katherine shuddered as she recalled the journey's first martyr. A bolt of lightning, a sudden stampede, and Nancy's father had been laid to rest in Nebraska ground. There had been time for a proper grave then, with a suitable service and heartfelt grief.

All that had changed when, one by one, they had begun taking sick. Thomas had been first. Then Mr. Masters. Tommy Nigel. Then Trudy Masters, Mrs. Corkindale and Nancy's mother, Lydia Baskin. The terrible pestilence had turned the once amicable group of travelers into a grim train of terrified individuals, each of whom had privately vowed to save himself and his family at all cost.

And the cost had been high. The dying were shunned, and the dead were hastily dispatched into shallow graves. In the end they had risked their immortal souls for another earthbound day. Katherine was certain that those who had abandoned two living human beings in this wilderness would carry the burden on their consciences for the rest of their lives, and beyond that, only God knew what they would face.

Katherine had assured them that she understood. She agreed that they had to hurry on. Too much time had been lost. They had to cross the mountains before winter set in. Katherine was surely a saint, they had said, burying her husband so bravely, then taking the sick woman and child into her wagon. Unfortunately, she lagged behind the rest of the party. She was forced to stop too often to care for them. She would find help at Fort Boise, they'd said. She wished them godspeed, and they wished her the same. There were tears in Mrs. Mueller's eyes, and Jane Simms had started to embrace her, but Jane's husband had prevented the contact. Katherine understood. They had to keep their distance and preserve their health.

"Katherine?" Katherine touched the child's hot face. "Are you sick, Katherine?"

"No, dear, I'm fine." She wondered how Nancy had even that much awareness left. "I'm going to take care of you, and you'll be fine, too."

Was it a sin to lie to a dying child?

"Don't let those . . . wolf dogs get me like they did—"

"I won't."

Another promise. Good Lord, how could she keep them all?

By late afternoon the pain had become Katherine, and Katherine had become the pain. It tore at her insides, while everything around her became disjointed. She had the fever, too. She knew she did. The six pairs of pointed gray ears bobbed up and down in front of her. The river undulated in and out of focus like the viper for which it was named. Heat pressed down on Katherine's head, rose from the earth beneath her and closed in from all sides. Harness clacked and clinked, wheels creaked and hooves clumped, all of the sound spinning like a toy top inside her head. She suddenly felt trapped, as if she'd been locked up with some cloying stench in the confines of a steamer trunk.

Katherine wasn't sure when she had stopped the wagon or how she had climbed down from the seat, but she knew the wagon was still close by. It would wait while she went to the river's edge and gathered the coolness against her face, breathed the freshness into her body. She stood high above the water. It shimmered in the sunlight, teasing her. So close one minute, so far below her the next. Her stomach was still rolling, like the wheels of the wagon and the rutted trail.

She sank to her knees and experienced, disjointedly, the sensations of vomiting and watching herself vomit, both at once. Her observer self chided her retching self, admonishing her to hold up her head, pull herself together and get back on the straight and narrow path. But the path wasn't straight. It surged and convulsed, then pitched her headlong into a slough of her own making.

Jed West had seen more wagons than he cared to count sailing along the southern rim of the gorge that contained the Snake River, but the one the Shoshone hunting party had described was not sailing. He could see the canvas ripple as the breeze passed it by, and the mules shifted occasionally in their traces. A woman and a child, Walks Before Many had said with his hands, and no sign of a man.

West approached the wagon with practiced wariness. He never presumed that his presence would be welcome. He knew from experience that no man set himself apart from his own kind without a reason.

There was no man with this wagon, but the dead child inside had not been deserted long. The mules had not begun to wander, which they surely would have after standing in the sun awhile. A faint moan drew West's attention toward the bluff. His horse's ears pricked as West nudged the big buckskin toward the scrub brush.

Like Phoenix rising from a puddle of slime, the woman pushed her head and shoulders up from the ground. Her spindly arms trembled, and she dropped her head forward and retched spasmodically. Apparently there was nothing left inside her that her stomach would reject, but West could imagine her pitching headlong over the bluff if she tried to stand. He swung down from his saddle and reached her with two long-legged strides. Easily lifting her into his arms, he judged that the woman weighed no more than a tumbleweed. She was woefully dehydrated, and he concluded that in her delirium she had sought the river, even though it ran well below her reach. He laid her on the ground in the shade of the wagon and offered her water from his canteen.

She sipped, groaned, and her eyes rolled back as she closed them. He'd missed seeing their color. He soaked a bandanna and washed the filth from her face and neck. The stench of sickness clung to the woman, but that was better than the stench of death that hung in the wagon. She groaned again when he unbuttoned her blouse to check for signs of skin rash.

One corner of West's mouth turned up in amusement when her hand fluttered briefly over the buttons he'd undone. Apparently her modesty was not unconscious with the rest of her. If she could see herself, she would realize that a man would have to be desperate indeed to strip down this wisp of a woman out of lust for her body. He pushed up her sleeves and assured himself that her skin was free of any rash. It was a good sign. She'd gotten too much sun, and she'd wasted away from the bloody flux, but she did not suffer from the fever that had taken the child. He poured more water over the bandanna and mopped her long, thin neck.

"Thomas?"

"No, ma'am. The name's West." Her onionskin eyelids fluttered open. West wondered what she thought she saw through those glassy, blue-gray eyes. "Jed West," he told her.

"Yes." She groaned and rolled her head toward the cooling cloth. "Going . . . west."

"Not on your own, you're not." He poured water into his hand and patted it over her forehead. "Where's the rest of your party?"

"Nancy?"

"There's a girl in the wagon. Is that—"

"Nancy," came the seemingly lucid reply.

"The child is dead," West said gently.

"Nancy's dead?" Her words were the weak issue of a dry throat.

"I'm sorry, ma'am. Where's the rest of your party?" he asked as he cradled her head and shoulders in one arm and trickled more water from his canteen into her mouth.

It ran out the corner, but at least she managed to swallow a few drops.

"Gone ahead." Her hand fluttered between them, then found a place to light in the loose folds of his muslin shirt. She gripped the cloth and looked up with sunken, soulful eyes, tapping the depth of West's pity. "My stomach hurts so."

"How long have you been sick like this?"

"Not long." She closed her eyes and sighed. "Must bury Nancy," she whispered. "Proper grave."

"I'll take care of her," he promised. Her hand was lost, like a sparrow trapped in the drapery of his shirt, but his chest swelled against its slight pressure. "Then I'm taking you up to my place. You don't need any more of this sun."

"I must go on . . . Oregon Country."

"This is Oregon Country."

"The Place of the Rye Grass," she said. "God's will."

"Not today, it isn't. Not likely for—" He cut off any predictions that might bode ill for her. Cleaned up, she was probably a pretty little thing, but she was frail. She couldn't handle any weight on her mind right now. He searched his own for words of comfort, but he realized that her grip on his shirt had slackened, and she had slipped just beyond the sound of his voice. Probably on her way to whatever kind of place she dreamed that spot on the banks of the Walla Walla River would be. Wai-ilatpu, the Place of the Rye Grass, the Cayuse called it. There was a missionary enclave there, but West had his doubts about whether any god had willed it so.

He dug a shallow grave with a shovel he'd found on the wagon. It wouldn't keep predators from the body, but the child was dead, and the woman would be, too, if he didn't see to her right away. He wrapped the small corpse in a quilt and laid it in the hastily dug hole.

"No!"

West spun on his heel as the shrill protest caught him off guard. She repeated the word more than once as she stumbled toward him, waving her bony hand like a wild-eyed apparition clamoring on behalf of a fellow corpse. Her hair could have been a nest stuck high on some gray-faced crag, and her half-buttoned clothes were as dark and dusty as any shroud. She fell to her knees beside the little hole, her hands snatching like ravens' beaks at the blue and yellow blocks of fabric that shrouded the dead child.

West leaned down and took a firm grip on the woman's shoulders. He hoped she hadn't gone mad on him now. He thought he could treat her illness, but he knew of no herbal remedy for madness.

"Don't trouble yourself now, ma'am. I'll take care of this, and then I'll get you to a place—"

"Deeper," she wailed. "This must be deeper."

"I don't know how you managed," he muttered as he tried to pull her away. "Give it over, now. You're using up what strength you've got left."

But she held her ground, digging at the dirt with one claw while she clutched the quilt with the other. "The wolves," she gasped. "They rip, and they tear, and they—"

"The child is dead, ma'am." *And you're not far from it.* "Nothing can cause her any more pain."

With an impossible burst of strength she wrenched herself from his grip and turned on hands and knees, suddenly kin to the very animal she feared. An unholy fire brightened her eyes as she poised herself to defend her charge. "She will be buried *decently*," the woman snarled. West watched in amazement as she reached with trembling hand for the shovel he'd dropped beside the hole. "I shall . . . do this job properly myself."

West grabbed the shovel, and for a moment there was a contest of her will against his physical strength. The man's power drained in the face of the woman's instinctive defense of a child.

"I'll do it," he said, and she searched his face for some assurance. When she found it, she yielded the shovel. He offered a supporting arm, and she gave way to it and let him carry her back into the shade of the wagon.

He moved the corpse aside, removed his shirt and dug. He cursed the sun and the stench of the heat-ripening corpse and the eyes of the crone who struggled to remain conscious only to supervise him. But he dug. Dirt and sweat lay thick on his back without a breeze to cool it. It was a relief to deposit the body and drop the first shovelfuls of dirt onto the quilt.

As he shoveled the last of the dirt atop the mound he'd built, he heard a breathless grunt and turned to find that the woman was pulling herself up, using the spokes of the wheel that had shaded her like the rungs of a ladder. West tossed the shovel aside.

"What in hell are you trying to do now?"

She grabbed for his arm as he reached to steady her, and she swayed against him. "We must pray for her now."

"If you keep this up, I'll be digging another damn hole," he grumbled as he swept her into his arms. "And then it'll just be me, and I'm not much for praying."

She rested her cheek against his grime-streaked shoulder. "Please. 'The Lord . . . is my shepherd.' You know the words."

Her voice was thready, and her breath felt like a dandelion puffball tickling his chest. Something inside him rose to the occasion of her determination and would not let her go it alone. He jogged his memory and recited most of the words, lending his voice simply in support of hers. The psalm came to him most naturally in French, but he followed her lead in English. By the time he spoke of dwelling in the house of the Lord, she had given out. He loaded her into the wagon and headed south for his mountain.

West had no name to call her, and she had not regained consciousness by the time he laid her in his bed, so he used the terms that came to him out of soft, shadowy memories. She was *le petit oiseau*, like the pretty little blue-caped tree swallow whose wing he had mended a couple of months back. He knew she couldn't hear him apologize when he stripped her filthy clothing from her. And he wouldn't have apologized except that, when the layers of cloth were gone, she looked even more pathetic than he had imagined. Her skin felt hot and brittle, like that of a white onion laid out to dry in the sun.

While he bathed her he made her promises that he hoped she couldn't hear because he wasn't sure he could make good on them even though he wanted to. He found himself wanting her to live. When she thrashed, probably in protest, he held her and sang a song that came to his mind's ear in his mother's voice. "Tell me, little one," he crooned huskily in French. "Tell me what troubles you."

Through the night he kept his vigil. He coaxed trickles of herb tea and saltwater down her throat and challenged himself to learn her name. Just her given name. For that word alone he was willing to sit at her bedside by the hour, administer his restorative brew, clean her, cool her, make his awkward music to calm her. He studied her and imagined what her name might be. Something biblical, like Ruth or Elizabeth, he decided. Perhaps she had been tutored by someone like the uncompromising sisters who had ridden roughshod over him in St. Louis. This woman's demands for hard work and prayer reminded him of his unhappy days as a student. The days when he had been called by a different name.

The woman's long slender fingers reminded him of his journey along the Mississippi to New Orleans and his two-week tryst with a sloe-eyed whore who'd played the piano. He couldn't remember the whore's name, but those soft, white hands were as unforgettable as that blissful fortnight. He touched his lips to his patient's hand—she would never know—and remembered the stubborn set of the whore's chin when she told him that if he had run out of money, he would have to sleep elsewhere. So ended another phase of his education.

This woman, too, was stubborn, but she was no whore. Even in her delirium, she had protested when he had undressed her. No matter how hot she was, she had wanted to be covered, and yet—he smiled whenever he thought about it—she was always willing to be soothed by his touch. He had bathed every part of her, and she had acquiesced to the relief he brought her. Be stubborn, he told her. Be as determined on your own behalf as you were for that child. Live, *ma petite fleur*. Live to tell me your name.

Katherine awakened slowly, her mind making its way through a thick haze. She first felt the heat of the fire at her back, and then she heard it popping. A man's face broke through the haze—dark-stubbled cheeks, dark eyes. His eyes encouraged her, kindled a spark in her and puffed on it like a bellows. When he saw that she was aware of him, he smiled, and his eyes fairly glowed.

"So you have decided to come 'round," he said. He sat before the fire and held her in his lap like a child.

"Who are you?"

"I've waited days to ask that very question, and now you've beaten me to it." Smiling at her as though she had just accomplished some wonderful feat, he shifted in the big, split-log chair. "Jed West. I found you down by the river a couple of days back."

"Found me?"

"You've been pretty sick, but I think the worst of it is over." With a nod he indicated the bowl he'd set aside. "You've been holding that broth down, which I take to be a good sign."

"A sign?" Thomas had always spoken of signs, and she understood them only in terms of Thomas's faith. Never hers. She never saw them first. She wondered about trusting this stranger's signs.

"You're doing better," he told her. "When I found you, you were out in the sun bareheaded and retching yourself inside out, and you had the bloody flux about as bad as I've ever seen. How long had you been like that?"

"I'm not sure." She glanced away. At the mention of dysentery—the bloody flux—Katherine felt the first emotion she'd known in a very long time. Embarrassment. This man was holding her in his lap and alluding to symptoms that a proper lady would keep to herself or die in the attempt to. "A week at the most," she confessed.

"A week is a long time," he said. "When did your party leave you behind?"

She considered the question, but she had lost all track of time. She wasn't sure what was real and what she had dreamed. It felt strange to be held in the arms of a man she had never seen before, but she hadn't the strength to move away. Her head was light and swirling inside with faces, strange scenes, snatches of a French lyric. When had they left her behind, and where? *Where* had they left her?

"You were sick when I found you," West supplied, "but luckily it wasn't with the fever that took the child. That looked like the typhoid to me."

"Nancy?" She remembered the small voice, the pathetic pleas for the mother who had died before her. "We lost her, too, didn't we."

"Wasn't much you could have done." His eyes brimmed with sympathy. "You wouldn't leave her until I'd dug the grave deep enough. I don't know where you found the strength, but you sure had your way over that grave."

"She begged me," Katherine recalled. "The wolves frightened her so. When her mother died, it was all we could do to throw a little dirt over the poor woman's body, and then—" She closed her eyes, wishing she didn't have to remember everything. "The wolves were right behind us."

"I figured the child was yours."

"No." She was drifting in memories and weightlessness. "Her mother was sick. Father dead. I...tried to..."

She was fading. He knew her exhaustion, but he wanted one more thing. "Tell me your name, *ma petite*."

"Katherine."

"Katherine." He smiled as he watched her drift off. "That's one I hadn't thought of."

When Katherine woke again, she could smell the morning dew. She turned her head and felt swallowed up in her pillow of soft fur. The cabin door stood open, and darkness had receded to the corners of the room. A mourning dove cooed softly beyond the mud-chinked timber walls, and the scent of brewed herbs made the cabin feel friendly. Katherine tried to lift her shoulders, but her efforts were feeble. As if he'd sensed her frustration, the big man who'd brought her to this place suddenly filled the doorway.

He stood there for a moment, one hand braced on the doorframe just above his head, blotting out the early daylight as he satisfied himself that she was awake. She remembered a roughening beard that wasn't there anymore. She returned his assessing stare, searching for the kindness she'd seen in his eyes—when? Yesterday? He ducked as he stepped over the threshold and crossed the floor with soundless steps. Katherine watched him dip a tin cup into a steaming kettle that hung just above the glowing coals in the stone fireplace. Then he came to her with the cup.

"Katherine what?" he asked as he sat beside her on the bed. He slipped his hand beneath her head and lifted it for a sip from the cup as if he thought she'd need his tea to activate her voice.

"Fairfield," she said before the cup touched her lips. She sipped, and when he took the cup away, she added, "Mrs. Thomas Fairfield."

He eyed her for a moment, and she wondered if her name changed the way she looked. "And where is *Mr.* Thomas Fairfield?"

"He'd dead."

If she'd said Thomas Fairfield had gone on with the rest of the wagon train, her husband would have been a dead man anyway. In the time West had spent ministering to this woman, he'd laid several curses on the heads of those who'd left her to die, and it had occurred to him that a husband might have been among them. More than once her gold wedding band had fallen from her emaciated finger, and each time he'd found it harder to slip it back on, simply because he didn't want to see it there. He told himself it disturbed him only because, whoever the man was, he had failed this woman, and his ring no longer belonged on her finger.

He slid his arm under her shoulders and propped her head against his chest. "Typhoid fever?"

"Yes. Like all the rest." She tried to shift away from him, but he held her fast. "I think I can manage the tea if you will only help me—"

"I've been helping you. Feeding you just like this." He held the cup to her lips. She hesitated, casting him a look that communicated her discomfort. He stared back at her, waiting. Finally she accepted the cup, and he continued. "Not always like this. At first I had to be pretty inventive about getting you to swallow."

The discomfort grew. She was wearing a flannel nightgown that had been packed in her trunk. She wasn't sure she wanted to think about the many liberties he'd obviously had to take with her. "What did you do?"

"From my mouth to yours." Her eyes widened, and he grinned. "While I stroked your throat and pinched your nose shut. You had no choice but to swallow."

"Oh, my." Had she been healthy enough, she would have blushed. "That seems so...so..."

"It kept you alive, didn't it?"

"Indeed it did, and I don't mean to sound ungrateful. It's just that I don't...that is, I'm not—" While she floundered, he fed her more tea. Finally she shook it off and sighed. "I feel rather foolish, Mr. West. I've cared for the sick myself, and I know full well what I have subjected you to."

"Out here we don't stand on ceremony too much. When you run across someone who's in trouble, you lend a hand either because you've been there yourself, or because you know damn well your time will come." He lowered her to the pillow. "I did what needed doing, and you're getting stronger."

She was quiet for a moment. Then, without looking at him she admitted, "I don't think I can get up."

"I'll get you whatever you need. Just tell me."

She couldn't tell him. Now that she was conscious, there were some things she had to do for herself. Even as she searched for a way to deny her weakness, tears of frustration sprang to her eyes. "I have to get up," she said desperately. "I know you must have been taking care of my...my needs in some way." She heard him slide the chamber pot along the floor beneath the bed, and she closed her eyes. "But now it's different, you see, because I am no longer—" She pressed her lips together tightly for a moment. "Because I am...aware."

"You would do the same for me," he said quietly. "You have for others."

"Please don't look," she whispered.

"I won't," he promised as he lifted her. "I've been helping you all along, and I swear I haven't seen a thing."

That afternoon he offered to wash her hair, and she accepted. They spoke little while he held her head over a basin and worked thin white suds through her hair. When she looked at him, he seemed to avoid her eyes, as though he were giving her leave to assess him without reproach from him. His nearly black hair fell in thick waves, reaching just past his shoulders, and his face was an attractive combination of handsome features—an aquiline nose, full lips and high forehead—and boldly chiseled bone structure. His voice was mellow, his speech more refined than that of most of the westerners she had met, but he had a lilting accent, which she could not help but find charming. She wondered about his parentage, but did not ask.

When he had finished rinsing her hair, he carried her outside. It was as though she had become an extension of him, and she tried to shake off the sense of security she felt when she was in his arms. It must have developed unconsciously, she told herself, and now she must wean herself from this dependency.

She winced at the sun's brightness, and he said, "Just keep your eyes closed. The sun will dry your hair quickly. Here," he said, pressing the tortoiseshell comb from her toilet box into her hand. "I brought in some things from your wagon when I took care of the mules."

"Thank you." She knew what things he meant. Personal things, like her nightgown and the chamber pot. She was becoming too accepting of these intimacies, and she had to start doing things for herself again. Especially those personal things. "The sun feels good," she said as she slit her eyes open to sensitize them to the light. "And it seems much cooler here than it was on the road."

He sat down with her on a striped trade blanket and wrapped her shawl around her shoulders. She struggled to sit up, but she needed his support, and after making a valiant attempt to comb her own hair, she let him take over that job, too. He heard the discouragement in her sigh. "You're doing well," he said as he used the comb to lift her long hair toward the sunlight. "Two nights ago I thought you might not make it. You'll gain strength as soon as your stomach can tolerate good red meat."

The very thought made her queasy. "I'm quite partial to your tea, Mr. West. It seems to have restorative powers of its own. I wish I could have shared it with the others who were so ill."

"You were lucky to escape the fever." He watched her hair fall bit by bit, like feathers, from the teeth of the comb. The color of honey, it glistened in the sun as it dried. "Why didn't they quarantine your wagon? Leaving you alone like that, your friends could have just as well put a bullet between your eyes."

"They were protecting their families," Katherine allowed. "We were slowing them down. They're all good people, I think, but they were frightened. I thought I could make it to Fort Boise."

"You would never have been able to ford the river on your own. They must have known that. Your faint-hearted friends are going to be late crossing the mountains. They're headed for snow." His smile was meant to be reassuring. "As I told you, you are the lucky one."

"It wasn't luck, Mr. West. It was God's will that you find me."

"Is that so?" He chuckled humorlessly. "It was the Shoshone who found you and saw fit to tell me about you. Warn me, actually. They said to stay away from the white woman in the death wagon."

"Why didn't you?"

He shrugged. "It had been a long time since I'd seen a woman of any kind."

Katherine glanced away.

"'Course—" West drew a deep breath and sighed "—you were some disappointment, but I figured, as long as I'd gone that far out of my way..." She flashed him a look of pure female indignation, and he laughed. There was a spark of the spirit she'd shown when she made him bury the child.

"The Lord led you out of your way, Mr. West. And the fact that the savages brought you word of my plight—" She sighed. "It must be a sign."

He lowered the comb, and his sense of humor fled. "What savages?"

"The Indians, of course. It's God's will that I carry on my husband's work among the Indians."

"He was a teacher?"

"He was a minister," she explained solemnly. "We traveled from Hartford. We were on our way to the Whitman Mission. I promised Thomas I would go on, and I think it's clear that God intends Thomas's work to become mine." She offered a thin smile. "Why else would I have been spared under such extraordinary circumstances?"

"Good question," West grumbled. A better one would have been, if fate had seen fit to bring a woman to his mountain, why in hell did she have to be a missionary?

Chapter Two

It had been almost two days since Jed West had taken Katherine out into the sunshine, and she was restless. She could hear the sound of his ax slicing along the grain of a piece of firewood. The wood cracked and splintered, and the pieces clattered as they were thrown into the pile. She had listened long enough, and she could anticipate the next sound within a couple of moments. Another piece of wood was positioned on the stump, and whack! went the ax. Within the past several hours, the man must have amassed enough wood to fuel the fireplace for at least a fortnight. Each time the rhythm of his work was interrupted for a few minutes, she waited, watching the door, but he was soon back at his chopping.

Katherine pushed the blanket back impatiently and swung her legs over the side of the bed. A wave of dizziness swept over her, and she dropped her chin to her chest and waited for it to pass. Amid the dark spots that danced before her eyes she spied her white wool shawl on the rough-hewn bench that stood beside the table. Four stumbling steps took her there. She braced herself on the table and snatched up the shawl as she waited for her vision to clear again. Her head felt as though it were full of whipped cream. She clutched the shawl to her breast and headed for the door. One deep breath of fresh air would clear her head as quickly as would a dose of smelling salts. Then perhaps the enigmatic man who had saved her life would indulge in a bit of conversation.

The door bolt rattled in its brackets, and the wooden pegs that served as hinges creaked in their worn sockets. Jed looked up from his work as Katherine stepped around the doorframe, clinging to it as if it were a tent pole and she the canvas with all her pegs loose. There was not a hint of a breeze, but had there been one, her hand would have anchored her, and all the rest—the voluminous nightgown over the willowy frame—surely would have been flapping weightlessly. She had only her own steam to move her, and that was flagging; she swayed, gripping the doorframe as her bare feet stumbled over the threshold.

Jed swung the ax once more and buried the blade in the stump. His unhurried stride took him to Katherine's side in time to catch her before she fell, but she objected when he bent to lift her in his arms.

"Please," she said, her chest heaving from her efforts. "I just need a place to sit and catch my breath. I thought I would watch you for a while, Mr. West."

He steadied her, then let her use his sturdiness as she would to support herself. "Watch me what?"

"Watch you carve up your firewood. I promise not to disturb you." She waved a pale, thin hand toward another tree stump. "There. I shall sit there quietly and watch."

"It's nothing so fancy as 'carving.' I'm just chopping wood, and you ought to be in bed."

She looked up to find the same hard look she'd seen in his eyes continually since she'd begun gaining a little strength. She had eaten everything he'd offered, whether she had the stomach for it or not, and she had tried very hard to make conversation, but he'd turned a deaf ear. She knew she must have been a terrible burden to him, and she wanted to show him that she was, indeed, making progress.

"I feel well enough to be out taking a little fresh air, Mr. West." She glanced back at the open door. "I've been lying abed for so long, and I was beginning to think I'd go mad if I didn't—" Hear another human voice. His, in particular, with its low tone and the lilting, velvety way he sometimes spoke. That was the truth of it, but the dark, unfeeling expression in his eyes prevented her from telling him that. "If I didn't feel the sun."

His expression softened. The sunlight had already taken a liking to her straw-colored hair, stitching a bit of silver through it. He remembered threading his own fingers through it, washing it and combing it dry, and he had half a mind to offer to do it for her again just for the chance to feel that cool, damp softness between his fingers. Her hands were cool and soft, and she was too unsteady on her feet to be self-conscious about bracing herself against his bare chest. But he was conscious of it.

"Sit here, then," he ordered more gruffly than he'd intended. "When you get tired, I'll take you back inside."

He settled her on the stump and pulled her shawl down tightly over her shoulders as if he were bundling a baby, but he avoided her eyes. Those eyes were like those of a calf sucking at its mother's teat. The stimulation tended to make him forget himself and think of her as a real woman, which, he hastened to remind himself, she was not. She was a missionary. He turned from her and went back to work, attacking the job with renewed fervor.

Then he thought he heard her laugh. He looked up and, sure enough, he could have counted her little white teeth. He scowled.

"Why do men always chop wood when they don't want to talk?" Katherine asked. She felt too light-headed to sit up straight, so she braced her forearms in her lap and leaned forward, hoping to minimize the weakness. It felt good to be outside. "I remember how Thomas used to—"

"You said the man was dead." Jed swung his ax and split an eight-inch log with a single blow. "Let him rest."

"I only meant—" The smile faded as she watched him toss the wood into the pile. Later he'd have to stack it, which would give him something else to do when he needed a reason to leave the cabin. "You saved my life, tending me in ways that I know were unpleasant for you, but you withheld no kindness from me when I was completely helpless. Now you refuse to talk to me."

"I've refused you nothing." He set another chunk of wood in place. "You need your rest, and I have work to do."

A forest to cut into little pieces, she thought, but she knew she would get nowhere if she made light of the task. "Are you a trapper, Mr. West?" she asked instead.

He flexed his back as he raised the ax, and his sweat-slick skin glinted in the sun. "I do a little trapping." Whack! Two chunks of wood fell away from the blade.

"Where is your home?"

"Right here." Thunk, thunk. Two more pieces were added to the pile.

"I mean, originally."

He eyed her for a moment. She needed to learn that it was dangerous to ask a loner like himself that question, or any that would naturally follow. But there was something in her eyes that made him answer. "Canada. Originally."

"Canada? How interesting! What brought you—"

"My travels brought me here."

He took a wide stance and held the ax in both hands, the end of the handle near his hip and the head close to his chest. His dark, waving hair, which reached past his shoulders, was tied back from his face by a leather brow band, and his richly tanned shoulders and chest were broad and thick with the muscle made from his labor. Buckskin breeches covered his slim hips, and he wore high-topped moccasins, which, Katherine had assumed, were simply what was available to him. Now, as he posed to fend off her questions rather than answer them, she reminded herself again that he had treated her kindly, handled her in the gentlest manner with the same hands that gripped the ax like a weapon. It was only his stance and his lack of proper clothing that gave him such a savage appearance.

"In truth," she said quietly, "I know so little about you, Mr. West."

"I haven't done you any harm. What else do you need to know?"

"I think, perhaps... that you do not plan to."

His fingers came away from the ax handle, then tightened again as he drew a deep breath. His face was expressionless. *Her eyesight improves with her appetite*, he told himself, *and her head is full of suspicion.*

"I don't," he said finally, and he planted the ax blade in the chopping stump. "Your virtue is safe."

"I wasn't thinking that way at all, Mr. West." She glanced away. She *had* thought about him that way. She had wondered about him in a hundred ways, much to her chagrin. But she was inclined to add a bit of truth on the heels of her fib. "You've given me no cause to—"

"That's right." He waved his hand in her direction, and his impatience made his subtle accent more pronounced.

"I brought a pile of skin and bones to my cabin rather than leave her by the river to die."

"You've given me more than shelter."

"I've done what was necessary to keep you alive. What does it matter who I am and where I come from?" He jerked his chin with the question.

"It doesn't, not really."

"I don't prey on sick women."

"Of course not," Katherine agreed as she pulled her shawl closely about her.

"And even if I did—" He turned from her with a disgusted grunt. "You don't have anything to worry about, Mrs. Fairfield. Your bones are safe with me."

"Mr. West—"

"I'll be right back," he said over his shoulder as he disappeared into the trees.

Within a few moments he returned from dunking his upper body in the stream that ran below the cabin. The bath had improved his outlook. "If you're hungry, I'll gladly quit this task and make us something to eat," he offered as he drew his shirt on again.

There was a hint of relief in the smile she offered. "I'm never hungry anymore, Mr. West. You don't give me a chance to be."

"I don't know what else to do with a pile of bones but try to feed her up." He stood near her and waited for her to squint up at him. He could have stepped to the side and blocked the sun for her, but he enjoyed his advantage. "I'm thinking it's time for something that'll stick to your ribs. Something like tripe, or maybe beaver tail. Good fat, the *savages* would say. You need some fat on you or you'll freeze this winter."

She noticed how hard the word *savages* came. He suddenly squatted next to her, and she was glad to lower her gaze and give her eyes a rest from the sun. "Perhaps I could make some bread," she offered.

"I doubt it." He permitted a spark of mischief to dance in his eyes. "I think you'll be eating whatever I choose to feed you for a while yet. Enjoy it, Mrs. Fairfield. Come winter, hard times are nearly assured up here."

"I've endured thus far."

"You've been lucky." He raised one dark eyebrow. "But I've said that before, haven't I?"

"Yes, and I've interpreted luck to be your way of describing God's grace. I expect hard times, as you say. I'm prepared for them." She was pleased with her confident tone, even though a small voice in her head reminded her that she had been far from prepared for the hardships she had faced on this journey. Now that she had seen the worst, she was prepared for more.

His laughter made her clench her teeth.

"Prepared for them," West mocked. "All eighty pounds of you, prepared for hard times."

"I believe I weigh more than eighty—"

"No, you don't." He lifted her into his arms as he stood, taking her completely off guard. Her arms went around his neck instinctively. "Eighty on the nose. I've been packing and trading for years. I know what I'm getting when I lift it."

Her nightgown had gotten bunched up, and he could feel the warmth of the backs of her knees. Some women were sensitive there, but he doubted this one was. All that kneeling had probably rendered her knees callused and calcified all the way around.

Unsmiling, she lifted her chin and glared at him. He enjoyed having her dignity at his mercy, and he bounced her a couple of times as he headed for the cabin door. "There's eighty pounds of missionary here—no more, no less. If I offered any more than ten beaver plews, I'd be getting the short end."

"Mr. West—"

"And beaver doesn't bring much these days."

He heard her sigh as he laid her on the bed, and he knew she'd worn herself out. That was fine. She'd probably sleep better, and sleeping, she couldn't ask questions. But he wanted to get some food in her first, and he headed for the flour box. If she wanted bread, he would make what his mother had called *vite* or hurry-up bread, along with some stewed fruit. This woman nibbled like a chipmunk, and he had to feed her often or she would never be strong. For one so small, she was a grand bother, he told himself as he added baking powder to a small mound of flour.

"What is the reason for your objection to missionaries, Mr. West?"

She wasn't asleep yet. The starch in her question told him that the sun hadn't wilted her much, either. He added a little water to his mixture and kneaded it with deft fingers.

"Who said I have any?"

"It's quite obvious. Your attitude changed when I told you that I intended to carry on my husband's work."

"Maybe I just don't like to see a woman taking on a man's job."

"Is that so?" She sat up so that she could see him spreading the sticky concoction in an iron spider skillet. "You handle that dough as efficiently as any woman."

"I do what's necessary. It's been a while since I've had a woman around." The dipper of water he'd used became a finger bowl. "One comes along, and she turns out to be a missionary. Half-dead one, at that."

"By tomorrow—" Katherine dropped her head back and closed her eyes, willing her prediction to come true. "I think by tomorrow, I should be able to handle the cooking, Mr. West. I'm not half-dead anymore, thank the Lord."

"You might also thank the woman who taught me to make the teas you've been drinking." He grabbed the skillet handle with a wet hand. Hurry-up bread reminded him of White Earth Woman, too. "Except that she *is* dead."

"Your...wife, Mr. West?"

"My wife."

"I am grateful to her. Were she here, I would—"

"You would tell her that her medicine—maybe with the exception of the tea that saved your hide—was no good, and that she should turn her back on the ways of the old ones and take up your Bible." He set the skillet over the hot coals in the fireplace, then braced his hands on his knees and stood, turning a cold glare on his guest. "My wife was a savage, Mrs. Fairfield."

"A savage?"

"I gave you your own term. She was Santee Sioux."

Katherine ignored his bitterness. She heard her own feeling of loss echoing in the hollow tone of his voice, and she asked quietly, "How long ago?"

Because it wasn't the response he'd expected, it took him a moment to answer. "Three years."

They stared briefly at each other, and then he busied himself again. He put a small amount of water into a kettle, added a little sugar and a few wild plums, then turned the slab of bread and moved the three-legged skillet away from the hot coals. He replaced it with the kettle and turned to her again as he straightened his back. He meant to turn away just as quickly, but the look she gave him was arresting. She cared about his loss, and he found himself admitting, "It doesn't seem possible that it's been that long."

She nodded, and her eyes suddenly glistened. "It's been only three months for me, but they've been the longest three months of my life."

"The wound is still raw," he reflected. He moved from the fireplace, approaching her slowly, though it had not been his intention to approach her at all. "As though someone has torn one of your limbs away."

"We had not been married long." She blinked furiously as she moved her hand over the red stripe in the blanket that covered her lap. "But I had known him all my life. Ever since we were children, I knew..." She lifted her chin and tried to stave off the tears by changing her focus. "How did she die?"

"She—" He stepped still closer. He found himself drawn to the femininity in Katherine's eyes, no matter that they were not brown, but blue. They mirrored all that she felt about her loss and his. "It was our first child. She was so—" Because she, too, was a woman, and he was only a man, he glanced away. "She died trying to give birth to the child she wanted so badly."

"And the baby?"

"Dead."

The word hung in the air like a dark, sticky web.

"Do you miss her still?" She closed her eyes and gave her head a quick mind-clearing shake. "That was an insolent question—surely, you do—but does it always hurt to think about her? Will I always—"

"No." Having lost touch with his doubts, he sat on the bed beside her. "It hurt when I refused to believe I could never have her back. I took pain as my mate, foolishly thinking it to be the last remnant of my wife. I refused to grieve properly and let her go."

"I have grieved in my heart until I cannot tolerate the feeling anymore," she declared softly. "I have prayed for some small measure of his faith, his capacity to do good works. But I fear I haven't the strength to carry on. I simply..." She stared steadfastly at her hand on the blanket as she shook her head again.

"Pile of bones or not, it was a strong woman who saw to it that that child had a 'decent' burial."

She looked up at him now, and he saw her gratitude. "You dug the grave, Mr. West."

"And you made damn sure I did."

Again she glanced away, and bitterness grafted itself to the despair in her voice. "He left me alone, out there in the desert. I followed him. I depended upon him, but he...he got sick and made everyone else sick, and then he left me there with *sick* people." Her hands became small fists as she spoke. "He brought me on this miserable journey and deserted me in the midst of strangers who could think of nothing but saving their own—"

Now the tears began to roll down her cheeks, and each halting word came hard. "Oh, Lord, I can't do this. Thomas *has* to go out there with me. We had planned...everything...together, and I can't..."

Jed touched her hand. Katherine looked up, and he saw that she was lost. He reached for her, and she leaned into his arms, whispering, "What shall I do now? I don't understand how I can be expected to...I don't..."

"What are you expected to do?"

"Go on," she said, struggling with a straining throat. "D-do what he would have—"

"Live your life, Katherine," Jed said quietly. "You must live your life."

She pressed her forehead against Jed's chest and rolled her head back and forth, sobbing and muttering her doubts. Her warm tears dampened his muslin shirt. She swore that she hated Thomas for leaving her, and Jed silently admonished himself to take no satisfaction in this. This was no true woman in his arms, but a grieving widow who would soon be the stiff-backed missionary again. His heart refused to heed his own warning, and he stroked her golden hair and allowed himself to feel her pain. His own had lulled itself into bittersweet memories, but he remembered a time when he had felt as bereft as Katherine did now.

He had refused to gash his legs and cut his hair as White Earth Woman's brothers had done, not because the missionaries had condemned the practice, but because he preferred to nurse his remorse. He fed it trade whiskey and kept it alive. He would drink himself to sleep, wake up in a cold sweat and run out into the night, calling her name, begging her to come back, cursing her for leaving him, pleading with her to forgive him. His wife's people thought him mad. They told him to go his way and take his whiskey with him. They had considered him to be one of them, and now they saw that he was not.

Nor did he find comfort with his father's people, who had taught him to read, write and speak his father's English properly. They told him that when he cut his hair, dressed in their clothes and ate his food with a fork, he bore little resemblance to his mother's people. But they had been wrong. His eyes mirrored the soul of his ancestry. Father's people, mother's people, wife's people. It was all there in the blackness of his eyes. Yet he lived apart from all of them. He had no people.

The madness the Santee had seen in him was real; it was the damnation he'd been promised so many times in school. It was the curse of the man who longed for some measure of peace while the very blood in his veins teemed with warring elements. Father's blood. Mother's blood. Even now, as he held this grieving woman in his arms, his own hot blood warred with his better judgment. Perhaps she knew little about him, but he had come to know her intimately. He had come to feel possessive of the life he had fought so hard to save. Even as he reminded himself that she was no longer his fragile little flower, he held her close. Missionary, he told himself. A meddling missionary. But still he stroked her hair.

"I'm sorry," she said, wiping her tears with her fingers as she pulled away from him. "I couldn't cry before. I've had terrible thoughts, selfish feelings, and I couldn't even weep for my husband until ... until now."

"With sickness all around you, you were probably unable to find the time to grieve."

"I was angry," she whispered. "I had no right to be angry."

"You have the right. You were deserted. Twice."

"But Thomas was not at fault."

"Perhaps not, but you were left without a man." He watched her draw away from him as she reclaimed her composure. That and the smell of bread and stewed fruit brought him back to reality. He moved from her and went to rescue the kettle from the fire.

"It's already September," he observed as he sliced wedges of flat bread. "Was your party late getting started?"

Katherine arranged the covers so that she could hold her food in her lap. "We were unable to travel with the party with whom we had made our arrangements. Thomas delayed our departure from Saint Joseph to help a keelboatman who had taken ill and was left by his friends to die—which, I'm afraid, he did, within a few days. But we had to wait for another wagon train. The wagon master was—" She shook her head. "I didn't like the look of him from the beginning. The last time we saw him was at South Pass."

"He deserted his party?"

"He did, and he took Thomas's saddle horse and Mr. Mueller's savings."

"He'll change his name and do the same next year." He handed her a wooden bowl. She savored the fruity steam and smiled. "I've seen too many stragglers," he told her, ignoring the sweet look in her eyes. "Desperation makes a man an easy mark. You should have wintered in Saint Jo."

"We couldn't do that. It was all planned. We had our instructions from the Missionary Board, and so much depends on our—" He walked away, and she finished quietly. "Others will follow next year if all goes well."

"All has not gone well." He helped himself to a wedge of bread and ladled the fruit over it. "Does that mean they will not come?"

"Once I have made the journey, I think—"

"I think they will keep coming whether Katherine Fairfield completes her journey or not."

"But I will complete the journey."

"You can't cross the Cascades before the first snow-fall." He set his bowl on the table and took a seat, facing her from across the room.

"Not even with a guide?"

"You don't have a guide."

She took that to mean there was no point in asking him. "Perhaps there's someone at Fort Boise. When we came through Fort Hall—"

"You might find someone." He brought a spoonful of hot fruit near his mouth, then glanced beyond it, catching her eye. "Someone who promises he can get any straggler through those mountains any time of the year. Especially a woman. In how many ways do you wish to be deserted, Mrs. Fairfield? And how many times?"

The frank stare lasted until West figured the point had been made. He turned his attention to his food. He was nearly finished eating when a small voice asked, "If I explained that I had been sent by the church, that I was doing God's work . . . would that make a difference?"

"I couldn't say. Depends on the man, I guess."

"I have no choice but to trust someone." She watched him finish his meal and push his bowl aside, and she remembered his reaction to the news that she was a missionary. "Even now I find myself alone with a man I hardly know. But the Lord knows you, Mr. West. He knows your heart, and He sent you to find me. I have to trust you."

"You don't have to trust me." He pushed his chair back abruptly and stood, gesturing as he spoke. "You can find some way to arm yourself. You've been sick and helpless, but now that you're gaining strength, you should be prepared. Your God helps those who help themselves, and I might not be the man you think I am."

"You said you had no plans to harm me."

"Perhaps I lied," he warned as he approached the bed.

Katherine clutched the bowl in her lap and kept her voice steady. "No. I don't believe you did. You are a Christian man, Mr. West. Anyone can see that." She ignored his burst of laughter. "You've taken such care in the way you've fed me and in the way you have given me—"

"My wife's tea. My mother's bread. Some of my grandmother's medicine." Each bit of information was punctuated with a pause as he anticipated the moment when his revelation would change the look in her eyes. "Cree medicine is highly respected, Mrs. Fairfield. Other tribes pay dearly for it, and Cree women guard their recipes." He sat on the edge of the bed, watching her closely as he continued. "But a grandson might wheedle and cajole the old woman who dotes on him to give up her secrets, just for him. My grandmother, if she still lives, is what you call a savage. She is one of the Cree people. I am Métis."

"Métis?"

"Mixed blood. My grandfather was Métis also—French with some Ojibway blood. He was a trapper in the Red River Country."

"And your father?" she asked.

"Ah, you would have liked my father, Mrs. Fairfield." There was no humor in his smile. "He was English. His blood was pure. He worked for the Hudson's Bay Company."

He raised his brow as he leaned closer to her. "Perhaps you are safe to trust that part of me. The English part. What do you think? With my French ancestry, I am more than half white. Perhaps I would not harm you." His dark eyes narrowed dramatically. "But there is still that savage blood. More than one determined missionary has tried to rid me of that blood. They have all failed."

"But you look..." She had noticed, perhaps even admired his unusual features, but she was not familiar with the savage tribes he mentioned, and she certainly knew no Frenchmen.

"I look like a Métis. Part Cree. Part Ojibway. Part French. Part English."

He seemed to want her to look at him, to learn the meaning of his claim by studying his face. She obliged, but she saw only the man who had held a cup of tea to her lips and gently coaxed her to drink small, life-giving sips. "No matter how much of you is savage, I am not afraid of you, Mr. West." She lifted her bowl and smiled tentatively. "And I like your mother's bread."

He raised one eyebrow. "Then eat it. I intend to sit here, just this close, until you do."

Chapter Three

Jed didn't mind sleeping on the floor. As long as there was no frost in the ground, the hard-packed earth was almost as comfortable as the straw tick and rope webbing that made up his bed. Of necessity he was a light sleeper, and night sounds frequently woke him, but lately he was not so much attuned to the predator's nocturnal cry as he was to the sound of his bed creaking whenever Katherine shifted in her sleep. Wide awake, he stared at the beams overhead and listened to the whisper of her breathing.

She had prepared their evening meal. Jed had spent the afternoon foraging to replenish his stock of roots and herbs. When he returned, the aroma of plum duff drew him to the cabin. Katherine's face was bright with anticipation, and when he started to chide her for using raisins that should have been saved for winter, the words wouldn't come. She wanted his approval, and the cheery light in her eyes along with the tantalizing aroma made him say things he hadn't known were in his head. Pea soup suddenly became a longtime favorite of his. She was welcome to use anything she found in his larder. Tomorrow he'd hunt down a couple of sage grouse and show her how to fashion a good spit.

Damn, where was he going to find any sage grouse? He would be forced to leave her alone for the better part of the day while he traveled to the sage flats and stalked birds, the way he had learned to do as a child. He still found the snare or the arrow to be more efficient than the rifle for bird hunting, but the hunt would consume more time than he wanted to spend away from Katherine. She was not strong enough yet, he told himself. Even if she were, she was still a woman in need of his protection.

She was a *missionary*. Damn his eyes, he kept trying to forget that. He shifted his backside on his wolf-skin pallet, straightening one knee while he bent the other one. The flicker of dying flames drew his attention. Shadows played on the rough-hewn table across the room, like a ring of children dancing around the empty whiskey bottle Katherine had filled with cuttings of rabbit brush. Their yellow blooms were fading now, but at suppertime Katherine had beamed with the satisfaction of "putting that bottle to a much better use than the one for which it was intended, Mr. West."

He agreed. Whiskey was intended to chase a man's despair into the corners of his mind, which wasn't so bad except when his judgment went with it. Too often his did, so he kept the obligatory mountain man's flask on the top shelf. He'd had some bad times with it, and now he used it only when the loneliness became unbearable. He had thought about taking a drink before he went to bed, but then he'd thought again. A cloudy brain would surely forget what a sensible man struggled to remember. She *was* a missionary.

Still, he wanted to look out for her. Missionary or not, she had a kindness about her—an artless eagerness to please. He knew she had had to walk some distance from the cabin to find those late-blooming wildflowers, but he had been unable to scold her for it. Her smile had been too sweet a contrast with the haughty tone of her voice. Her words smacked of Mrs. Thomas Fairfield, the missionary, but the pleasure she took in preparing the table to impress him seemed suspiciously feminine.

He had gotten himself in a bad fix, and he couldn't decide what to do about it. Get rid of her, something sensible said to him: see her safely to one of the Hudson's Bay Company's outposts and let her hole up for the winter with the pilgrims and merchants with whom she belonged. A fleeting primitive inclination had him showing her what a real woman's purpose was, then letting her stay or go as she pleased—but he quickly discarded that notion.

The man he was, even through the worst times, would never allow him to see to his needs with an unwilling woman. And though his heart had protected itself with calluses after his wife's death, his instincts as a husband were still there; he was a protector. Katherine trusted him. He would not permit himself to harm this or any woman.

She made him feel soft inside, but he was determined not to let it show. Hardness on the outside was not difficult to maintain, but when it became a throbbing masculine reality, as it was now, it was difficult to endure. In the dead of night the quiet rustling in his bed had roused him from sleep, then aroused every male nerve in his body. Again she turned in her sleep, this time with a small, womanly sigh, and again he shifted, cursing his male flesh. This was absurd! It was unnatural to suffer thus with her so close by and with no husband, no wife to give either of them cause to abstain. She was without a man, and he was in need of a woman.

She trusted him.

And, damn those blue eyes, she was a missionary. Missionaries were bent on changing men's lives, and Jed West's life had seen enough change. Once a missionary started her meddling, there was no going back to the way things had been. You couldn't be Indian; you couldn't be white. Where was the place for the man who was both? The missionaries had never had a good answer for that question, but they had surely not suggested that sharing a bed with one of their kind might be part of it.

Jed tossed the wool trade blanket aside and sat up. Early morning was the worst time for a man to lie near a woman he couldn't have, but it was a good time to hunt. He reached for his moccasins.

"What's wrong?"

Her voice was languid with sleep. He tried to ignore the way it drew him toward the bed. "Nothing. I promised you grouse."

"This early?" She lifted her head, and her long, yellow braid fell back from her shoulder with a soft sound.

"I'll have to do some traveling," he explained as he wrapped the lacing around one tall moccasin. "I may be gone for a while. It's time to scout out some places where I might set traps come winter." He paused, appreciating the way the predawn shadows softened those dark circles that persisted around her eyes. "Don't venture out after flowers or anything else today. Not alone. Do you understand me?"

"Yes. But will you take me out sometime, just to look around? I do enjoy—"

"When you're stronger, I'll let you ride with me. For now, you have your books and your sewing. Stay close to the cabin."

"I didn't go far yesterday," she told him. "Just to the stream and a little beyond."

"No farther than the stream, and don't be dawdling down there, either. Don't want you running into a rattler. They're denning up this time of year, and they'll strike at anything that moves." He hung his possibles bag over his shoulder and reached for his rifle.

"I'll be cautious," she promised.

"Just stick close and rest up while I fetch us some tasty fowl. Make yourself some yarrow tea. It's good for female complaints."

"I don't have any complaints, except—"

"You've got missionary complaints, I know, but I've told you I don't want to hear about those. I've got no teas to remedy any of that." He unbolted the door. "You take it easy, and I'll be back before nightfall."

Katherine found that she could not sleep once Jed had left. Dawn light glowed around the edges of the window frame. She got up, unlatched the plank window and pushed it open. Its creaking hinges harmonized with the warbling mountain bluebird, who sang praises to the autumn sun's waning warmth. He would be leaving soon, Katherine thought, and so would she. The morning's golden hue intensified as a reminder more than a promise and gave her a strange feeling of dread. She'd begun to feel safe with Jed.

She dressed and made herself a helping of hasty pudding for breakfast. The cornmeal mush warmed her inside, and she wondered what Jed had taken along for his morning meal. He was always more concerned about what she ate than he was about food for himself. But she was not as frail as he thought she was, nor was she as useless. Moreover, she was tired of being the convalescent. Her clothes and her bedding were stale with sickness, and Katherine had had enough of it.

Fresh air, clean water, lye soap—that was a fine ticket. Katherine propped the cabin door open and beckoned the pine scent inside. The sun had banished the dew and warmed the morning, and Katherine vowed to follow suit, banishing musty air and dreary thoughts. She carried blankets and fur pelts outside, draped them over limbs and bushes and beat them with a straw broom. Then she carried water up from the stream, heated it and washed not only her clothing, but what she could find of Jed's. It was a day to make the most of the sun.

Surrounded by cottons and wools, flapping in the warm breeze like an array of multicolored flags, the mountain cabin could have been a New England cottage on wash day. She'd left only one dress, and that was the one she wore. Flushed with the pleasure of having accomplished so much, she threw caution to the warm autumn wind and stripped down to her chemise.

It was only when she stopped working that Katherine's sense of purpose began to fade, and she had nothing else to buoy her energy. She sat on the bed with a hot cup of tea, pulled off her shoes with her free hand and massaged her aching feet. Ah, those arches; they were the worst. She closed her eyes and sagged back against the wall, certain that she would never be able to get up again.

Jed stepped through the open door and found her that way. Oddly, he noticed first that her feet were bare, and that one dangled just above the floor while the other was propped up on the bed. There was something endearing about those small, bare feet. She looked like a rag doll that some child might have left on his bed. Damp, fine, almost colorless tendrils framed her face, while the bulk of her hair was caught up on the back of her head. The cabin's interior was dusky in the late afternoon, but a damp sheen over Katherine's fine, fair features turned her face into a beacon beckoning to him from the dark corner of the cabin. Then he noticed the white chemise with the white pantalets peeking out beneath it. Incredibly, she was not dressed.

He walked over to the table and plunked down his string of gutted birds. Her eyes flew open at the sound, and she made a valiant effort to meet his frank stare with a dignified one of her own as she patted the bed, absently fishing for some piece of fabric with which she might cover herself. The straw tick was bare. Every last scrap of cloth had been hung outside. She was too tired to flutter with embarrassment, so she sighed, resigning herself to the fact that she'd been caught in her underclothes.

"I didn't expect you back this soon," she said.

"Truly, I didn't mean to leave you alone this long, but I ended up setting out snares for the birds. It takes time, but it works."

"There's tea," she offered. "But it might not be the right kind for a hunter's complaints."

He lifted his chin toward the kettle and sniffed. "Yarrow." He was grinning when he turned to her. "I've got no complaints. Bagged four pretty little hens."

"I shall be pleased to pluck them after I bring in the laundry," she offered as she scooted to the edge of the bed.

"You've already worn yourself out. I'll take care of this." He dipped himself a cup of tea. "I told you to take it easy today."

"I'm tired of taking it easy."

"Well, you wore yourself out. Feel better now?"

Sitting with her arms crossed over her chest, she rounded her shoulders as if she were trying to curl up into a nondescript ball. "What I feel is . . . humiliated because I didn't foresee—"

"What difference does it make now? I've seen you." He sipped his tea, eyeing her across the rim of his tin mug. "And I've seen you before this," he added, knowing full well that it was not the same. The woman who sat on the edge of his bed with her arms wrapped around herself in a hug born of modesty was hardly the scarecrow he'd reclaimed from death's door.

"I don't think . . . I doubt that my dresses are dry yet. I laundered your things first."

"My things?" Jed grinned. "Were they the worst?"

"No. They were less cumbersome."

He set his cup down and left the cabin, returning in a moment with several articles of clothing. He tossed all but one white shirt aside, and that he took to Katherine. She stood slowly, and he slipped his shirt around her shoulders.

"The dresses are damp."

"I hope by nightfall . . ." She lifted one arm into the sleeve, turning her nose into the collar. It smelled sun dried.

The shirt seemed to swallow her up, and Jed held the shoulders so that she wouldn't disappear from his sight as she slipped her other arm into his sleeve. It made him feel possessive of her to see his shirt cover her slight frame; *his* shirt sheltered her embarrassment. He smoothed it over her shoulders, and when she raised her eyes to him, he lost himself in them.

His kiss was in his eyes, and she saw it coming. He gripped her shoulders. She made no move to step away, though he gave her time. What she saw in those eyes, dark as molasses and promising some sweet kind of sustenance, summoned her in a way that no man ever had. She saw hunger, and she needed instinctively to exchange nourishment.

She lifted her chin, he dipped his, and their lips met halfway between her need and his. Her kiss was untutored, and he did not pause to wonder why. He reveled in the chance to teach as his tongue traced her lips' soft seam, searching for some small rent. He put his arms around her and drew her close. He felt her hands at his waist, touching tentatively. She was afraid to reach, but she could not turn away. He persisted with his tongue, coaxing gently until her lips parted, and he slanted his mouth over hers.

Katherine trembled. His kiss awakened some wild thing inside her, and it tugged on her, stroked her, demanding to be set free. She couldn't move, couldn't draw breath as Jed breathed fire into her. Oh, Lord, it would get the better of her. Jed's mouth was too wonderful, and it felt too good to let him hold her in his arms. He slipped his hand to the small of her back and pressed her against him, grinding his sex against the place where the wild thing dwelled, and she moaned into his mouth. *Set it free. Set it free.* He answered with one quick plunge of his tongue, then another.

He took a wider stance, enforcing greater intimacy as he bent to nibble her neck. "You need me, too," he whispered.

"No," she said, but her groan told him, yes.

"I won't hurt you."

"I know," she said desperately. "I know you won't."

"I will give you pleasure, Katherine."

"I don't want pleasure. I don't—"

"That's not what your body tells me."

"I will burn in hell if you do this. Lord, oh Lord."

Jed was stunned. His heart pounded in his ears as he looked down at her. She pinched her eyes shut, and what little color she possessed drained from her face. "This hell of yours is madness, Katherine. You need a man, and I need a woman.''

"Then we shall slide into that pit together, because this is wrong, and our sin will—''

"I thought to make a woman of you,'' he said quietly. "You look like one—more so all the time—but you are still the missionary.''

"Yes.'' Her eyes flew open. "Yes, I am. And I know you to be a good man, Mr. West. You came home to find me like this, and naturally you thought—''

"*I* thought?''

"But you must remember, Mr. West—''

"I kissed you the way you wanted to be kissed.'' She closed her mouth and stared at him, and he saw the guilt in her eyes. It was a joyless victory. He'd made his point at the expense of her pride. "The way we wanted to kiss each other,'' he added softly.

She turned away. "It is a weakness in both of us, then.''

"Perhaps you're right.'' Wanting her was indeed a weakness, and taking her would be a mistake. There would be no end to the problems she could cause him. "But there was no sin in what happened here,'' he said as he stepped back from her. "Only folly.''

Katherine was left to sort out her own confusion when Jed left the cabin. Lord, it was just the way it had been with Thomas. Worse! Thomas had been her husband, and he had been willing to spare her the inconveniences her mother had warned her a woman must suffer in the marriage bed. He had promised that she would bear no children before they reached the Whitman Mission safely, and she had been grateful. She had witnessed the misery a woman with child might endure on the trail—Jane Simms's miscarriage and the untimely death of Arthur Franklin's young wife. But no matter how chaste Thomas's kisses or how restrained his touches, that awful wildness in Katherine had too often raised its head, and she would ask him not to stop. He would pray with her then. Oh, how she would pray. *Make me worthy of this man, Lord. Take the terrible lust from my woman's heart.*

She muttered the same such prayers as she gathered the laundry, beat a bowl of cornmeal batter and plucked and singed the birds Jed had killed. *Forgive me. Forgive him. Forgive us our trespasses.* It wasn't Jed's fault. It was hers. Many times he had bared his torso while he worked, and she had looked upon him with shameless admiration. He had ministered to her in his way, touching her only to care for her, but she had begun to enjoy the way it felt when he sat close to her, held her, touched her face or lifted her in his arms.

We are human, Thomas had told her. *We have the same weaknesses that others have, but we have the means to conquer them. We must not be deterred from the path God has chosen for us. It is for us to spread the word.*

Jed returned at dusk. Katherine was trying to decide how best to truss one small carcass for roasting when Jed joined her next to the table. His hair was damp, and he smelled of night air. It made her shiver just to stand this close to him.

"What are you doing to that poor bird?" he asked.

Katherine's back stiffened. "Nothing that will offend her any more than you have already done."

"Are you so certain of that?" He took the bird from her hands and split it down the backbone with the big Hudson's Bay Company butcher knife she had laid aside on the table. "We owe her the dignity of being properly prepared," he instructed as he performed the same operation on the other three birds. Katherine watched while he seared them over the coals, skewered them out flat, pinning slices of bacon on both sides, and impaled them on a long stick, which he had soaked thoroughly to prevent it from burning. They looked like four denuded bats, hovering over the fire with wings outstretched.

Jed stood and backed away from the fire. The heat felt good. It had been a warm day, but by sundown the autumn chill had claimed the air, and the small lake he'd bathed in had been downright icy. He glanced at Katherine, who stood in the corner, dressed now in blue calico, with her arms folded tightly under her bosom. He noticed that she had made the bed and replaced the fur pelts that served as rugs. She'd made a neat stack of his clothes and set it in his chair. His sleeping pallet was back on the floor, perhaps a little farther from the bed than he'd had it, and she had added a feather tick and a pillow. He didn't own either.

"I hope you'll find them comfortable, Mr. West. I would like you to have them."

"Your husband might not approve of me sleeping on his pillow."

"It wasn't Thomas's," she said crisply. "It's mine."

He wouldn't insult her by refusing her gift, but his lips twisted in a wry smile at the thought of sleeping in her bed while she slept in his. As a schoolboy he had learned to count on these missionaries to make everything complicated. Then he noticed a licorice scent in the room and spotted a bunch of sweet goldenrod on the table, another on a shelf and still another in a crock near the hearth.

"I happened upon those close by," she explained quickly. "I didn't go far. I thought the scent of the leaves would—"

"It makes good tea," he told her, as though there had to be a practical use for everything she brought to his cabin.

"I'll make some. I have corn bread ready, but those birds..." Katherine took a deep breath, pointedly savoring the spit-roasting bacon and grouse. "Our supper smells delicious."

He had cooled his ardor in the lake, and now she was trying to warm him up with flattery. He ignored her as he hunkered down to tend to his birds.

"Mr. West?"

She had crept closer. Out of the corner of his eye he could see the hem of her dress and the black toe of one shoe. "Jed," he said without looking up. "I'm no 'mister.'"

"Jed, then," she agreed quietly. "I want to apologize for...for giving you cause to...for giving you such a very bad..." She launched each false start with a deep breath as she twisted her hands in her skirt. "Impression of my moral character. Not being properly dressed when you came home, well, how can one excuse such a thing? But I...on the trail, you know, propriety sometimes gets lost with the need to be practical, and a woman finds herself—"

He'd been angry with himself as much as he had been with her. The joke was on him. He had tried to make love to a missionary, of all things. She didn't know what in hell—or heaven—she wanted, and he didn't have the time or patience to help her find out. But, damn, supper did smell good, and so did the cabin, what with the sweet goldenrod and the fresh laundry and the bedding all aired out. A man couldn't help but enjoy those things. He turned his head and grinned up at her.

"You're right, Katherine." He'd decided to let her share in the joke. "A man shouldn't get overly excited when he finds a woman sitting on his bed in her underclothes. Chances are, she's just being practical."

Her voice became high and thin, like a kitten's cry. "I wanted everything clean. I had been wearing—"

"That kiss, though." Jed pulled the spit from the fire and made a project of testing the birds while he threw out his casual observation. "That kiss wasn't the practical kind. I've gotten many a practical kiss, mostly from whores, and yours wasn't like that."

"Wh—whores?"

He stood, nodding, satisfied that supper was done. He might have had Katherine herself on the spit the way she was squirming. "I've been up and down the Mississippi trying out those practical kisses, back a few years ago when I was still pretty green. You haven't practiced enough to do any practical, honey-put-your-money-where-your-mouth-is kind of kissing." The satisfaction was still there when he looked up from his birds and smiled. "You kissed me because you wanted to, Katherine."

"You kissed *me*."

"That's right."

"I wasn't—"

"Near as I could tell, we were both in on it. At least, we were until you started preaching hellfire and damnation. That's where you go your way, and I'll go mine." He set the spit on the table. "You said something about corn bread?"

"Oh, yes." She jumped as if he'd given her an order. Her hands fluttered from shelf to shelf, gathering plates and the bread she'd wrapped in a cloth. "In fairness, I fully intended to apologize for not being properly dressed when you came back to the cabin this afternoon, but I do believe that when a gentleman makes advances—"

"There's the problem, you see. I am no gentleman." He took a seat at the table and helped himself to one of the birds. "I'm a savage."

"Métis," she corrected quietly as she sat primly on the edge of her chair.

"Métis." Jed sank his teeth into roast grouse and tore the meat off the bone. After he'd worked on it for a moment, he eyed her pointedly. "What about my grandmother? Is she still a savage?"

"She is Cree, I believe. I would assume that, being married to a Frenchman, she was ... instructed in some form of Christian faith?"

"She was." He broke off a piece of corn bread and discovered that it was still warm inside. He looked up at the woman who'd made it. "Aren't you going to eat?"

"Yes, of course," she said, helping herself to one of the birds. "Then your grandmother embraced the teachings of the missionaries."

"She saw good medicine in the stories they told. But the priests didn't approve of her medicine, which, she said, her people needed. Her medicine was a sacred gift, and no one could convince her otherwise. She let my grandfather bring his Jesus things into her lodge, but when he was sick or the traps were empty, he went to her for medicine."

"And did your mother continue these practices?"

He waved the notion away. "She didn't have that power."

"Because of her mixed blood?"

"Because she did not receive the power," he repeated, his patience strained. "Some do, some don't."

"Surely your grandfather saw to her proper baptism."

"Mine, too. We had no problem with that. There was room in my grandfather's life for all good things." Jed smiled, remembering. "He taught me to hunt and trap. On a portage from one lake to the next I would follow along with the few things he would let me carry, while he hefted the birchbark canoe high above his head and sang the songs of the voyageurs. I hoped one day to have a man's shoulders and a man's voice, just like my grandfather's."

Katherine watched him devour the bread and felt good because she'd made it. She'd forgotten that the food was there for her, too. She wanted to hear more about Jed's family. His grandfather's shoulders could have been no stronger than Jed's.

"You sang to me," she recalled. "In French, I believe. It was the most soothing voice, and even more—"

She glanced away quickly. She had almost compared Jed's low, mellifluous voice to Thomas's rather tinny hymn-singing, but she stopped herself.

"I'm told it's not good French. Impure, they say."

"Who says this?" she asked, relieved that her small inconstancy had gone undetected.

"The missionary teachers, who said that I must speak my father's English." He glanced at her plate. "Your food is getting cold, Katherine."

Another spark of admiration flashed in Katherine's breast as she took a bite of the meat. It tasted wild and smoky, and she took a moment to savor the unique flavor. "You speak two languages, then."

"I speak Cree fairly well, also, thanks to my grandmother," he reported as he finished off the chunk of bread.

"Three languages!" she marveled, then caught herself again. "English is, of course, the most useful. But the French sounds so..."

"Among the Métis, the Cree and the French tongues have blended." He was working on the grouse again, separating the meat from the fine bones. "I didn't know that until I was taken away and made to go to school."

"Who took you away?"

"My father." His hands stilled. "The Englishman."

"Surely he wanted what was best for you."

He looked up, letting the grouse fall back to his plate. "How can you be so sure? How could *he* be sure? He took me to St. Louis when I was ten years old, turned me over to the missionaries there and told them to take the savage out of me. That was the last I saw of him."

"He never returned for you?"

Jed shook his head. "I was told that he 'corresponded' with the school. I think that meant he paid them to keep me there."

"And your mother...didn't object to—"

"My mother had no say in the matter. My father would come to our camp on the Winnipeg, which is our Cree name for the Red River. He would stay as long as he had business there, and then we wouldn't see him for a year, maybe two. It was during one of those visits that he decided he did have a son—two, in fact, but my brother was younger. He decided the elder of the two would be required to speak his language properly, read his books and learn about God in a different way." He raised a greasy finger to punctuate his point. "I spent eight years of my life in that pursuit. Truly, I spent the first two of those years looking for ways to escape."

"You ran away?" She imagined a younger Jed, a child capable of being frightened, and her voice reflected the kind of maternal sympathy no woman could hide.

"Many times. But I was always tracked down and brought back." With a shrug, he turned back to his plate and pulled a chunk of breast meat from the bone. "Which probably meant more 'correspondence' was exchanged."

"You were so young. You must have felt..." Good God-fearing people, she told herself. They would not have neglected his needs. "But they took good care of you, I'm sure."

He was staring at the meat in his hand, and he seemed not to hear her. "I remember looking at a map, understanding for the first time what it represented, and asking the teacher to show me where my mother was. He said that such places were not marked on the map. Such wilderness was poorly charted. It was known only to trappers and savages." He glanced up. "My mother and my grandparents."

"But they were kind to you," she insisted. "The people at this mission school."

He considered the statement, for she had made up her mind already. She wanted to believe, and he wanted to be truthful. "I don't know," he said finally. "Their ways seemed so strange to me that I couldn't tell what they intended. They held with beating a child with a switch or denying him food until he had 'learned his lesson.' It was hard for me to learn that way." His smile betrayed remembered sadness. "But they kept trying to teach me."

With a quick shake of her head, she tried to push the sadness aside with adult insight. "Perhaps those lessons come harder to boys than girls. Even Thomas felt the sting of the schoolmaster's hickory stick on occasion."

Even Thomas. Jed suppressed a disgusted chortle. "No *savage* would ever strike his child," he responded instead.

"You mean the savages' children never misbehave?"

He wondered fleetingly if the woman would ever set aside that word. "They behave like children," he said with studied patience. "They are permitted their childhood until the time comes for them to be men and women."

"And they never do anything wrong? Nothing deserving of punishment?"

"When I lived with my family, whenever I did something wrong, my mother asked me to stop. My uncles and my grandfather would talk to me about what I had done and explain what was expected. That was all that was necessary. I wanted to be like them, you see?" He couldn't tell from the look in her eyes whether she saw the way it was or not.

He pushed back his plate and sighed. "When my father took me to St. Louis, we hardly spoke during the entire journey. I didn't know what to expect. I had never seen a city. Soon after we arrived a stagecoach nearly ran over me, and my father snatched me up by the front of my coat and shouted in my face."

"Surely you understand why. He didn't want you to get killed."

"I understood two things," he told her, indicating the number with his fingers. "City streets were dangerous, and my father was angry with me, not the thing that had threatened my life. That anger made me want to leave him. At the school, there was more anger, and so much talk of sin and guilt. I couldn't imagine that this hell they spoke of would be any worse than wearing hard shoes that didn't fit and stiff collars around my neck and living in constant fear of that switch."

The look in her eyes had softened now, and he thought he might have gotten through.

She wanted to touch him. She wanted to reassure him somehow. "It seems . . . it was cruel to take a child from his mother and leave him with strangers, but surely—"

"Surely, surely," Jed mocked. "My father was not a savage, was he, Katherine? He was an Englishman. If what he did was cruel, there must have been some civilized reason for it. Surely."

"You were his son," she said quietly. "I think he must have been trying to—"

"When I became a man I searched for my father. I had done what he required, and I wanted him to see that the school had done its job. I was like him. I could speak his language, read and write. If they would hire me, I could keep the books for the Company, just the way he did." With a wry smile, he shook his head. "But I was too late. He had done his job well, and the Company had called him back to London." He paused as he remembered the final insult. "He had returned to the wife and children he'd had there all along."

"He had . . . *two* wives?"

"At least. Although—" he tried to shrug the whole matter off "—my mother had none of the 'civilized' trappings. No documents, no ring. She had lived with him and given him two children. That was all."

All thought of defending the Englishman vanished. Katherine felt betrayed by him, as Jed had been. She spluttered, struggling to devise the best possible reprisal. "He should be . . . he ought to be . . . horsewhipped!"

"Horsewhipped?" Jed tossed back his head and laughed. When the first laugh died, he glimpsed the fire in her eyes and laughed again. "Perfect! My own avenging missionary. I can just see you taking after my father with one of those stinging switches, Katherine. Teaching him his lesson. What an idea!"

The prospect made laughter bubble in her own throat. "You don't think a buggy whip would do?"

"Ah, no. It must be a snappy switch, and you must not let him off until he has groveled on his knees, confessed and done his penance."

"And what must that be?" she asked, delighted with the notion.

"He must tell his prune-mouthed British wife about his Métis wife, and his milk-faced brats must hear of their brothers."

"It's only fair," Katherine chimed.

"Yes!" Suddenly he realized how pretty she looked when she laughed, and he sobered. "Yes," he repeated quietly. "It *is* only fair."

With the change in his mood, Katherine's mirth faded, too. She saw the vacant expression in Jed's eyes, and she assumed his regret was for the loss of his father.

"What are your thoughts, Katherine?" He raised a challenging eyebrow. "Is there a bastard where there was once a savage, or are they one and the same?"

"I think there is a good man, whether he calls himself Christian or not. Those other words—" she waved them away, just as he had done moments ago "—are just words. They have nothing to do with the man you are."

"You are an interesting woman, Katherine." The womanly look in her eyes warmed him inside, and he returned his own masculine version. "Your smile is no more a missionary's than your kiss is that of a whore."

Her eyes widened, and she opened her mouth to protest, but he laughed, and she forgot the words. There was nothing left to do but laugh with him.

Chapter Four

Once Jed had heard the sound of Katherine's laughter unleashed, he wanted to hear it again. It started slowly, deep in her throat, as though she were trying hard to pinch it back, but its brightness escaped through her eyes. Jed loved to coax it free. He liked to tease her. She would never admit it, but she begged to be teased. He could make the most outrageous claim, and she would willingly walk into his trap. If she would share nothing else with him, he resolved that the missionary would learn to laugh with the mountain man.

He loved to sneak up on her, too. He had moved a chair outside for her and left her sitting in the sun to read while he went foraging. She had hardly moved. Beyond the flutter of golden aspen leaves he could see the sun catcher at work in her hair. Had Jed been sitting in her place, the snapping of that last twig would have brought him to his feet, but her ears were not fine-tuned. The carpet of brown pine needles challenged him to tread lightly as he stepped into the sun.

"Look what I found!"

Katherine's head popped out of the book. Cocooned in her shawl, she reminded Jed of a long-necked doe distracted from a meal of willow bark. But instead of bolting for deeper woods, she smiled.

He held a buckskin pouch aloft. "Something sweet," he hinted.

"Surely not . . . sap?"

He barked a laugh as he strode across the cabin yard. "Surely not. That's the only guess you're allowed until you taste what I have here." He knelt beside her chair, and untied the drawstring on the pouch. "Close your eyes and give me your hand."

She raised one eyebrow in mock suspicion. "Is it wise for me to trust you in this?"

"You'll have to decide." His grin was full of mischief. "I think you'll like the treat I've brought you."

She shut the book and reached for the bag, but he held it away.

"Close your eyes."

She flashed her suspicious look one last time before, smiling slightly, she complied. He guided her hand to the bag.

"It's alive, isn't it?" she accused.

"Don't you trust me?"

Her hand inched its way inside the pouch until all four fingertips encountered the viscous substance at the bottom. She opened her eyes and beamed at him. "Honey?" He smiled as she withdrew her hand, fingers dripping. "Where did you find it? I hope the bees were gone for the day. Mmm."

He watched her lick her fingers one at a time. She savored her forefinger as though she were sampling stick candy, and she had three more flavors to go. One golden drop of honey winked in the sunlight as it prepared to escape from the tip of her little finger. On impulse, Jed caught it with his tongue. He glanced up and saw the surprise in her eyes as he took her fingertip in his mouth and flicked his tongue over its fleshy pad. Her little quiver made the tip of his tongue tingle.

With her stomach aflutter and her finger in her mouth, Katherine froze. She watched Jed lean back slowly and smile. The sweet shine looked even more appetizing on his lips than it was on her own finger, which she had sucked clean. She licked the other two quickly, fidgeting under his mischievous scrutiny.

"You make a good honeycomb, Katherine. A man could taste to his heart's content and never suck out all the sweetness."

She licked her lips inadvertently as she stared at him.

He broke the spell by turning to the pouch in his hands. "It's tricky, getting honey from selfish bees," he said as he considered the prize. "You can tell them all about the children waiting at home and the wife who needs a little sweetening, but still they want to keep it all for themselves."

"Children?" A quick laugh relaxed her shoulders. Jed was so good with a tall tale. "What children?"

Jed's eyes were suddenly full of fun. "Six of them, waiting outside the cabin with their little tongues lolling like puppies. Old Man Coyote would have had those bees dropping tears of honey into his pouch with a story like that. It didn't work as well for me." He turned his wrist to show her the five small welts, each with a red prick at its center.

She sat up straight and reached for his hand. "They stung you! Does it hurt?" She stood and pulled him to his feet with a quick tug. "If we rub some salt on them, it might still help."

They went inside, and Katherine made a salt-and-water paste and began rubbing it into Jed's bee stings. He smiled as he leaned his hip against the table and watched her. He'd already applied the juice of the aloe, and the pain was gone. "Whose medicine is this?" he asked.

"My mother used to do this." She glanced up at him. "Who is this Coyote?"

"A sly old trickster. Laugh at him if you will, my grandmother used to tell us, but pay attention to his methods. They may be useful to you."

"Trying to charm the bees seems to have gotten you stung."

"But it got me a cache of honey." With twinkling eyes he nodded at their hands, his resting lightly in her palm while she tended it. "And some other good things."

He glimpsed the regret in her eyes as she released his hand and turned away. "We must try to... to avoid these familiarities, Jed. They start so innocently, and before we know it, we are..."

"We are what? Covered with honey and salt and smiling at each other?"

"It's the *way* you smile," she said quietly, as though someone might be shocked by the secret. "It's almost like... like the way you kiss."

He laughed. "You may think your own smile is tight-lipped and bookish, Katherine, but you ought to see it from my side of the table."

"Then I must not be doing it right. The smile that I intend is... charitable." She watched him hang the honey pouch on a wall peg, and she knew her explanations sounded feeble. "While it may sometimes appear otherwise, Jed, it's Christian charity that I mean to express."

"Charity." He thought it over and nodded. "I've had some experience with Christian charity in the past, and yours is different. I like yours better."

Katherine tucked a wisp of hair behind her ear and sighed. Perhaps her clothes were not plain enough. She wished for a black and white habit that would leave only her hands and face exposed. Along with that, she could have done with an end to these flutterings in her stomach that had nothing to do with chaste charity.

As if he could read her thoughts, Jed folded his arms across his chest and grinned. "Don't let it trouble you, Katherine. Your virtue is still safe with me as long as you hoard it the way the bees do their honey. I've had my share of stingers today."

"Have you, now," she bristled, not without satisfaction.

"I thought we might take a short ride this afternoon," he suggested. "Unless you want to stick close by the hive."

"I would welcome an outing."

"Then I will be charitable, Katherine, and take you—" he gestured toward the door with a flourish "—out."

Katherine watched him saddle the big buckskin gelding, and she realized she was in for another awkward moment. There was only one horse. Her mules had to be picketed in a string and moved twice each day for grazing. She wasn't sure how far away they were. She could imagine herself riding astride, which was awkward enough, but she and Thomas had never ridden double. Not even when they were children. Jed turned, smiled and beckoned her with a jerk of his head. Temptations seemed to present themselves in battalions with this man!

But Jed gave Katherine the seat in the saddle, and he sat behind the cantle. At least she didn't have to hold on to him and press her cheek against his broad back. His right hand was busy with the reins, and his left was free to touch her shoulder before he pointed to a tree to call Katherine's attention to the black-billed magpie's long green tail feathers. Or he might touch her knee and point out a porcupine waddling through the brush. His mouth was ever close to her ear, ready to whisper a mountain creature's name or simply to keep her blood astir with the warmth of his breath.

They followed a cliff edge trail, and the buckskin's easy gait was marked by the swishing of his hooves in the fallen leaves. Whenever they ducked a low-hanging branch, Jed's chin rested momentarily on Katherine's shoulder. She could almost feel his smile. She welcomed his suggestion that they stop for a rest beside a clear, blue lake. She would take some comfort in putting some space between them.

They sat on a mossy carpet in the shadow of white granite spires that the mind could easily make into the walls of a castle whose battle-loosened stones had been strewn down the mountainside. Golden serviceberry leaves fluttered in the breeze above Jed's head, and their soft shadows played over his face, which was as hard and angular as the granite formations above them. He stretched out, bracing himself on his elbow, and Katherine wondered how he managed to grow more handsome with each day they passed together.

"Tell me more about your travels," she suggested, breaking a long, easy silence. "You have lived among the Cree and the Sioux, and you attended school in St. Louis. Where else have you been?"

"I spent some time in New Orleans," he began. He hiked his brow to acknowledge, "That was where the boy became a man. Then I joined up with some trappers, spent a couple of seasons in Ute Country, south of here. Went back to St. Louis, hired on as a translator with a surveying party. Learned all about how they make those maps I'd once been so curious about. I ended up back on the Red River."

"And were you reunited with your family?"

He nodded. "For a time. My grandfather had died. My brother had become a man. My mother was old before her time—at least in my mind she was. She'd been a young woman when I'd seen her last. I decided to stay and do what I could to make her life easier. That, of course, meant trading with the Company."

"Hudson's Bay," she said, clarifying for herself.

"It smacked of following in my father's footsteps, which I was loath to do, but I longed to live as a Métis again, and the Métis hunt and trade with the Company." In Jed's world, "the Company" needed no clarification.

"But your father was not a trapper," Katherine recalled. "He was more of . . . an administrator?"

"He was an Englishman." Jed's tone hardened. "He looked out for the Company's interests, and the Company looked after him."

"So you need not have felt—"

"I wanted nothing to do with the Hudson's Bay Company. I was accustomed to hunting where I pleased and selling my catch where I could get the best price. Not so for the Métis in the North. There is only the Company."

"Is that why you left?"

He shook his head. "I left because I got into a scrape with one of the Company men on a foray through Sioux Country. A man named Thomas Simpson, who had friends in high places. He had a low opinion of the Métis and had made many enemies, but he was an ambitious man. He liked to explore. Always looking for new territory, new bands of Indians to trade with. In the end he was always forced to deal with us. The Company depends upon my people to be their middlemen. Anyway, my brother, Jean-Paul, was along, and—''

He broke a twig off an overhanging branch as though it had suddenly gotten in his way. He'd already told more of the story than he'd ever discussed with anyone. He remembered the look in Jean-Paul's eyes when Simpson had insulted his parentage for the last time.

''And there was a fight. Simpson was killed.''

''Did you kill him?'' Katherine asked timidly.

''His arrogance killed him.'' He offered a level stare and waited for more questions. Remarkably, she accepted his answer. ''After that trouble, I knew I couldn't go back, so I stayed with the Sioux.''

''And met your wife.''

''And married a fine woman.'' He looked out over the clear blue lake and smiled at the memory of White Earth Woman's face. He had been angry, and she had gentled him. Like clear water, she had cleansed him.

Katherine's eyes were as wide and as blue as the lake. Enough of old memories, he told himself, and he smiled warmly. ''This may be our last chance for a bath, Katherine. What do you say?''

''A bath?''

He sat up. ''In the lake. The air's still warm enough. Won't be too many more days like this.''

''Oh, but, Jed, we'd have to take our—''

''Clothes off.'' The prospect brought him to his feet. ''Most of them, anyway. Put them aside with your foolish modesty. You've got nothing under there I haven't seen, Katherine.''

She stood, ready to argue. ''But I don't intend to have you see any of it again.''

He shrugged. "Suit yourself." With one quick motion, he stripped off his buckskin shirt. "I never pass up a chance for a bath," he told her as he tossed the shirt aside and smiled at the way her chin dropped. "It's my Cree blood," he explained as he shucked his pants. "I don't know how you civilized people stand each other."

Jed's laughter echoed off the lake's sheer rock headwall as he tossed aside his buckskin breeches and ambled down to the water wearing only his breechclout. Katherine huffed and puffed, muttering with indignation. She started after him, then backed off when he dunked himself and emerged with a rousing yelp. She stepped closer, watching him dive and splash around like a sleek otter. His antics were almost jubilant. She undid the top two buttons on her high-necked dress, hesitated and glanced Jed's way again.

The water was clear and deep—too deep for Katherine. Jed disappeared, and the ripples he'd made had drifted ashore before he surfaced again, tossing a spray of droplets off his long hair. He was having a glorious time, while underneath her layers of clothing, her skin was beginning to itch. She paced the shoreline, grumbling more. The itching was all in her mind, she told herself. She was meticulous about her ablutions, and his carefree gamboling was quite obscene.

"Katherine, bring the soap from the pouch that's hanging over the saddle horn."

Soap, too? She stomped up the hill, praying for deliverance from yet another temptation. A bath with soap!

"After I've washed, I'll get out, dry off and turn my back," Jed promised when Katherine returned with the soap. "How would that be?"

"Risky," she said as she tossed the soap.

He caught it just above his head. "You think I'd peek?"

"I think I'd sink." She clasped her hands behind her back and looked down at the scuffed toes of her black shoes. "I can't swim."

"Can't swim? Of course, you can swim."

Without looking up, she shook her head vigorously. She heard the water slosh around him as he pushed closer to shore.

"Take off that dress and come down here. Can you float?" She shook her head again. "Come on. I'll show you how to float. Just keep a few of those underclothes on for your modesty's sake."

"But they'll be wet," she complained as she dispatched three more buttons.

"They'll dry." He stood calf deep at the water's edge and offered his hand. "River crossings are dangerous, Katherine. You haven't even got a fighting chance if you land in the water and can't swim. Come." He beckoned her with a gesture. "No more traveling until you learn."

The steep drop-off permitted no easing into the water. If it had, Katherine would have changed her mind after the first contact between her warm flesh and the icy water. She shrieked, teetered and toppled into Jed's waiting arms. Within three feet of the rocky shore the water was waist deep, but Katherine was already thoroughly soaked.

"Ohh!" Her squeal bounded across the water and bounced off the rocky headwall. "It's too cold!"

Jed laughed. "You'll adjust quickly. Here." He took her hand away from her face and put the soap in her palm. "Let's do this before your lesson."

They passed the soap back and forth between them while Katherine muttered between clacking teeth as she hurriedly washed hair, skin and underwear. By the time

Jed tossed the soap ashore, Katherine had worked up a lather of her own, and her shivering had subsided.

Jed smiled, noting how closely she stuck by him. He liked having her on his home ground, and he told himself it was only because it was so satisfying to turn the tables and have a missionary at his mercy. But she was not the missionary at the moment. She was as uninitiated here as he had once been in her world, and she was waiting for his instruction. He sank at the knees and let the water level climb up his chest as he put his arm around her shoulders.

"Lie back in my arms," he told her. "I'll hold you until you come to trust the water."

She tipped her head back, then caught herself and jerked up. "I don't think I can..."

"Easy. I've got you, Katherine."

She relaxed one muscle at a time, continually testing the look in his eyes for any hint of mischief. The water was cold and hostile, but the proximity of Jed's warm body comforted her. The look in his eyes promised security. Then his arms started to melt away, and she grabbed for his neck.

"You promised to hold me!"

"I am."

"You were letting go," she accused. "I felt it."

"I wasn't going anywhere." The death grip she had on his hair made it impossible. "You're not over your head here, Katherine."

"But almost."

"I won't let anything happen to you. Let's try again."

She let him guide her into position, watching him warily all the while. Other people were able to swim, she reminded herself. She liked rowboats. She enjoyed fishing.

She loved to bathe. Perhaps she could swim, at least a little.

"You must trust me now, Katherine." The wide-eyed look of suspicion she shot Jed made him smile. She had no idea how tempting were the small breasts that rose above the water like two mounds of wet, white clay; her lack of awareness enhanced the enticement. Nature had done the work of an artist, molding cloth and flesh into hard peaks that would taste like melting snow. He might lower his head just a few inches and slide his tongue over the nearest one and...

"All right." Katherine closed her eyes. "I trust you."

Jed swallowed hard. Her hair swirled around her face like a drift of golden aspen leaves. When had the bony waif become such a beauty?

"There's a water spirit," he told her quietly. "In the beginning, all land was pulled from her depths, and since that time she buoys the land we walk upon. Her power puddles in her lakes and races through the veins of earth, which are her rivers. Trust *her*, Katherine."

His voice was as deep as the primal water in his tale. Even when his arms left her, his voice was still there, and she knew those strong arms had not gone far. It was the voice that buoyed her carefully and let her rest in its reassurance. No spirit, her heart told her. No water. The same voice that had kept her alive with French lullabies now kept her afloat. With her eyes tightly shutting out the water that lapped against her temples, she gave a thin-lipped but triumphant smile.

"*Voilà!* You see, *ma petite*? You are as light as a feather. The water—"

The spell was short-lived. She jackknifed, grabbed for his neck, and he caught her in a protective embrace. This time she steadied herself without grabbing handfuls of his hair. They grinned at each other, two slick-haired water creatures bobbing with their chins just above the water.

"I did it, didn't I? I floated!"

"You did."

"But you helped."

"I let go. You were on your own."

"But only for a second."

"You were floating, Katherine. Pretty as you please." Her eyelashes were spiky, and a drop of water rolled off the end of her nose. Beneath the water their bodies brushed against each other, and she was as pretty as *he* pleased.

She laughed. She still had no idea how pleasing she was, and he hoped she wouldn't guess. "What is the next step?"

"Next we get out and dry off." He touched her pouty lower lip with his forefinger. "Your lips are turning blue."

"I'm not cold now."

"Yes, you are," he argued as he carried her out of the water. "You just don't know it yet."

"I did well, didn't I?" she marveled, forgetting all but her achievement.

But Jed was acutely aware of the arms that lay easily around his neck and the cool, wet cloth pressed between her skin and his. "You did very well," he assured huskily. "Next summer, you will be diving like a beaver."

"Next summer?" She stared, then drew herself up as though recognition of who he was and who she was was just dawning on her. He lowered the arm supporting her legs, and she slid along his body until her feet touched the ground. His heart settled with them.

"I'll be—" She stepped back and hugged herself against a sudden chill. Her voice reflected the coolness. "I shall be in the Place of the Rye Grass next summer."

"Perhaps someone there will teach you."

"Oh, no, I don't think so." She shook her head quickly. "I hardly think there would be time for such things, what with all the work that must be done among the . . . the Indian people there."

"All the more reason." He snatched up her dress and moved farther up the slope to retrieve her shawl. Her pathetic shivering drew him back quickly. "The people in that country—the Cayuse, the Yakima, the Flathead—they love the water. They are fishermen. The women—"

He draped her shawl over her shoulders, and she pulled it snugly around her. "I don't intend to embrace their ways. I intend for them—"

"To take up yours?" He handed her the dress. "Best you learn to swim, Katherine. You may be netting salmon next summer to earn your keep."

"Oh, no, not salmon. I intend to become a fisher of men."

"Best you learn to swim," he repeated, then nodded toward a screen of serviceberry bushes. "Take your wet clothes off before the chill takes hold."

"I think it already has."

Jed turned away as Katherine disappeared into the bushes. He gathered his own clothes and sought no hiding place as he stripped away his breechclout and slipped into his buckskins. If she caught herself spying on him, he knew she would scold herself and hide her face. Every time she caught herself being a woman, she took refuge behind a wall of shame, and then she became righteous. The cycle angered him. How often would it be necessary to prove to himself that she was not truly a woman? Best to be rid of her, he reminded himself; but he had built up an immunity to his own reminders.

Katherine emerged shyly and spread out her wet clothes to dry in the sun. It felt strange to be dressed only in the outer half of her costume. Jed lounged on a large, flat rock, sunning himself like a mountain cat while he nibbled on pinches of something from a pouch. Katherine followed the urgings of her empty stomach and moved to join him.

"Come around the other side," he invited with a directional gesture. "That's the way up."

She negotiated the natural rock steps, and he gave her a hand at the top. "Hungry?" he asked as they sat down together.

"Oh, yes."

He offered the pouch. "Pemmican. Dried meat ground with tallow and cherries. It will fight off that chill."

It tasted gamy and sweet. Katherine chewed slowly, letting her tongue adjust to the unusual texture. The second bite was better than the first. "I can see how it would," she said finally. "It's very rich."

"Winter food," he said. "Hunters' provisions. Fewer of your people would end up boiling their horses' hides for food if they carried pemmican on this westering of theirs. The fur companies trade for it."

She watched Jed help himself to another bite. Boiled horsehide? People couldn't eat leather.

"Those people who deserted you will run into winter, sure as hell. They'll run out of flour and fatback, and the game will be scarce. They'll eat anything," Jed predicted. "But, of course, you have nothing to learn from the Indian."

Katherine glanced away. "I don't mean...that I have *nothing* to learn."

"Mon Dieu," he marveled. "A crack in the wall."

"But these heathen spirits you speak of, Jed. They're—"

"The water spirit?"

"You are a Christian man," she insisted. "Your enlightenment was hard won, and you must not slip back into the darkness by—"

"I am Métis, Katherine. Not English, nor French, nor Cree. My blood is mixed. If I try to be English, they remind me that I am Cree. If I try to be Cree, they tell me I am French. I am all of these, or I am nothing. Don't try to tell me which part to choose. I've tried, and I've learned. When I deny any part, I slip back."

"But you cannot be Christian *and* heathen."

"Why not?"

"Because . . . it isn't right."

"Then I won't be right," he decided as he rested his head in his hand and considered the wisps of white clouds above his head. "But I'll be whole."

Katherine tucked her shawl behind her head and let the rock's hoarded heat warm her back while the sun warmed her face. It was hard to understand a man like Jed. He was not like Thomas. Whenever Jed's inconsistencies bewildered her, she tried to recall the comforting singularness of Thomas's mission. Thomas was purity itself—pure of blood, pure of mind, pure of soul—like those white clouds that slid across the blue sky. Thomas would have known what to say to Jed, but Katherine could think of nothing but trivial things.

"Is your name Jedediah, like the prophet?"

"My name is Jed," he said.

His words sounded guarded, and she wondered why. "Surely you must have been christened something more—"

"Jed West," he clipped. "Nothing more."

"But your brother's name is Jean-Paul," she recalled, attempting to pronounce it with the same fluid accent Jed had used. "It sounds as though your grandfather might have named him."

"He did."

"Did your father name you?"

"My father called me 'boy.'" She turned her head and found him staring at her. "What's wrong with just Jed?"

"Nothing. I only wondered whether there was more."

"No more than what you see, Katherine."

What she saw was Jed. In that moment there were no other names. There was no other man, and there were no more memories. The only eyes in the world were dark and compelling, arresting. All thoughts but one: he was going to kiss her. She lifted her chin and parted her lips willingly. She didn't want to think about anything else but the taste of him on her lips.

He shifted to his hip and took her in his arms. He willed her arms around his neck, and suddenly they were there. He felt at once powerful and tender. He pressed his body against hers and eased his tongue past her lips, showing her how gentle his invasion of her body would be. He moved his hand along her back, kneading as he went, bidding her relax. He would be good to her. His hand cupped her buttocks, and he applied only a subtle pressure. Her hips settled against him, and he groaned and sought her breast.

Oh, she felt wonderful. So full and tight and tingly. His hand molded itself to her breast, and she felt it swell, giving him more to hold. His palm made slow, dizzying circles, and her nipple became tight and achy inside her single layer of fabric. Then his fingers shaped it into a nub. She pressed tighter, hoping to relieve the delicate throbbing she felt between her thighs. She whispered his name.

"Not here, *ma petite*." He kissed the quivering pulse point on her temple. "This rock would leave you bruised."

Not here, rang in her ears. *Not now. Not yet.* She pinched her eyes shut, and her face burned hot with shame.

"I would love you more gently, Katherine. On the mossy bed beneath the—"

"My flesh is weak," she confessed. She would not open her eyes. She could not look him in the face. "Oh, this terrible feeling! It's worse with you than it was with Thomas."

"Terrible feeling?"

Katherine nodded furiously. "The feeling that comes when you... when you..."

"When I touch you?"

"Or kiss me. Or... or just..."

"There's nothing wrong with that feeling, Katherine."

It was the low timbre of his voice that comforted her more than his words. She tightened her arms around his neck and hid her face beneath his chin. "Not for a man," she whispered, "but a woman should never let that feeling happen to her. It's wrong. I'm sure of it. A woman—"

"It isn't wrong." Jed found himself holding her the way he had when she had grieved. It made him uncomfortable, but he did it anyway. "A woman feels pleasure, too. You were married, Katherine. Surely you—"

"Thomas was concerned for my safety. He said the journey would be difficult enough, and that if I were to become... if he were to... get me with child..."

"He never..." He felt the shake of her head against his neck. "Not even once?"

"Thomas was a saintly man."

"He'd have to be."

"He *did* love me." She would not tell this man how she had been kissed by her husband, and how she had shamefully turned to him in their bed and asked for more.

"He was right," Jed admitted. "A man's seed can grow to cause a woman's death."

Katherine's face emerged from her place of refuge, and she saw the shadow of remembered pain in his eyes. "Oh, no, Jed." She forgot herself and touched his cheek. "You were not the cause of her death. You gave her your child. You had no way of knowing—"

"She was my wife. She wanted that child."

He held her, but he avoided her eyes. *Look at me,* she thought. *I'm a woman, too.*

"I tried to help her when the baby wouldn't come, but I failed. Perhaps if I had been a 'saintly man'..."

"Oh, Jed, there is always the terrible specter lurking with the joy. Every woman knows that." Without thinking she brushed the damp hair back from his temple. "I never knew my own mother. My younger brother lived, but she died giving him birth. My father remarried and gave us a stepmother."

He drew back, but not altogether away from her. It took two of her small hands to hold one of his. They sat together in silence on the big, flat rock and watched the sun's slanted rays burnish the lake's soaring headwall. Katherine cradled Jed's hand in her lap and thought about how easy it was to be close to him, to comfort and be comforted.

"I cannot spend the winter with you, Jed," she said finally. "I must be moving on soon ... for both our sakes, I think."

"I can't take you to the Whitman Mission before spring."

"I know. But you can take me to Fort Hall."

"You would winter there?" She nodded, and his voice hardened as he withdrew his hand from hers. "I won't harm you, Katherine. You cannot think that I would—"

"If I stay, we both know what would happen."

"Then perhaps it's right that it should happen."

She knew—if she allowed him to—he could convince her that it must happen; but never would she believe that it was right. She closed her eyes and drew a long, slow breath. "I have Thomas's work to do. I can't be another man's woman. You have no use for missionaries, and I—"

"I can't stay at Fort Hall, Katherine, and there would be no one to protect you. At least here, you have no one to contend with but me."

"I have been to Fort Hall. At least there is another woman there."

"You wouldn't be safe there. There would be men who—" Her innocence rankled. It made her more vulnerable than any grown woman had a right to be. "You're safe with me. Maybe not *safe*, but better off than you might be—as safe as a woman can expect to be in this country."

"I know." But she was not safe with her own feelings. Her resolve was slipping. She was losing sight of her mission, and she could not let that happen. "Still, I cannot stay with you, Jed. If you would take me to Fort Hall, I would pay you whatever—"

Jed's back stiffened at the proposal. "I have said no." He stood and pulled Katherine to her feet. "Now, there's an end to it. Get your clothes. I have my own work to do."

Chapter Five

The last of Indian summer passed with September. Early October brought thick morning frosts. A wafer of ice covered the water in the rain barrel until noon, and the last of the berries were exposed to the night's hard freeze. Katherine had learned to forage for edible wild plants, and now she helped to smoke fish and jerk venison in preparation for winter.

Late autumn was the beginning of Jed's busy season. It was the time when he hunted for fur and meat. He traded both. With his Indian partner, whom Katherine had not met, he traded in the fall and spring, but he did as little business as possible with the Hudson's Bay Company. Katherine discovered that the best way to put a damper on a conversation with Jed was to mention a Hudson's Bay Company outpost, particularly Fort Hall or Fort Boise, and *most* particularly in connection with her wish to spend the winter at either place. At the suggestion, he would become reticent or simply walk away.

It angered her when Jed walked away, and he did it more and more often. Sometimes he used the old wood-chopping ploy, but other times she would look up from her work and find him staring at her, and then he would be gone for a while. She wanted to tell him that she struggled, too. If she wished to leave him, why should it anger her when he left her alone? She knew why, of course. The weakness she felt for him brought her to the verge of tears at times, and when he looked at her the way he often did, his dark eyes hollow with hunger, she wanted to confess her own longings and regrets. But she knew there were things best left unsaid. It wouldn't do for him to know that she hurt inside whenever he guided her hands to teach her the technique for filleting meat or stretching a hide. They were mundane tasks made exquisite by the touch of his hand.

That sweet ache was reason enough for her to leave, but when Jed announced that he would be tying a bell on her lead mule and turning the team loose for the winter, Katherine panicked. What if they strayed too far to be found in the spring? What if the Indians stole them? Without the mules, how would she complete her journey?

Let them go, a part of her said.

She told herself not to listen.

The mules would take care of themselves, Jed said, and nobody else would want them.

That wasn't true, Katherine told herself as she slipped away from the cabin in the late afternoon. The team and wagon were her link with Thomas's mission; she couldn't risk letting her husband's dream die. She would show Jed that she was capable of tending to the mules herself. They were her responsibility, after all.

She found them picketed a couple of miles downstream from the cabin. They did consume a lot of grass, and soon that grass would be covered with snow. Maybe she didn't need all six, she reasoned as she untied the first lead rope. Maybe four would be enough. Maybe one, if she could ride him. If she could just keep one...

"Come on, Jack," she coaxed as she leaned into the mule's shoulder. "You're stepping on the rope. Step back, please."

Politeness failed to impress Jack. He planted his hoof on Katherine's foot. Pain shot through her already shoe-pinched toes, and she screamed. Jack hopped off her foot and kicked up his back legs, sending Katherine on a roll off the embankment and into the swift, icy stream.

Katherine sputtered and shrieked as her dress and coat soaked up their fill of water. She scrambled to find footing, but the current and the weight of her clothing dragged her down. She bumped along, swallowing water with every terrified sound she made until she was washed against a rock that was large enough for a mooring. She hugged it with both arms as she coughed and gasped for breath. Her knees dragged against the rocky streambed, and she thought if she could stand, the water would only be waist deep. She could wade out. It wasn't necessary to be able to swim. She assessed the distance. Oh, Lord, the bank looked so far away, and there was so much water—such fast-moving water! She could do it. God help her, she *could* make it.

The current knocked her over on her first try, and she was lucky to get her arms around her rock again. Lord, it was cold! Already her head pounded with it, and her fingers were numb. She had to stay calm and try to think. She'd lost one shoe. If she could rid herself of some of the rest of her clothes...but for that she would need a free hand, and she didn't have one. Lord, Lord, she didn't dare let go.

Yes, she did. She dared what she had to dare, and she wasn't going to die on this rock. She found her footing again and tried to balance herself between the rock and the current. One hand. That was all she needed.

In her sodden black coat she might almost have been mistaken for a small bear by anyone but Jed West. His blood had been pounding in his veins long before he caught up with her, but the sight of her tangled in yards of fabric in the middle of the stream was heart-stopping. He swung down from his saddle and tore off his coat.

"Hang on to the rock, Katherine!" He peeled off his shirt, panicking the moment he lost sight of her. "I'm coming after you," he shouted as he tossed the shirt aside. His moccasins went next, followed by his pants. By the time he skittered sideways down the embankment, he was tossing off woolen drawers. He hit the water stark naked.

Her face was all eyes and wet hair. She reached for him before he was close enough to catch her, and he dived for her. The current took them both, but Jed reached for Katherine's anchoring rock and stopped them both from slipping downstream. He steaded himself, slung her over his shoulder and slogged ashore.

She coughed and gagged as he let her slide to the ground. He made sure she wasn't choking before he tore into the buttons on her coat. "Help me, Katherine," he pleaded, his chest heaving with his effort to catch his breath. "Got to... get these clothes off. You'll freeze."

She shivered violently, fumbling for her fastenings, but her fingers were numb and useless. An eerie lightness settled over her, and the worry that she couldn't seem to do anything right became less pressing. She wondered how her teeth could be so noisy, and when she started to comment on it, she realized that Jed's teeth were chattering worse than hers.

"Where are your c-clothes?"

He managed to pull off her coat and tackle the dress despite his terrible shaking. "They're dry. Try to get yourself out of this. *Vite!* Qu-quickly. We need...f-fire."

She grabbed his arm as he drew away, and he saw the unreasoning fear in her face. *Dieu,* her face was milky, her lips blue. "Do as I say." He forced himself to speak calmly. "I'll build a fire."

Jed collected a few sticks along with his clothes. Out of the corner of his eye he watched Katherine struggle with useless fingers. He pulled his pants back on and pulled the rest of her clothes off almost simultaneously. He wrapped her in his coat, which was cut from a four-point wool trade blanket, and he pulled his buckskin shirt over his head. His strike-a-light pouch was in the possibles bag hanging on his saddle. The sun had already slipped below the horizon, and the temperature was dropping.

He willed steadiness into his hands as he struck the flint and got a spark. Dry grass tinder gave itself up to a life-giving blaze. Jed turned to find his woolen drawers still lying on the ground, and he snatched them up and offered them to Katherine, who had curled herself into a ball inside his green and black coat. Wet yellow hair, terror-stricken blue eyes and purple toes were all he could see of her. He reached under the coat, pulled out one leg and jammed it into the gray drawers.

"What kind of fool thing are you trying to do here, Katherine? You nearly got yourself killed."

She couldn't stop shivering, and she'd already bitten her tongue twice.

"Damn it, answer me! Have you lost your mind? What are you doing out here?"

"M-m-moving the m-mules."

"I told you I'd look after them. What the hell . . . how did you manage to land in the water?"

"M-mule stepped on my f-foot."

"Look at you." He shook his head in disgust. "With all those wet clothes weighing you down, you were as helpless as a turtle on its back." He moved her closer to the fire and sat her down with her back to the flames, which he hoped would dry her hair quickly. "Rub your legs and feet."

"What about you? Your lips are b-blue."

"If we both take a chill over those mules, I swear I'll skin 'em out for moccasin soles." He positioned himself between Katherine and the cold night wind, and he reached behind her to spread her hair over her back.

"Jed, you c-can't let my m-mules go. I have no other way t-to...t-to..."

"Be quiet about those mules now. Nobody's going anywhere except back to the cabin as soon as I get you dry and figure out the best way to bundle you up." He shivered. "Damn, it's cold."

The ride back to the cabin seemed endless. Jed caught the wind in his face, and Katherine huddled behind him while the buckskin horse picked its way through the dark woods. They did not speak of what she'd done or of how cold they were, but the image of her body being swept away by the icy current burned vividly in Jed's mind, while the aftershock of a close brush with death coursed through Katherine.

The embers in the fireplace came to life with added fuel. Katherine dressed in a flannel nightgown and brought a blanket to lay over Jed's back while he poked the flaming logs into place.

"Sit here," he ordered, and she knelt next to him on the fur rug. He put his arm around her and brought her under the blanket with him. They shivered together.

Jed took her small feet, one in each hand, and gently manipulated her toes. Pain shot from her toes to her knees, and Katherine stifled a whimper. Jed would be angry with her now, and he had a right to be. She blinked back stinging tears.

"I know it hurts." With both hands he caressed her feet in a way that would have been almost erotic if she weren't in such pain. He had cut up his saddle blanket and bound her feet, but now her pain became his own.

"I thought if I could handle the mules myself, you wouldn't turn them loose," she said, as if he had demanded an explanation.

"I would find them in the spring," he said quietly. "They have to be free to forage through the winter or they'll starve."

"But I thought . . ." She had thought of leaving. Every time the thought of him stirred her baser instincts, she tried to replace it with the only noble idea she seemed capable of conceiving—that of continuing her journey. And he knew that. She glanced up at Jed and wondered why there was no anger in his eyes.

"You're probably wishing for one of those switches," she said. "I've behaved like a schoolchild today."

"Move your toes for me." He nodded when they wiggled against his palm. "Good. The pain will pass soon." He looked steadily into her eyes. "A man might punish his wife for being unfaithful or lazy. You are neither."

"Nor am I your wife."

"And you're no child, although you seem willing to impress me as one. Why won't you be a woman, Katherine?" They looked at each other for a moment. Katherine couldn't answer, and Jed didn't want her to. If she had reasons, they wouldn't please him. "In any case," he said finally, "I have no thought of punishing you. It's good to have you safe."

Katherine was stunned. Her chest felt tight, and her throat tingled with an emotion she couldn't name.

"Thank you," she said, her voice husky. She swallowed hard. "It *is* thanks to you that I'm safe."

"And perhaps your god, who led me to the right place."

Her eyes widened. "Do you believe that?"

"Of course." He smiled and brushed a wisp of hair back from her forehead. "How could I not believe it? This was the second time."

"So you see? I'm to complete this journey. I'm meant to do Thomas's work."

"I would read the signs differently," he said with a chuckle. Time would tell. They had all winter. "You're still shivering."

"I can't stop trembling on the inside." She wrapped her arms around her middle. "I think it must be the fear."

"I think it must be chills. My people always bathe until the ice prevents it, but your method was unusual, Katherine."

"Perhaps some tea," she suggested, shifting her feet underneath her. "And there's corn bread from—"

"Stay by the fire," he said, and he tucked his half of the blanket around her.

Within a few moments he had brewed a hot drink, and he returned to Katherine's side with two steaming mugs and a plate of corn bread. "This is strong medicine," he warned, "so sip it slowly and eat something with it."

She tasted from the mug while he took his corner of the blanket back. "What is this?"

"Something to warm you inside."

"Spirits?"

He laughed. "Some say so."

"I don't hold with—"

"It's mostly tea, Katherine. Trade whiskey has its uses, and chasing a chill away is one of them." He sipped from his cup as he watched the fire across the rim. He had intended his advice for himself, as well. Sip slowly and eat. Meditatively he added, "It's also useful for getting a season's worth of furs from the Cree for whatever the traders wish to spare."

Katherine scowled. "The traders get the Indians intoxicated before they trade with them?"

"I don't deal in whiskey anymore, and I seldom use it myself. Not since . . ." Not since he had tried to drown his grief in the stuff and discovered for himself that it would be the death of him. "But it's common practice to start a trade meeting with a gift of whiskey or rum. My grandmother said that life had changed so much that people wouldn't know how to get along without trade goods anymore. But the whiskey is the worst."

"Bad for the Métis, also?"

"Too often it is, unless the Métis is half-frozen after giving his coat away. Then it serves a medicinal purpose."

"It's the devil's own brew." She shivered again and took another sip. "But it does feel like fire inside, and right now—"

"Right now you must eat." He broke off a piece of bread and held it to her lips. "Otherwise you will soon be flying high as the moon."

With the tip of her tongue Katherine gathered crumbs from the corner of her mouth. A sip of tea made the bread slide easily down her throat. She wondered at Jed's sly smile. "You shouldn't be half-frozen," she chided. "After all, your people bathe in the rivers until ice covers them." She giggled. "I mean the rivers, not the people. I would hate to see you covered with ice, Jed."

His smile reached his eyes. "You would be safe with me then."

"I am safe with you now."

"Perhaps." He helped himself to a piece of corn bread. "But if what happened today is any indication, you're the one who's likely to get me into trouble. I had no blanket, nothing but the clothes on my back."

Her smile faded, and she glanced down at her cup. "I know I've caused you trouble, Jed. I do hate to cause trouble. My stepmother predicted that I would never be anything but a burden to a man, and I'm afraid it's true."

A sip of fortified tea helped her continue. "I was a burden to her, you see. My father is a merchant, a very busy man. After my mother died, he needed a wife, and Abigail needed a husband. She did not need another woman's children, a fact which she pointed out to me many times. She also said that schooling was wasted on a girl, that I was too plain to be of interest to anyone but a preacher, that if I married Thomas I would be poor and miserable and that we should not come looking for charity from my father." The recitation ended bitterly. "I was never able to please my stepmother."

"Did your father approve of this journey?"

"He approved of my marriage. He said that if he were a younger man, he would go westering himself."

"To be rid of his wife," Jed surmised.

"Oh, no, Abigail is very beautiful, and my father dotes on her. No, he believes there are fortunes to be made here, and he says that with the American settlers coming in droves, the Oregon Country will soon become a territory of the United States. The British presence is limited to trading posts and—"

"And the few Métis families that the Hudson's Bay Company has managed to resettle." Jed raised his cup in acknowledgment. "Your father is right. The Company has set limits on trapping in the North Country, but along the Snake River they've encouraged their people to trap everything in sight. They want to drive out the American trappers and the free traders. They don't see that it isn't the trappers they must worry about. It's the settlers. This joint occupation of the Oregon Country that the British and the Americans have cooked up is about to come to an end. The American settlers will see to it."

"But I thought you hated the Company." Katherine frowned as she studied the enigmatic expression on Jed's face. "The British claim to this land is Hudson's Bay's claim, and the United States is simply extending . . ." She looked at him, puzzling. "Whose side are you on?"

"I'm on Jed West's side."

"But which country?" she insisted.

"Which country?" He finished his chunk of bread and licked the crumbs from his thumb. Then he looked at Katherine and wondered whether his explanation would mean anything to her. He shook his head. "I don't belong to a country. I belong to the Métis, the people who hunt and trap and trade in the Red River Valley."

She could not know what it meant to be one of them. The need to return to his people had burned in him throughout his boyhood. He had known when he was home again. Like the Plains tribes, the Métis followed the buffalo in the summer. He remembered the excitement of the great hunts, the smoky taste of the celebration and the squeal of wooden wheels as the caravan of meat and hide-laden Red River carts snaked its way to a trading rendezvous.

"I want to go back someday," he confided solemnly. "I have never belonged anywhere else."

The sound of his yearning made her heart ache. "Why can't you go home, Jed? Is it because of this man who was killed?"

"It isn't a matter to trouble yourself with, Katherine." He shook his head, giving the dream a final dismissal. "It's an old grief, best left to die if it will."

"If it will?" She leaned closer to him. "Were you accused of this killing? I don't believe you are a murderer." She watched him sip from his cup, and he kept his eyes on the fire as though he hadn't heard her. "Was it your brother who killed that man?"

"Simpson was—" Jed scowled at the flames. "Simpson was who he was. That's all that matters." He turned to her, and the fire blazed in his eyes. "I want you to forget that I told you any of this."

Katherine blinked. "Why have you trusted me with...even this much?"

"I don't know." He knew that he wanted to tell her even more. He wanted to tell her the man had not died by his hand. Katherine would believe him. She believed him already, but he wanted to give her his word. The word of a fugitive mixed-blood who had no country. He tossed the blanket from his shoulder and stood abruptly. "How is the fire coming?"

"The fire?"

He smiled and reached for her cup. "The one inside you. Does it need more fuel?"

"Oh, my." She laid her hand over the tucked yoke of her high-necked nightgown. "I'm feeling warm in some places. My face, for example." Her bright-eyed giggle surprised them both. "This tea of yours makes me giddy."

"Then we'll go easy. Eat some more bread."

Katherine took a pinch of bread from the pan, tipped her head back and dropped it into her mouth. While she ate, the fire teased her. In it she saw outlandish images of a beautiful, sun-burnished man without a stitch of clothing to protect him from the cold. "You were certainly quite something today," she told the fire absently.

"Quite what?" Jed sat beside her again and handed her another cup of steaming brew. The light in her eyes delighted him, and he wondered whether he should have been more generous with the whiskey. It wouldn't take much more to give him the same advantage the trader had when he offered the whiskey first, then the bargain.

"*Not* savage," she assured him solemnly. "I would not say 'savage.'"

Amusement agitated one corner of his mouth. "What would you say, then?"

"Quite civilized, I think."

He laughed merrily. "I was buck naked, Katherine. Is that what you truly meant by *quite something*?"

She shook her head, waving the notion away. "You did the civilized thing. You always do. You are a gentleman, Jed West, no matter how you dress." Her eyes flirted with him as she sipped her tea. She giggled again. "No matter how you *un*dress. No matter how you wear your hair or what kind of river spirits you worship, I say you are a gentleman."

"I shall add you to my list of references."

"Do." She sat up straight and cradled her cup in both hands. "Should the occasion ever arise . . . should I ever be called upon to witness for you, be it at the very gates of heaven, I shall speak loud and long on your behalf, Jed West. Truly. I shall put my whole heart into it."

"That's comforting."

He set her aglow. She loved the way he smiled at her through his dark eyes. "But I could do a better job if I knew your Christian name," she teased. "I've thought and thought of what it might be. There's more to it than 'Jed,' although Jed is a wonderful name. But there's more.'' She tipped her head to one side and considered the question. "I cannot guess what it is, but I think it must be French, and it must roll off the tongue the way some of your words do sometimes.''

"The way yours are right now?''

"No, no, you have a lovely way..." She smiled dreamily. "You have a voice that sounds like...like a river flowing deep in its channel.''

"Hmm. Heaven's gatekeeper should be impressed when he hears this.''

"It's a soothing sound. I remember hearing it when I was sick.''

"Do you remember what I said?''

"Most of the time I didn't understand, but it didn't matter. As long as the voice was there, I knew I was not alone.'' He had been as close then as he was now, but she had known only the voice. Now her head was filled with the buckskin and wood smoke scent of him and the beauty of his expressive eyes and the memory of the way his lips tasted when he pressed them against hers.

"I remember what I said.'' He took her cup from her hands without taking his eyes off hers. "I asked you to live and tell me your name.''

"And I did.'' She was so heady with the sense of him that she thought it was within her power to choose life anew, even now. "It's Katherine.''

"Your face invites a kiss, Katherine.''

"I know.''

He set their cups aside and lifted his hand to her forehead, touching her hairline with tentative fingertips. She raised her chin, and her blue eyes dazzled him. A kiss was all she invited, he told himself. Something to soothe her, the way his voice did. And all he wanted was to feel any part of her skin against any part of his. That would be enough.

She closed her eyes in hopes that his lips would touch hers straightaway, but they did not. She felt the soft brush of his nose and the warmth of his breath against her cheek, his cheek against her lips, then his lips lightly sweeping her forehead. She could not breathe for wanting his kiss, but the feel of his face was everywhere on hers, and the heat of it made her tingle with fever.

"Your skin is soft," he whispered. "Everywhere."

She had no thought of protesting; when at last he took her lips with his, she had no thoughts at all. His tongue sought hers, and she parted her lips to accommodate him. Breath, heat, tingling, fever—such headiness. Life thrummed everywhere inside her. Everywhere!

They reached for each other, seeking to hold and be held, and their kiss spoke of needs that neither would confess aloud. She was unaware that she had moved into his lap. He was aware of nothing but the sweet taste of her mouth, the feel of her long back and the feminine swell of her hips beneath her flannel nightgown. He ducked his head, searched for the pulse in her neck with his lips and knew the runaway excitement in her blood.

"My skin is warm," she said softly. "You've made it warm."

"I'll make it as warm as it is soft," he promised, and he whisked his shirt over his head and tossed it aside. "Everywhere."

"Everywhere." She wanted that, yes, and she wanted to warm him, too. He loosed the buttons on her nightgown, and she remembered the way her nipples had ached in the cold, but now—oh, such an aching as this she had never felt. She glimpsed his wistful smile before she tasted his lips again. She savored his tongue, and she sucked his very breath when his hand, his fingers, his thumbs, just his thumbs brought her nipples such an irresistible ache.

"I'll keep the wind from you, Katherine."

"Oh, Jed, your hands..."

"I would feel yours, too." He took them from his shoulders and placed her palms against his chest. "Follow my lead. Warm me."

His chest was hard, and his skin was hot. He laid her back on the plush fur carpet and touched her, kissed her, laved her breasts until her head spun with yearning. He pushed her nightgown above her hips and caressed her belly. Of their own accord her hips moved with the motion of his hand.

"There's a warm place for me here, Katherine," he whispered. "Your hips invite me inside."

"But will you come?"

He gave a low chuckle. "Your hips promise to see to it that I do. But *I* promise... not too quickly."

"Yes, quickly. Before...before..." She strained against his hand and buried her hands in his hair.

Before the whiskey wore off? he wondered. Before she changed her mind? Before someone pecked out heaven's window?

"Don't leave me like this again," she pleaded.

"Again?"

"Don't wait. Please."

"Katherine, look at me." But her eyes were shut tight, and her mouth trembled. Had the whiskey done its worst? Did she beg for release from a dead man? Jed touched her hair and passed his thumb over the damp sheen on her forehead. "I'm not your husband, Katherine."

She opened her eyes and looked longingly at his face. "I know who you are."

"I won't have you pretending I'm someone else."

"There is no one . . . Jed, please."

Tomorrow she would tell him there was. There was the memory, and there was the memory's mission. And then Jed would become the subject of her nightly confessions. He wanted her, but not this way. He wanted no whiskey fog filling her brain. She whimpered and touched his belly the way he had asked her to only moments ago, but he stayed her hand. If tomorrow she but touched his face, he swore he would make her his.

But he'd brought her this far. He moved his hand lower and found the warm, wet cove she'd offered him. She stiffened at first, but his intimate caress had its way, and she gave herself over. For tonight, that would serve.

"Jed—"

"I know. I'll take care of you, *ma petite*."

He always did.

Jed lay awake long after Katherine had fallen asleep in his arms. In the interest of moderation, he'd done himself several disservices this night. He hadn't gotten drunk or availed himself of his bed or satisfied his needs with a willing woman. Had he taken advantage of some combination of those opportunities, he would have been dozing contentedly. He wondered where he had come by this troublesome conscience of his.

She was the missionary, after all. She was the one with all the regulations. He'd pulled her away from death's door more than once. Surely he had a right to expect something in return. Deliverance, he thought, and he considered the woman in his arms. Deliverance was her special province.

Deliver me, then, Katherine. Deliver me from loneliness. Deliver me from exile. Be my woman and let me love you the way you need to be loved. It is not your destiny to make over other people's lives. None but mine. Make my life over, Katherine.

At daybreak Katherine discovered that she had moved to the bed, but her last recollection was of the fur rug near the hearth. And the fire. And the warm pillow Jed's shoulder had made. She sat up and looked around her. Jed was gone.

Oh, that whiskey was the devil's brew. It made her head ache and her stomach feel queasy, but it hadn't erased the memory of the way she had behaved. She deserved this punishment and more. There was a wickedness inside her. She was a daughter of Eve. Jed had reminded her that he was not her husband, but that had not mattered to her. Guilt pressed hard against her chest as she heaved herself from the bed, washed and dressed. She pulled her hair back painfully tight and pinned it into a plain knot. For further penance she added nothing to flavor the gruel that she prepared for breakfast.

A gust of cold wind chased the hearth-side warmth into the corners of the cabin. Katherine set the spider skillet on the table. The flour sack she'd twisted around the handle slid to the floor as she watched Jed close the door. They exchanged an age-old look between a man and a woman who shared concerns.

He had come home.

She was waiting with food on the table.

He was a welcome sight.

She'd been on his mind all the while he'd been gone.

It was more honesty than Katherine could tolerate long, and it was she who turned away first.

"I took the mules upstream and tied a bell on the lead," he told her. "They won't be hard to find. They've been feeding here long enough to make this their territory."

He tossed his brown fur cap on a peg and shed his striped wool coat. He was hoping for a greeting, even a comment from Katherine as he sat on the edge of the bed and unlaced his knee-high moccasins. He reached under the bed for a low-top pair. He was waiting, but she was silent.

"It's bitter out there this morning," he told her finally. "Cold enough to snow."

"Breakfast is ready," she offered in a small voice. She listened to the chair legs drag against the earthen floor. It was only gruel. She held her breath, almost hoping he would complain.

"A hot meal waiting on the table. Can't ask for more than that on a day like this."

Her slow sigh seemed to her suspiciously like relief; she deserved no relief. "I made tea."

"Let's have some honey with it." He tipped his chair onto its back legs and reached for the pouch, which hung close at hand.

"You must have gone out during the night," she said as she took her seat. She served up the gruel with a wooden dipper, filling his bowl to the brim.

"I did." He sipped tea and enjoyed the warmth of it as it slid down inside. "Couldn't sleep. I decided to take care of those damn mules before they caused us any more problems."

"You needn't have troubled yourself during the night," she said tightly.

Jed looked up from his bowl. "Did something happen while I was gone?"

"No."

He added honey to his tea and dribbled it over the gruel. The rich, golden color reminded him of the way her hair had spilled over his arm the night before, and he smiled. "I picked you up off the floor and put you in bed before I left. You were sleeping pretty soundly."

"I was besotted," she said with disgust.

"You were tired. You needed rest." He watched her dip her spoon into her bowl. *You needed more than rest, Katherine.* He watched her toy with the thick mush, and he waited, but she did not look up at him. He forgot his food, his drink, his next breath. Instead, he watched and willed. *Tell me how it was with you, Katherine. Give me leave to tell you how it was with me.*

"You might have taken a chill," she said quietly. "Going out again after... after the evening's ordeal."

"Ordeal?"

"I noticed that your hair was frozen stiff when we got back to the cabin last night."

He'd suffered overmuch from stiffness last night, and the notion that she'd taken notice of the least discomforting aspect of it made him smile. He imagined her touching his hair and laughing. "It didn't get quite dry."

"And you gave me your hat."

"But I kept my moccasins, and your feet nearly froze."

Her spoon clattered against her bowl, and her eyes were wide with an urgency she could not name. "You gave me almost everything else you had, when you would have been within your rights to... to make me... to leave me without—"

"You were in need, Katherine," he said, his voice a steady counterpoint to hers. Their eyes exchanged a poignant acknowledgment. "I could not leave you that way."

She sighed. "No, I don't suppose you could."

They ate in silence. Katherine cleared away the dishes, cleaned them, stacked them, and when there was nothing left to keep her busy, she turned to the fire. She could not look Jed in the eye. He moved quietly, but she felt him standing close at her back. She wanted to feel his hand on her shoulder. Oh, Lord, even the mountain of shame she felt was not enough to put a stop to the awful yearning inside her. His touch might lift the shame. Or redouble it.

"Do you wish to finish what was started last night?" she asked stiffly.

"I have made no such demands on you, Katherine."

Her shoulders sagged. "I know. I was the one who—"

"I was the one who brewed the tea."

"It wasn't just the whiskey." She turned to him. "There was such wantonness in me, Jed. I tempted you, and you . . . you took yourself out into the cold night, while I slept, too intoxicated to feel the full measure of disgrace for what I—"

"Are you saying that I disgraced you last night?"

She shut her eyes against the judgment she saw in his. "I disgraced myself. I dishonored my husband's memory."

"I, too, was once married." She looked at him now, and he watched her digest a thought that had never really crossed her mind. "It's not the same to you, is it?"

"Of course it is. But it's been some time for you, and Thomas . . . You didn't know him, Jed. He was too good for this world. Too good for me."

"My wife was *of* this world, and we were good together, but your presence in my bed has nothing to do with her."

"Oh, Jed, we have no right—"

He caught her by her shoulders and brought her face closer to his. "Is it because of who I am? What I am?"

"It's because of who I am." She hung her head, and her words were nearly lost in the dip her dress took between her breasts. "Because of what I am *supposed* to be."

"Pure in mind, soul and blood," he summarized as he released her.

"I was sent by the Missionary Board. I cannot replace Thomas because he was ordained, and I am just a—" She shook her head, refusing to let her gender excuse her from her duty. "I must be prepared to do what I can. And what has happened between us . . . these feelings . . ."

He waited, but she pressed her lips together and refused to say more. "What feelings?"

She shook her head, sadly this time. "Whenever Thomas would . . . whenever we . . . he would manage to mutter a prayer for both of us."

"I don't want to hear about Thomas."

"And then he would find some wood to chop or tend—" she laughed convulsively "—tend those mules. He never wanted—"

"I wanted, Katherine. Make no mistake. *I* wanted you." He reached for her again, and her slight shoulders trembled in his hands. "I have seen to the mules, and there is plenty of firewood. The effects of the whiskey have worn off. If you ask me now—"

Not even burning tears could distort the beauty of Jed's face. His lips were within reach of hers, and it was as much for her own ears as for his that she recited, "It would be wrong."

Teeth clenched, he turned away from her. "They've poisoned you, Katherine. Those damnable missionaries. They tell you everything is wrong. The way you dress is wrong, the way you eat, the way you wear your hair." He faced her again, lifted a helpless hand and confided softly, "The way I spoke, the color of my mother's eyes . . . none of those things was any good."

Her throat burned. She wanted to touch him. She wanted to reach up and touch his cheek. She wanted to tell him how dear to her was the sound of his voice, the way his hair glistened in the sun, the way his eyes glinted when he smiled. But it would be the wrong thing to do, she resolved, the wrong thing to say because she would be in his arms in a flash, and her weak flesh would be her downfall.

"I was good enough last night," he said.

Katherine closed her eyes and whispered. "My husband is hardly cold in his grave."

"I would make you *my* woman, Katherine."

"No." She turned away just before a menacing tear escaped to her cheek. Her recitation was rusting, but she stubbornly managed to repeat it. "It would be wrong."

The door closed quietly at her back.

Chapter Six

The plan Katherine had spent the day devising and revising had to be tested aloud. It was time to put an end to the heavy silence she and Jed had shared since morning, but she dreaded telling him of her intention. She already felt the loneliness it would bring. Closing her Bible in the middle of Exodus, she cleared her throat.

"I've decided to leave for Fort Hall in the morning."

Jed looked up from the rawhide web he'd fashioned within a curved willow frame. At his back the logs shifted in the fireplace and disturbed the ominous stillness with a soft thud. Jed tied a knot and jerked the long ends tight. "You plan on stealing my horse?"

"No. I'm about to ask you if you would help me gather up my mules. I'm taking the wagon."

"Why Fort Hall?"

"It's closer than Fort Boise." She knew it made little difference to him which she chose. Both outposts belonged to the Hudson's Bay Company.

Jed turned the snowshoe frame and braced it against his thigh for leverage. "Take you six days if you're lucky. Longer after the first snowfall," he said as he started weaving a new row.

After a moment of uncomfortable silence she proposed the rest of her plan. "I would pay you to drive the wagon for me."

"I'm not for hire."

Katherine got to her feet, hoping for some kind of advantage over him while she asserted her right to carry her plan through, one way or another. If the book in her hand wouldn't suffice, perhaps height would. "Then I shall have to drive myself. I cannot stay here through the winter."

"But you don't mind wintering at Fort Hall."

"The man who runs the post has a wife, I believe. I would not be the only woman there."

"The Sioux have a name for those who like to camp near a fort or a trading post in the winter. They're called 'loaf-around-the-fort people.'" He spared her a disdainful glance. "I don't spend much time around trading posts."

"I'm not asking you to stay, Jed. I'm only asking you to take me there. By spring—"

"You're afraid you would be damaged goods by spring—" he lifted a mocking eyebrow as he whipped a long rawhide strip through a hole "—if you stayed with me."

She stepped closer, entreating him with an open-handed gesture. "The truth is, the longer I stay, the more difficult it becomes for me to go."

"Why should that be, Katherine?"

They looked at each other, and all the answers flashed from her eyes to his and back again.

"You have been good to me," she said quietly.

"Have I? This pressing need to leave, to spend the winter with anyone but me, is no testimony to that claim."

"I do trust you," she insisted. "You know that." It sounded feeble even in her own ears, and she desperately wanted him to believe her. "I trust you more than—" More than whom? Herself, certainly, but who else? What else? Jed West had become her deliverer and her refuge. The truth was blasphemous, but a lie would have been transparent, and both unnerved her.

She knelt beside him, her blue skirt spreading like a water ring over the earthen floor. "I have begun to care for you in ways that a woman, unless she is free to marry, must not permit herself to care for a man." She hugged the book beneath her breasts. "And I am not free."

"No. I see that you're not. You stand with one foot in this world and the other in the next, and you cannot function fully in either place." He looked at her dispassionately, as though he were sizing her up. "Still, you're a woman alone, and there's a scarcity of your kind around here. If you don't want a man, you'd best get acquainted with some kind of weapon for your defense before you go to Fort Hall."

"I don't think I could use a weapon."

He sighed and shook his head as he set his work aside. "I wasted my time bringing you up here. I should have known that the wolves would get their due in the end."

Moonlight flooded the sage flat as the embers of the camp fire burned down to a warm glow. Jed hunkered down near the heat and separated the coals with the end of a stick. Tonight he would sleep inside the wagon with Katherine. The temperature had crept lower each night they'd spent on the trail, and the only thing the season lacked now was snow. That, too, would come soon. Cold winter nights made the coyote's howl sound lonelier and a bed with no woman in it feel emptier.

This would be the last night he'd spend in Katherine's company, and he wasn't going to spend it on the frozen ground. She had nothing to offer him but body heat and, by God, that was better than nothing. She'd been so damned careful around him the past few days, making sure she didn't sit too close on the wagon seat, didn't brush up against him when she dished up their supper. Tonight he would put an end to her little pretense. She would lie close to him, and he would claim that closeness as payment for this fool's errand he'd taken on at her request. They would keep each other warm, and tomorrow night, when they were miles apart, they would both remember how it felt.

She walked up behind him, and he stiffened, preparing himself for another purely functional exchange of words—words that would ring hollow in the infinite darkness. He could speak as coldly as she could—indeed, they had matched each other for icy stubbornness on this trip—but come bedtime this night, he would make her aware of the difference between a dead man and a living one. And then he would leave her to her own devices. *Gladly.*

"We'll be there tomorrow, won't we?" she asked. She'd been watching him tend the fire for what she knew might be the last time, and she realized the trembling deep within her bosom was not caused by the cold.

He detected her tone of regret, but he steeled himself and answered simply, "Yes."

"Perhaps you'll come to Fort Hall in the spring to trade your furs."

His chuckle was humorless. "Would you have me pay you a social call?"

"I would be ... pleased to see you any time."

"You see me now." He watched her eyes follow him as he stood. "Are you pleased?"

"Yes." His angular features were bathed in moonlight, and the night breeze ruffled the fur on his cap. It thrilled her to see how dangerous he looked and know that she was with him. "The time runs out so quickly now. I wish I could make it stand still for just a few more hours."

"Why?"

"Because I'm afraid."

"Your god will protect you. If he's so determined to have you meddle in people's lives in his behalf, he'll protect you."

"Thomas's faith was stronger than mine. I tell myself that I'm in God's hands, but still I'm frightened of what's to come." She sighed. "The memory of Thomas's fate is too fresh in my mind."

"Well, you've taken your safety out of my hands." He turned away from her and kicked dirt over the coals. "After tomorrow, it won't be my worry."

"But you'll be my friend, won't you, Jed?" She caught herself and quickly modified the urgency in her tone. "I mean, just for tonight if we could put aside the strain we've created between us and spend one last night talking about anything and everything the way we—"

"You're playing with fire, Katherine. I don't need a friend. The only time I've knocked on a door to call on a woman was to do business with her. She satisfied my needs, and I paid her price." She started to turn, but he grabbed her arm. "Name your price, Katherine. I'll pay it."

"Please don't, Jed. You know I wouldn't—"

"You want nothing between us, and I'm letting you have it that way. I've done right by you, Katherine. You can't say I haven't."

"I know."

"But you, my pretty little bird, you don't know what you want." Without thinking, he tightened his hold on her arm. He wanted to shake her. "By the time you figure it out, it'll be too late."

"It doesn't matter what I want. I have to finish this journey." Her wide eyes pleaded for some kind of pardon. "Haven't you ever started on a path and felt that you had to see the end of it?"

"I've been down a number of paths and taken many detours. Sometimes the detour becomes the true direction."

"My true direction is west, Jed. God wants me to go there, and I cannot deny Him."

He took hold of her upper arms. "God? Or your dead husband?"

"Both." Within his grip she squared her shoulders. "I am to be the instrument by which Thomas's work may be carried out. I truly believe that." Jed released her abruptly, and she stepped back to catch her balance.

"Do you see this?" He snatched an ax from the ground where it lay and brandished it near her face. "*This* is an instrument. It has no will of its own, so I use it to do mine. But you are no instrument, Katherine. You are a strong woman, and you deserve to exercise your will, live your life and discover your own passions." He touched the ax handle to her forehead. "There is a battleground inside this head of yours. If I could kill your ghost for you, I would. But a ghost must be released from the heart that harbors it. It must be laid to rest."

"He doesn't haunt me."

"Does he possess you, Katherine?"

"No!"

"Then let him go. Weep, wail, curse, howl at the moon—"

"I have done my—"

"No, Katherine, you have not broken his hold."

"He has no—"

"Do it, Katherine. Let him go."

"His vision must live. I cannot . . . my true direction is . . ."

"Bury yourself, then." He tossed the ax away from him. It clattered against the ring of rocks that made the firepit. "As I said, after tomorrow, I won't give a damn about your direction. You can jump in the man's grave with him for all I care."

She cringed inside when he turned away again. "I don't believe that, Jed." She wanted some piece of him to be hers. She reached for his sleeve, but it slid from her grasp. Quietly, she said, "You're a good Christian man, who loves his neighbor the way the—"

"No, don't call me that." He stood still as a statue and directed his anger at a dark, distant peak. "It's a curse on your tongue. You use it to have your way with me, to bind me to you in an impossible union, the way you bind yourself to a dead husband. You say you cannot be my woman, and I tell you I cannot be your neighbor."

He turned to her, and she saw his struggle to calm himself. Finally, he spoke in a hushed voice. "But here we are, each wanting, and while neither of us can move the other, time stands still." He lifted his hand to touch her cheek. "But only for one night."

"I cannot think that after tonight I won't see you again."

"I cannot think of spending another night on the ground beside your bed." She held her breath as he took her face in his hands. "I have decided to sleep with you tonight." Her lips parted for protest, but he added quickly, "It's the best way to keep warm."

They shed their coats and bundled together in blankets inside the wagon. Jed's breath warmed Katherine's cheek, and she thought of the soft feather tick she'd quietly left behind for him in the cabin. She told herself to lie still, resist the temptation to whisper to him. She took comfort in the sound of his heartbeat, and she was nearly content. But sleep would not come.

Katherine's breath warmed the hollow of Jed's neck, and he remembered the snowshoes he'd been netting for her. He promised himself he would finish them and have them delivered to her at the fort. His fingers itched to caress her. Even for a moment. Just her shoulder. He closed his eyes and listened to the wind whistle down the night sky. But sleep would not come.

"Jed?"

"Hmm?"

"I can't go to sleep."

"Are you cold?"

"Just my fingers and toes."

"Put your feet between my legs."

"Jed—"

"Shh. Just do it. Here. Put your hand inside my...there. And this one, so. Better?"

"Mmm."

She snuggled in close. He had tucked her hands inside his soft chamois shirt—one under his arm, one at his side—and he'd captured her stockinged feet between his calves. The cold was banished from her extremities. Against her cheek she felt the nubbly patch of beadwork that decorated his shirt.

"Jed?"

"Hmm."

"I noticed this shirt when you put it on this morning."

"Did you?"

"I confess, I did. It's beautiful. Did your wife make it?"

"No. My wife's patterns were different. This beadwork has only recently become a favorite Cree design. Flowers and curling vines."

"Your grandmother?"

"My mother made this one."

She assessed the bumpy texture with her fingertips, following the circuitous trail as she recalled the reds and greens, the pinks and blues in the floral pattern. She had not known him to wear such ornate clothing and wondered why he had chosen to do so now. Strangely, the delicacy of the flowers only enhanced his masculinity, and she wondered what the austere style of her clothing did for her image in his eyes.

"I wear mostly plain clothes." It was almost an apology. "No baubles. Nothing fancy."

"I know," he said with a note of sympathy.

"But sometimes I think, what harm could come from wearing a few ribbons or a bit of lace?"

"What harm comes to mind?"

She thought for a moment. "Perhaps the risk of turning a man's head."

"Your head was turned by my shirt, and here we are." His chuckle rumbled in his chest. "Would I have escaped your notice in my plain wool shirt?"

"No."

"Just so, Katherine, your undecorated dresses make you no less attractive to me."

"When I was sick I was unattractive."

"You were a scarecrow."

"You see?"

"A stubborn little bag of bones who fought for her life the way a runt fights to get to a bitch's teat. Each time I thought I'd lost you, you would dig into your last shred of life and claw your way back."

"That could not have been me, Jed. I'm such a bloodless creature. I've never been that tenacious."

"Yes, you have. You would have died if you hadn't been."

"My stepmother predicted that I couldn't last a week on this journey. She said I would make Thomas turn back."

Jed had no comment to make about Thomas. They lay still for a time, Jed resenting Thomas's intrusion and Katherine regretting it.

"Jed?"

"What?"

"Tell me your given name. Tell me what your mother called you."

There was a long moment of silence.

"Girard."

"Girard. I knew it would sound like music."

"I've put that name aside, the way a man leaves his boyhood name behind. I needed a new name, and I took one from a dead trapper. I'm Jed West."

"Why? Why did you change your name?"

"It doesn't matter, Katherine. You asked to know my given name, and I have told you. But I am no longer that man. That man vanished in Sioux country. I ask you not to repeat the name to anyone."

"It was because of that Mr. Simpson, wasn't it?"

"I trust you not to speak of that business to anyone, either."

"I won't."

"The Sioux believe that a ghost becomes restive when its name is spoken aloud. I have not spoken that name in years."

"You're not a ghost, Jed. And the man you were is part of the man you have become."

The man he had become. Since Katherine had dropped into his world and made unsettling ripples, he had begun to take a look at this displaced man. This hermit. This nameless, landless, bondless orphan. He was a man who had been pieced together from diverse swatches of humanity. He had spent his life trying to create a place for himself, some niche where no one piece of him was less acceptable than the others. What he'd found were an isolated cabin and a few fleeting weeks with a woman who refused to change her course for the sake of loving him.

But she had touched his reclusive soul, and he believed he had touched hers. It was only a spark, but it was something. He pressed his lips to her forehead and memorized the scent of pine and wood smoke in her hair.

"Did they call you by another name when you were a little girl?"

"No. I was always Katherine. No one had a pet name for me."

"Shall I give you one?"

In the dark she smiled and whispered, "Yes."

"I think you would make a pretty Kate. A bonny sweet Kate."

"I like that. It sounds like something from a child's rhyme."

"I don't know about that, but I remember that one of my grandfather's partners used to call his rifle 'bonny sweet Kate,' which he said was his sister's name."

"Are you naming me after a woman or a rifle?"

He smoothed her hair back from her temple. "I am recalling my grandfather's good friend, who was a Scottish mixed-blood."

"Scottish? But your grandfather was French."

"We are truly a mongrel lot, aren't we? There is sometimes a problem with the warring churches who want to save our souls—the Protestant missionaries who came with our English fathers and the Catholic ones who followed the French—but in the end we are Métis, and our Cree and Ojibway mothers feed us and dress us and make the lodges that cover our heads."

"And teach you stories of river spirits."

"The stories, yes. I loved the stories—the winter talk after the snow had covered the ground. Remember the one I told you about the beginning, when the earth was brought up from the water's depths?"

"I remember."

"The one who brought the bit of mud from the bottom of the water was a brave soul who succeeded where others had failed."

"Who was he?"

"Earthdiver." Jed spoke the name with remembered reverence. "I used to listen to that story and imagine myself as the earthdiver—the one who was part of both the land and the water—the only one who could bridge the two. I would hold my breath as I listened to the storyteller, and I would feel the water around me. It was murky, and the deeper I dived, the less I could see. It didn't matter. I knew when I touched it that I had found what I was searching for. I could feel it embedded under my fingernails. Sand. Mud. A small mound in the palm of my hand. It was my task to bring it into the light."

"Your task?" He spoke of light, and she had a sudden, inexplicable sense of the light. It drew her deeper into his vision.

"In the mind of a young and idealistic daydreamer, yes. But I still had to swim back. I thought my lungs would explode, and the watery depths were full of obstacles. Each time I heard the story, I fancied new and more terrible hazards."

"Did you make it to the surface?"

"I haven't yet." He laughed. "I guess I don't want the story to end. But it's been a long time since I've even thought of it."

"Oh, Jed, it's a wonderful story."

"What?" he teased. "A pagan tale of river spirits?"

"Yes!" She paused. "No. I really wasn't thinking of it that way."

"Perhaps there's a chink in your righteous armor." He shifted his position slightly. "Anyway, it's just a story. There are no great tasks left. The earth is made. A man has all he can do to find a place for himself in it."

"Do you think you might ever... travel a little farther west?"

"You mean, as far as the Whitman Mission at the Place of the Rye Grass?"

"There's important work to be done, Jed, and a man like you could be instrumental—"

"Already you've forgotten what I said about instruments."

"I'm a poor one. I speak only English, and I know so little about the people and their needs. But you—"

"They need to be left to live their lives in peace. These white pilgrims who travel across the land bring starvation and disease. I've seen it among the Cree people along the Red River and the people of the Missouri River—the

Arikara, the Mandan and the Sioux. The first one gets sick, and soon hundreds are dying."

"Disease will take its toll, Jed. Everywhere."

"Whole villages," he told her. "You cannot know until you've seen it. You cannot imagine."

"My husband died that way, too. I know."

He would not argue the point. Perhaps she did know. The loss of a mate could seem like the loss of an entire village, or even the world. He buried his fingers in her hair and caressed her temple with his thumb, hoping to ease all that from her mind.

"Enough of ghosts and ancient tales," he whispered. "Sleep now, bonny sweet Kate. Sleep in my arms."

Fort Hall boasted four log buildings and a partly constructed palisade. One long, narrow building served as a stable. A split-rail corral stood behind it. Dogs, pigs, chickens and goats made way for Katherine's six-mule hitch as she headed for the largest of the three cabins. She wondered why no one came out to greet her. Surely they'd heard the dogs yapping. She secured the reins with a loop around the wagon's brake handle and hollered, "Hello, the house!"

A stout, moon-faced woman in a rabbit-skin cap peered around the corner of the cabin. "Land sakes, a woman! You ain't alone, are you?"

Katherine pointed southward toward the foothills and recited the explanation she'd rehearsed for Jed before they'd parted company. "My party left me behind. A man named Jed West saw me safely here."

"You plan on staying the winter?"

"If it's all right with the agent here. I haven't much choice. I hope to move on with the first westering train that comes through in the spring."

"Jump down." The woman wiped her hands on her skirt as she ventured forth. "I'm Louise Granger. My husband's in charge here. Come on." She pointed across the yard. "He's down to the bar, jawin' with Jim Bridger. Your party left you behind, you say?"

The two men watched Katherine as though the very way she strode across the yard were a source of amusement. She felt uneasy even before she introduced herself and told Frank Granger that she had been to Fort Hall before, but she had kept to her wagon to tend a sick passenger.

"You were with that bunch had the typhoid fever pretty bad?" he asked. Katherine nodded, and Granger eyed her suspiciously. "You sick, Miz Fairfield?"

"'Course she ain't sick," Bridger put in, grinning. "Look at her. She's chipper as pork pie."

"I had a life-threatening bout with dysentery, but I was aided by a Mr. Jed West. I believe you may know him."

"Know of him," Granger allowed. "He's got an Indian partner I see once in a while, but West don't come around here himself. Kind of a mystery man."

"I know him," Bridger said. "Known Jed for a long time. He tended a gunshot wound for me once. He found you on the trail, did he?"

"Actually, a party of Indians discovered my plight and alerted Mr. West. I was quite close to death at that point. It was a blessing that—" It was the first time she'd heard herself put it quite that way. The hunting party she'd initially feared had, indeed, been a blessing. "That the Indians saw fit to seek help for me."

"Miracle is they didn't take a nice big chunk o' that pretty hair you got." Granger elbowed Bridger, but Bridger denied him his laugh.

"Granger, you're talking to a lady here."

Louise was pleased to have a bit of information to supply. "She's an emigrant bound for the Whitman Mission."

"Missionary, are you?" Granger asked.

"Yes. The Whitmans were, of course, expecting me this fall. I hope I can work for my keep, Mr. Granger. I haven't a lot of money."

"From the looks of you, you'll have to learn how. Won't be no more emigrants passing through till summer." He took quick stock of her team and wagon. "I can let you have room and board, trade for them mules. Come summer, I'll sell 'em as recruited and maybe get you passage with a family."

"Recruited?"

"You take in a worn-out team, feed 'em up, and they're recruited," Granger explained. "Next season, another emigrant gets this far, team's worn out, he pays my price, and he leaves his team to boot."

"I'd sooner have my team and wagon, Mr. Granger. To depend upon another family—"

"You'll do what you have to, Miz Fairfield. You got yourself in a fix. Got a bed up in the loft, three squares a day, and you help with the chores. Louise is generally pretty slow in gettin' things done around here."

It was Jim Bridger who helped Katherine turn out her team and unload some of her belongings from the wagon. He was tall and wiry with the leathery look of a man who had lived in the mountains for most of his life. He told Katherine he'd built a way station of his own in Utah Territory to the south.

"Don't like to stay in one place too long, though. More settlers coming through every year. Country's changing too fast. Men like Jed and me, we got to search harder and higher every year for places that ain't trapped out, ain't spoiled by some farmer's plow.''

Katherine handed down a carpetbag, which she'd packed with her necessities, and she took the bedding she would need. Bridger set down the bag and reached to help her down from the wagon. "Have you known Jed long?" she asked.

"Long enough to know the kind of man he is. I owe him my life, same as you."

"Then you know—"

"That's he's a mixed-blood? Sure. That's the natural way of things, ain't it? Got me a young 'un by an Indian woman.'' He picked up the bag and took the blankets from Katherine. "Nothing wrong with that."

"A child is a blessing, Mr. Bridger."

"'Course, them Métis people up in Red River country, they're kind of a different breed. Been there a long time, you know. It's almost like they're a new tribe—one that wasn't there before the white man came. They got their own ways. You probably know what I mean."

She knew Jed, and listening to this man talk about him seemed to bring Jed closer. She nodded as they walked together slowly.

"Yes'm, they're a different breed, all right. And there's trouble brewing 'twixt them and the Brits."

"What kind of trouble?"

"Well, the Hudson's Bay Company runs the whole show up that way. A man can't trade with nobody else, see. They got their rules. They outfit Indian hunters, and the Métis are kind of the middlemen. Damn good hunters, them Métis. They supply the forts with meat. But they want to be free to trade as they please. And they got this council up there, mostly run by the Company, and from what Jed says, the Métis are about the only ones don't get much say on this council. The council decides what they can do and what they can't. Word is, them Métis been gettin' pretty itchy over it.''

"Of course, none of this affects Mr. West, now that he—''

"It affects him plenty." Bridger touched his temple and narrowed one eye. "Mostly up here. I don't know too much about the particulars, but I know he's had his own trouble with the Company, and I know he's touchy about going back home. Treaty or no treaty, Hudson's Bay Company is still around.''

"Treaty?''

"Haven't you heard?" He glanced down at her and realized it was a stupid question. "'Course you haven't. Just got word myself, even though it was all signed and sealed months ago. America has jurisdiction over the Oregon Country now. Everything south of the forty-ninth parallel. Next thing you know, them settlers, they'll be agitating for territory status, and then where will the wilderness be?''

The mountain man's worry was lost on Katherine. "Then the Hudson's Bay Company is no longer the law of the land.''

"Not officially, no, but old dogs don't go down easy." He stopped several yards short of the cabin door and lowered his voice. "You watch yourself around Granger. Myself, I don't like to see the way he treats Louise, slow-witted as she is. Ol' Frank said he wasn't hitchin' up with no Indian woman, so he advertised back East. Louise come out from Missoura.''

"She seemed to be pleased by the prospect of female companionship.''

"Reckon she would be. But you—" He gave her a conspiratorial look, as though they'd had something in common before they met. "You just watch yourself. Think I'll head out and see what my ol' friend Jed West is up to."

With Jim's departure went Katherine's sense of real contact with Jed, leaving her desolate. She faced spending the winter with a man who offered little more than a grunt in response to any comment put to him, and a woman who had the mind of a child.

Most of the chores fell to the two women. They hauled water and wood, fed the livestock, mucked out the barn, prepared food, kept the fire burning through the night and began the cycle again the next morning. At the end of the first week, Katherine was exhausted. With a fortnight under her belt, she'd gained a second wind and considerable resolve. Her mission would begin with the Grangers.

Louise did her best to attend to Katherine's nightly Bible readings, but her thoughts obviously strayed. Granger sipped his trade whiskey while he listened—or appeared to listen. Katherine could feel his eyes on her while she read. Being regarded thus by the man made her feel greasy, as though she were rendering lard, getting smeared with it, choking on the stench. When she looked up from the page, his eyes glittered at her like shards of glass set in the folds of a sow's ears. Even though the whole atmosphere smothered her, Katherine hesitated to retire each night, for then she would often hear the sounds of Granger's temper. More than once she had seen the purple proof of his cruelty somewhere on Louise's body. Louise attributed every bruise to her own clumsiness and asked Katherine not to worry about them.

It was cold in the loft, where Katherine slept. After her first midnight confrontation with a rodent, she had scrubbed the area and made a clean straw tick. But she was more successful in battling mice and other pests than she was in fending off the chill at night. Granger's racks were filled with fur pelts, but he offered none to keep her warm. Jed had given her a wolf pelt, and she clung to it each night beneath her blankets. It was her only tangible piece of him.

She remembered their parting on the hill above the fort. She had climbed down from the seat and followed him to the back of the wagon, where he'd already untied his horse. Neither of them had spoken. She had seen the challenge in his eyes; one word of hesitation from her, and he would not have permitted her to stay. As she huddled in the loft, she envisioned the kiss she had secretly wanted him to press upon her that day. She tasted it on her lips. Regret was not a word, but a kiss not shared.

Katherine cursed her faltering resolve. She had no right to Jed's kisses, and she knew he would not have ridden away if he had permitted himself to kiss her. He had offered her a long moment of silence—a chance to change her mind. When the moment had passed, he had mounted his horse and disappeared over the knoll.

The wolf pelt was her best source of comfort now. Here in this bleak place Jed was like a shadow. These people had heard his name, dealt with his partner, but no one knew him except Katherine. In the dark, he filled her mind. She remembered the rich mahogany sheen of his hair and the way the light in his dark eyes betrayed the depth of his feeling. She listened to the wind, and Jed's low, soothing voice came to her through a crack in the wall's chinking. At times when guilt nagged her, she tried to remember her promise and the man to whom she had made it, but she had trouble conjuring a memory of Thomas's face. It was Jed's image that somehow soothed her cold feet and her blistering hands.

He was a merciful man.

"I told you to keep them damn chickens out of the barn!" Granger slammed the door behind him, threw his cap on the floor and waved a stick. "You hear me, woman? You know what I found on my saddle this morning?"

Katherine lifted her chin slowly and took pains to ease her Bible closed. She leveled the most contemptuous stare she could manage. "There are two women here, Mr. Granger."

"Only one who don't obey her husband," he accused, brandishing the stick in Louise's direction. The woman cringed in the corner near an array of steel animal traps. "Ain't that what the book says, Miz Fairfield? Woman's meant to obey her husband. I won't abide no chicken sh—"

His move was quicker than either woman anticipated, and he struck Louise across the shoulders with a loud whack. Katherine shouted unintelligibly and flew from her chair, her face suddenly hot, her mind red with rage. She reached for Louise, and the stick came down across the back of her hand. A warning of the next blow flashed across Louise's terror-stricken face. Katherine's shoulder burned wildly, but she cared for nothing except the helplessness in Louise's eyes.

"I'll help you," Katherine promised. "We'll make him stop this." Her vow became a shriek as she whirled on Granger, her fingers poised like claws. "Stop it now!"

Granger was momentarily taken by surprise. He tried to shove Katherine aside, but she hurled herself against the arm that held the stick.

"Git back out of the way!"

"Stop hitting her! Just stop—"

The door swung open, and an Indian man stepped inside. Granger lowered his hand. Katherine stumbled backward, her chest heaving as she stared at the stranger. His black eyes were as expressionless as the two holes in the wolf face he wore on his head. He held his buffalo robe together with a hand that was missing its first two fingers. Calmly he closed the door and let the robe slide off his shoulders, revealing the pistol he held at his side.

"What are you doing here, Half Hand?" Granger squared his shoulders and stepped away from Katherine. "I outfitted you a month ago."

"Come for more tobacco."

"More tobacco? You eatin' the stuff?"

"What I do with it is my business." There was a silent question in the brief look he gave Katherine. Apparently satisfied, he tucked his pistol in his belt and eyed Granger. "You selling tobacco, or not?"

"'Spose you and your partner can get twice the price for it back in them hills, but that's the way of the business, ain't it? What are you paying with?"

"Made Beaver."

Granger nodded. He wouldn't refuse the Company's own brass coinage. "How much you need?"

The fight was over, and the women said nothing of the incident as they went about their chores. Katherine managed to recover her dignity without disclosing the awful way she quaked inside. If the man called Half Hand had not arrived when he did, she didn't know what she would have done. Her rage had swallowed up all reason.

Half Hand left the post immediately after his business was concluded, and Katherine wondered about the concern she could have sworn she saw in the single glance he had spared her. Granger had mentioned Half Hand's partner, but Katherine refused to speculate on the remark. She had to put the day behind her and get herself back on the path God had chosen for her. Toward evening she decided to practice her much neglected capacity for humility by making certain there were no chickens in the barn.

Granger followed her there.

She had hung the lantern on a hook, and his shadow fell across her face as she shooed a hen along in front of her broom. She looked up, and the chicken squawked on its way out the door.

Granger's eyes glittered. "You got better sense than the missus, and you're a looker to boot. I wouldn't have to be so hard on somebody like you."

Katherine squared her shoulders and tightened her grip on the broom. "I've agreed to help with the chores, Mr. Granger. There's no need to wave your stick at anyone. Just explain to us what needs to be done."

"Well, Miz Fairfield," he said, scratching his bristly jaw as he looked her over, "I was about to do just that. I was about to show you just what needs doin'. See, I've learned a thing or two about women over the years." Katherine took a step back, but he grabbed the broom handle and gave it a quick jerk, pulling her toward him. She let the broom go. He tossed it aside and grabbed her arm.

"High-headed bitch like you needs breakin' in. Once you been bridled and mounted, you'll be a different woman." Granger loomed over her, his face made more sinister by the shadows. "Come summer, you won't be doin' no preachin'. You won't even be apt to talk much. You'll be skulkin' around like that ol' hen you just whacked. Knows her place when the cock's around."

Katherine could smell his rank breath. Her mind raced with images of kicking him somewhere—anywhere, *every*where—and she was trying to screw up the courage when a familiar voice split the cold night air.

"Let her go."

Granger turned, and Katherine jerked away from him. Jed West stepped into the barn.

Granger's eyes widened. "You got some claim on this woman, mister?"

Jed looked at Katherine. "You want to stay with him, or come with me?"

"I . . . Jed." That was her answer. Lord, his face, his sweet face. "We have to take Louise with us. He beats her. He's—"

"She's got the same choice." Jed jerked his head in the direction of the main house. "Get what belongs to you."

Katherine left the barn and ran, lifting her skirts and stretching her legs as she hadn't done since she was a child. She headed for the main cabin.

"So you're ol' Half Hand's partner." Granger made an effort to recover his bogus bearing in the presence of a man whose power clearly exceeded his own. "The mountain hermit, Jed West."

"We're trading the team and wagon for two good horses, Granger. Got any objections?"

"Not a bad deal, but you ain't takin' my wife."

"I won't *take* her, but if she wants to come, you'll give her a horse and provisions." Jed kept his rifle low, pointing it at no one, but it was primed and ready to fire. "Let's take a walk on over to the house and ask your woman what she wants to do."

Katherine had already put the question to Granger's wife, and Louise's answer was as firm as any she was accustomed to giving. "I can't leave my man, Katherine. He's all I got."

"He hurts you, Louise."

"Not all the time. Not generally when there's folks around, and not when I don't make too many mistakes." Louise handed Katherine the Bible she'd left on the bench they shared when Katherine read to her. "I don't want to leave here. This here's the best home I've had. I'm the agent's missus here." She offered a hopeful smile. "That's somethin', ain't it?"

Katherine tossed her carpetbag on the floor. "I ought to tell Jed what he did to us. Jed would—"

"No." Louise touched Katherine's arm. "That ain't what you read me from the book, Katherine."

"The book doesn't tell us to turn the other cheek to the likes of him."

"I been with him for a long time, and he never hurt me too bad. I reckon I'll stay. I just got to remember to keep them chickens away from Frank's saddle."

"Oh, Louise—"

"It's all right, now. You go on with your Mr. West. He's the one took care of you when you were so sick, wasn't he?" Katherine's nod brought another smile. "He must be a good man. Better'n Frank." She lowered her voice at the sound of footsteps outside. "But Frank's all I got and all I'll ever have."

Jed followed Granger into the house. Katherine's heart fluttered wildly, and this time she knew it wasn't from her fear of Granger. It was pure joy. Jed had come for her.

But Louise laid a hand on Katherine's arm again and stared at her curiously. "Lord-a-mercy, Katherine. Your Mr. West looks like an Indian!"

Chapter Seven

The season's first snowflakes drifted out of the black night. Only the plodding of three horses disturbed the quiet. Fighting cold and drowsiness, Katherine imagined hearing the flakes settle on the ground. She had ridden behind Jed in silence for more than an hour, and before that her comments had met terse response. She felt like the runaway child whose father was saving the inevitable tongue-lashing until they got home. Katherine understood Jed's anger. For her sake he had put himself within reach of the powerful Hudson's Bay Company.

She wasn't sure what the consequences might be, but she knew he had taken a risk. She wanted to battle his dragons the way he had done for her, but his foes were shadowy. She wondered what weapons they carried and how they might know him. Were there old handbills with Jed's likeness tucked in the records at every outpost?

"Louise thought you were an Indian," Katherine ventured as she coaxed her mare's head even with the buckskin's nose.

"Did that bother you?"

"No, but if you're worried about Granger suspecting your identity... well, now they think Jed West is an Indian. Not a Métis."

"Granger is Hudson's Bay Company. He recognizes a Métis."

"Would he have reason to recognize you?" She waited for an answer, but he offered none. She lowered her voice, as though the night might have ears. "Are they looking for you, Jed?"

"I don't know."

"How long has it been?"

"Seven years."

Katherine tried to imagine what might have happened seven years past. A well-placed company employee who disliked the Métis, Jed's hot-tempered younger brother and Jed had traveled the plains together.

His arrogance killed him.

But not Jed. Jed was no murderer. What had he to fear after all these years? Whatever it was, it bred more fear; Katherine was afraid to ask.

Two inches of snow lay on the ground by the time they reached a tipi, which stood tucked in a stand of ponderosa pines. No one was about. It was like finding an empty house in the woods. Katherine followed Jed's lead in dismounting and unloading saddles and packs. She did her share of the work until their belongings were stowed, the horses picketed and firewood arranged in an ash-filled fire pit.

"Does anyone live here?" Katherine asked.

Jed struck a spark with his flint. "Half Hand left it for us and went on up to his people's winter camp."

"He's your partner, isn't he?"

"He is." The firewood became a small flaming tipi, illuminating their faces.

"You sent him to Fort Hall?"

"Half Hand said my company had been none too pleasant recently. Ever since Bridger spent two days in our camp smoking up Half Hand's tobacco and telling me I was a fool to leave you with Granger. So Half Hand took a notion to check things out and set my mind at ease. Didn't work out that way. What he saw didn't set too well with him." Jed rubbed his hands together and held them close to the fire, nodding at her. "Didn't set too well with me, either, Katherine."

"You came quickly." Katherine scooted closer to the fire and took off her shoes. "You couldn't have been this far away when you got the news."

"I rode in a lot faster than we just rode out."

"It's dangerous to ride too fast in the dark," she said. Then she thought, tell him something he doesn't already know. Something important.

"This is dangerous country," he reminded her.

Her toes were beginning to tingle. She stopped wiggling them and smiled at him. "I was so glad to see you."

"Considering what I walked in on, I imagine you'd have been glad to see—"

"*You.* I was glad to see you. It was like a miracle." She took off her coat, carefully set it aside, then quietly confessed, "I've missed you, Jed."

"I've been out of my mind," he said, shedding his coat and tossing it over hers. "I was crazy to let you—"

"No, I should have listened to you."

They sat knee to knee on the fur pallet near the fire. She folded her hands and tucked them in the folds of her skirt on her lap. She looked like a porcelain doll he'd once seen in the window of a store.

"You wouldn't listen because you're afraid to be with me." He knew it, and he hated it. He untied the knife scabbard at his waist and laid it aside.

"I was afraid I wouldn't see you again. I tried not to miss you, but I did. Sometimes at night it got so bad—"

He waited until she looked up at him. His intensity smoldered. "How bad, Katherine?"

"I remembered the sound of your voice," she said timidly. "I pictured the way your hair waves when you've just set your hat aside, and I remembered watching you wield an ax and thinking how gentle your hands can be. And sometimes, deep in the night, I thought I heard the sound of you sleeping next to my bed, the way you..." She closed her eyes against her boldness and shook her head. "Oh, Jed, I imagined things I shouldn't think about."

He cupped her chin in his hand and made her look at him again. "Think about them now. Fill your mind with them. I've thought of nothing else."

"I want to go home with you."

"Home?"

"To the cabin."

He took her shoulders in his hands, searching his mind for some promise he might offer her. He could find nothing worthy of a woman like her. "There's nothing there."

"You live there. It's a good home, Jed."

"I have no home, Katherine. The cabin was a place to stay. This is just another place. Another man's lodge."

"Is this where we're going to stay, then?"

"Where do you want to be?"

"With you."

"Because I'm the lesser of two evils?"

She lifted her chin. "Because I want to be with you."

He drew her to him with his eyes and covered her mouth with a kiss that promised pleasure—the only promise he had to offer. There was nothing tentative in the way she kissed him back. It was an open, welcoming kiss, one that would hold him to the promise his kiss made. He would give her more. His body would bring her pleasure. He'd told her that before. It wasn't a trade. It was a gift, and she was willing now to accept.

He tumbled her back on the pallet, whispering, kissing her and whispering again. "Why? Tell me why."

"Because I love you." She plunged her fingers into his hair and reveled in the free-fall feeling that came with saying the words. "But you knew that."

"No."

"You knew it before I did, Jed, yes. Oh, yes."

He unbuttoned her bodice and unlaced her woolen undergarment, greeting her neck, her collarbone, the high swell of her breasts with his kisses. She shrugged out of her sleeves, and, in one quick move, he had her out of the dress.

"I knew if I ever got you back, I'd make love to you," he told her. "That's all I've known for certain since you left me."

He took her layers of clothing from her until there was only the last—the cotton that protected her skin from scratchy woolens. He kissed her and stroked her, for she was like a wild, wary colt who had half a mind to shy away. When Jed tugged on the ribbon between her breasts, she put her hand over the bow. A last-minute entreaty flashed in her eyes. His eyes asked her indulgence as he moved her hand, placing it on his chest. Two buttons made their impression on her palm.

"I want you to know me, Katherine, so you'll known there's nothing to fear." He dipped his head near her ear and whispered hotly, "Undress me."

"I . . . I couldn't, Jed."

"Try." He eased the ribbon loose and let the backs of his fingers rest between her breasts. "Try one button at a time. While I—" The first button slid from its mooring, and she dropped her hand to the second one. He smiled against her neck. "While I kiss you...and kiss you...and kiss..."

His shirt fell away as easily as potato peeling, and her fingers skittered against his skin. He was hard and warm and satiny. Filled with wonder at the very feel of him, she whispered his name. Glorious sound, she said it again until he covered her mouth with his. There was a fluttering, deep in her abdomen, as though a swarm of gypsy moths had found the brightness his touch kindled inside her.

The way she said his name made him swell with the need to answer her, go to her, come inside her. He could deny her nothing now unless she asked him to let her go, and that he could not do. Not now. He could deny himself anything else but this one fulfillment. In this place, in this moment, he would be one with her.

He suckled at her breasts until the peaks ached so sweetly that she arched her back to invite him to continue. He made her moan, made her blood run hot. He took the last of her clothes and replaced them with his stroking hands. She tried to remove the last of his, but her fingers trembled. He guided her hands, taking them to himself, coaxing her to learn first by touch. Her untutored exploring sent him near the brink, and he groaned. She jerked her hand away with a murmur of apology.

"It's all right," he whispered. "I need you, Katherine. Let me show you how bad."

Her mind eddied around the word. "Bad?"

Words had stopped making sense. "I'll make it good," he promised. "I'll make it sweet for you, *ma petite amie*. So sweet you'll hardly feel..."

Already he'd made good his promise. So good. He stroked her thighs until she wept between them, easing the way for his deeper touch. She called out to him as she pressed her face against his shoulder and rode the swelling wave he'd made for her.

Now was the time to go to her.

Now was the time to welcome him inside.

He met her as the wave crested, caught her on the breaking curl and drove her higher, pushed her higher with rolling hips and sang out with her as they sailed.

The flames cast a golden glow within the conical confines of the lodge. In their fur bed Katherine felt a new sense of warmth and security. The thought of the snow piling up around them only made her feel more snug, like a burrowing creature who has made her nest for the winter.

Jed's slow, fingertip investigation of her contours had made her shiver with delight. She knew she probably wasn't supposed to enjoy his attentions this much, but there was not a prayer in the world that would stop her after what they shared tonight. Then she felt his hands again as she closed her eyes and allowed herself to feel beautiful wherever he touched her. The curve of her shoulder—a touch and a kiss—the long path down her arm. He made a tingling spot in her palm with a tongue-flicking kiss, and she smiled.

"What's this?" Jed puzzled over the back of Katherine's hand.

She hadn't noticed the bruise, and it forced her to remember Granger. She glanced away, willing the memory to leave her. Granger was behind her now. She was with Jed, whose concern for her gleamed in his dark eyes.

"Did Frank Granger do this?"

"I was trying to stop him from hurting Louise. I don't know what came over me. I just couldn't let him—"

"Is there more?"

"No," she said too quickly. Then she added, "Nothing serious. It's over now."

"Turn over," he ordered gruffly. He found another welt high on her back, and the expletive he muttered in French seemed incongruous with the tender kiss that was meant to chase away her pain. "I should have killed him for you, Katherine."

"No." She turned to him and took his face in her hands. The firelight burnished his skin, and his black hair glistened against his shoulders. There was more sorrow than anger in his eyes. "You are no killer, Jed. You would not kill a man unless he threatened a life."

"If I had been there—"

"You were there when I needed you most, and I knew when I saw you that I was safe once again. You would not let him hurt me anymore."

"I would not let anyone hurt you. If you stay with me..." He slipped his hand between their bodies and touched her feminine mound. "Did *I* hurt you, *ma petite*?"

"I'm not sure. There was such an exquisite feeling, I'm not sure which part was pain and which was pleasure."

"There'll be no more pain. I promise."

She touched her nose to his shoulder and said quietly, "I want the pleasure, Jed."

"You shall have it. All I can give you."

"We should be married."

He smoothed her hair back from her face, the way he had when she was sick and hardly knew him. She knew him now, but he had known her for a longer time.

"You are the wife of my heart. What would you have me promise you, love? I'll take whatever vow you say."

"Do you love me?"

"I left you at Fort Hall because it was what you said you wanted, but I couldn't go far from you. You had my heart, Katherine." He mocked himself with a laugh. "Yes. I am as besotted a fool as I ever was—drunk with love rather than whiskey."

She smiled. "Love is better for you. But you must promise to be faithful to me, also. You must forsake all others as long as we both shall live."

"As long as we're together, I'll have no other woman." He loved the way the firelight struck sparks of gold in her hair. "And you? Can you promise to love me as I am?"

"I love you, Jed. Just as you are."

"I'll permit no other man in my bed, Katherine. Not even the ghost of one."

"I know."

He covered her breast with a possessive hand. "You belong to me now in a way that you never were his."

"He was so sure of everything. There was a season for everything, he said, and our time would come when we reached Oregon Country."

"Perhaps he wasn't so sure of himself." Katherine started to protest, but he added, "There's no shame in that. He was young, and he had an innocent bride who was counting on him in more ways than he could handle all at once. No man is born with experience." He cradled her against his side, figuring he'd given Thomas his due, mostly for Katherine's sake, and that was as generous as he cared to be. "Is your grief past now?"

It was not a notion she wanted to entertain just then, but Jed deserved reassurance. "I thought of you these past days, Jed. Not Thomas. I knew that he was dead, and that it was you who lived in my mind and my heart. And you were somewhere in these mountains. Even while I tried to be at peace with the choices I had made, my real hope was that you would come back for me."

"And so I did."

She lay quietly in his arms for a time before she gave voice to the question that had begun to throb in her brain. "What shall we do, Jed?"

"I don't know. Love each other as we've promised. Beyond that . . . I have nothing else to give you, Katherine." He sighed. "We are so different. Our lives until now, our people, our beliefs. Like two different worlds. This love might destroy us both."

"But we have to try, don't we?"

Try what? He'd done his damnedest not to love her, and he'd failed miserably. "Would you object to wintering with Half Hand's people?"

She glanced around her and thought it strange that she should seek refuge in a tipi. She imagined a whole village filled with dark strangers speaking a foreign language. She had planned to visit, to bring God's word, but not to stay.

"Can't we just stay here?"

"We'll travel north and find his band. We'll be safer with them than we would be on our own. That's why I traded the wagon. It would only hinder our mobility now."

Safer with them? In their village instead of a missionary outpost, with its proper house and its chapel? "Maybe we could still go— If we're going to travel anyway, maybe we could—"

"I will not go to the Whitman Mission, not even for you. I could never belong there."

"I only thought . . . for safety's sake."

"You would be safe there, Katherine, but I would not." He kissed the corner of her forehead, and the way her soft skin felt against his lips made his heart ache. "It begins again already. I am what I am, Katherine. You said you wanted to be with me."

"I do." She pressed her face into the pocket of his shoulder and inhaled the pine and musk scent of him. "I do, I do. Let's not talk about those things now." With a hard, quick hug she suggested, "Let's make more promises."

"Ah, you would have me sewn up tight in your woman's pouch."

"Indeed, I would. I want you safely out of any other woman's reach."

He chuckled. There were just the two of them now, and the rest of the world be damned. "You're the first one who's stumbled upon me in a very long time."

"You stumbled upon me, and there are surely more where I came from."

"Will they be on their way next spring?"

"Probably." She propped herself up, bracing against his chest, and tucked her hair behind one ear.

Oh, she was a pretty sight now, with her eyes full of fun. "You mean I would have more to choose from if I waited a few months?"

"Perhaps."

"I'll watch the westward march from any hilltop, pick out a healthy one this time—"

"I'm healthy!"

He grinned as he traced her arm with his forefinger. "A good swimmer. I'll watch near a fording place, just to make sure."

"I fully intend to learn."

"There's that missionary tone. I'll have to watch out for that, too."

"Find yourself a mute, Mr. West. You won't have to worry about any tone at all."

"On the other hand, that tone presents an interesting challenge." With a quick movement he reversed their positions. "I can sometimes subdue it with a kiss."

He lowered his head to kiss gently, his tongue offering teasing suggestions. She rubbed herself against him like a cat, and he growled and laughed and hooked his leg over both of hers.

She gave him a saucy smile. "There must be something about me that you would not wish away, Jed."

"I would wish nothing away." He kissed her eyes, the tip of her nose, then rolled to his back, taking her with him in his arms. "I would not change you, Katherine. You're a fighter, even though you never throw a punch. Few women could match your courage, and likely no man could come close to it." His hug was possessive. "It takes courage to love a man like me."

"And patience to love a woman like me."

A quiet moment passed while they promised themselves they were up to the challenge.

"Jed?"

"Hmm?"

"Where is my 'woman's pouch'?"

"Have you misplaced it, *ma petite*?" His hands moved over her body again. "Let me see if I can find it for you."

The journey north to the camp of Half Hand's band took several weeks. Jed used lodge poles to make a travois, and they were able to take the tipi, robes and supplies, along with the few personal belongings they had permitted themselves. They traveled long days when the weather held, short days when it did not. Katherine remembered her covered wagon with more fondness than she'd actually felt when she'd ridden in it the previous summer, but she never spent too much time in a saddle.

Jed made her a pair of high-top moccasins lined with fur, and when she became too saddle-sore to ride, she walked, leading her horse.

Her pluck and determination earned Jed's admiration, and he showed his respect by not pampering her. When she winced, he felt her pain, but for the sake of her dignity, he offered no words of sympathy. She was doing fine. When they made camp, he provided whatever salve or infusion he thought might help. In the case of the salve, he enjoyed putting it where it would do the most good.

They camped with two bands of Nez Percé before they reached Half Hand's people. Half Hand was the only one who spoke much English, but Jed preferred to get his message across with a little Nez Percé and a good deal of sign language rather than rely on Half Hand to translate for him. Katherine was a curiosity at first, for none of the villagers had seen a white woman before. She let Half Hand's daughter, Cry Of The Blue Jay, touch her hair, while his wife, Red Blanket Woman, took a close look at her eyes. Katherine passed muster, and she and Jed were given a place within the small eight-lodge community. Jed encouraged Katherine to help him erect the tipi so that it might be observed that she did a woman's job without complaint.

Once he was settled in, Jed established his routine easily—one that seemed to Katherine to be no routine at all. He and Half Hand hunted and trapped when the mood struck them. Sometimes Half Hand's brothers would join them, sometimes not. Katherine became a fair hand at making meat, but she was not as efficient as Red Blanket Woman was at preparing skins. When Katherine's fleshing knife got the better of her and tore into the hide, Red Blanket Woman would take the knife from her hand and finish Katherine's piece, then go back to her own. The displacement rankled, and Katherine would take to her Bible. Let the others laugh and chatter about the way she couldn't do anything right. She, at least, could read.

It was different when she and Jed were alone. When she had his complete attention and he spoke English and he buried his nose in her hair and called her his bonny sweet Kate, ah, then she felt warm. When he made her a set of snowshoes and took her past the frozen creek to a place where no one could witness her awkwardness, then patiently showed her how to walk on top of the snow, she felt loved. And at night, when he wrapped her with him in his blankets and prolonged their lovemaking until his need overwhelmed him, she felt necessary.

Christmas had come and gone with little notice, and Katherine felt as though she had missed a whole season. She had made a special meal and brought pine boughs into the lodge—efforts Jed had acknowledged with appreciative comments, but no inclination to celebrate. Next year they would be someplace else, she decided. The mission, if she had her way. And next year there would be candles and carols, maybe even a wedding, and none of these storytelling sessions in a tongue that was completely foreign to her.

"The women come to hear the stories, too," Jed ventured one evening as they shared the soup Katherine had prepared. "It would please me if you would come this time."

"I can't understand any of it. You know that. And since the women are not permitted to sit with the men, I can't share the benefit of Half Hand's knowledge." She stared into her wooden bowl and felt her face grow hot. "I don't like feeling stupid."

"No one thinks you're stupid. They know you have another language."

"That's right. I have another language." Shoulders squared, she sipped at her soup. Jed plucked the meat and wild turnips from the broth with his fingers, but Katherine had learned that, in the absence of a spoon, she could sometimes capture a chunk discreetly as she sipped. "It would behoove them to take an interest in our language, Jed."

"*Our* language? You mean English."

"That's right. I've tried to teach Red Blanket Woman just a few words, so that we could communicate, and she simply turns her face away. She won't even try."

"She's tried to teach you things, too, but you ignore her as well."

"Teach me what? When I do something wrong, she just takes it out of my hands and does it herself." She adjusted her lap robe in a huff. "The way Abigail always did. As if I'm such a ninny, I can't do anything right."

"Red Blanket Woman wants to show you. She expects you to watch and take the job back when you understand. But you always back away and leave it all up to her."

"If she could just *tell* me . . ."

"Even if you spoke the same language, she wouldn't tell you. She would show you." Finished with his soup, he set his bowl aside and leaned closer, hoping she would take heed soon. She had come to this land for this very purpose, but since they had taken refuge with Half Hand's people, she had kept herself apart from everyone but him. "If you wish to talk with people, you must listen," he told her. "If you would teach, you must be willing to learn."

"But all this hand talk seems so . . ."

"So what?"

She threw up her hand, and for lack of a better word she blurted, "Uncivilized. It isn't proper to gesture profusely that way. It isn't..."

He laughed at her civilized gesture of frustration. "I never thought it was proper to look an elder in the face when he spoke to me, but in school I soon learned that if I didn't, I would get my ears boxed."

Suddenly smiling, she reached over to lift his hair back from his ear. "Indeed, I see the effect. This one looks as though it had quite a mauling."

"That happened last night," he confided as he slipped his hand beneath her coyote lap robe and touched her knee. "When a certain proper lady nibbled at it until I thought I might burst through my skin."

"I did not."

"No?" He drew back in mock surprise. "Must have been your sister, then."

"I don't have a sister, and if I did—" She knew that her coy smile always made his eyes dance and tempted him to tease her more. "I wouldn't let her get anywhere near your ear."

"Why not? Because she might tell me all about the way you used to climb trees and skin your knees and shake your fist at the boys when they called you a—what was it? A ninny?"

"That was my stepmother's word for me." He started to rise, but she laid her hand on his arm. "Jed, don't go."

He would have stayed without hesitation—there would be many more nights of winter talk before spring came again—but she could not continue this way. Unless she tried to make her way among these people, she would soon languish with heartsickness for her own. And then she would be lost to him. He smiled and took her hand. "Come with me, Kate."

Part of her wanted to. She had missed Christmas, and, even though no one else seemed to know that, she might have felt as though she were attending some festivity if she went to the story-telling. But the prospect of feeling like an outsider loomed large in her mind. She hated feeling invisible.

"N-no. Not this time." She gave only a slight tug, and he released her hand. Too easily, she thought.

"If you change your mind, you know where I'll be." He reached for his woolen coat. "I won't be gone long."

Lord, she wanted to understand these people. Jed learned so easily, but then he was a man. Like Thomas, who had ministered to people wherever they needed him, be it saloon or salon, Jed adapted because he knew so much. Thomas had learned from books, and Jed had learned from life. Katherine was afraid she wouldn't learn these important things either way.

It wasn't as easy to teach as she'd thought it would be. Red Blanket Woman had not repeated words after her the way she'd envisioned. She had not been anxious to listen to Bible readings. Katherine had had better luck with poor, hapless Louise. What good would Katherine ever do anyone under these circumstances? She could be Jed's wife. His woman, she amended hastily, since there had been no real marriage. And if she ever learned to tan a hide, she might be his helpmate. But what *good* would she ever do?

The night was dark and quiet. Katherine stole from her lodge like a thief in the night, afraid to make a sound. A camp dog sniffed at the bottom of the heavy buffalo robe she held tightly around her shoulders, then skulked away. The walls of the big council tipi glowed with the warmth of the fire and fellowship inside. She counted the shadows of the people, the women on the left, the men on the right. She tried to guess which one Jed might be, but she couldn't. He blended right in. She could hear the crackling of the fire, the low rumble of voices and the ready laughter.

She cast a wishful glance at the community of winking stars in the black sky. She wanted to belong. It would feel good to blend in, maybe even to twinkle a little bit. But how could she when she couldn't understand a single word, and she did everything differently? She didn't even look like them. Or *they* didn't look like *her*.

The snow crunched beneath her moccasins as she drew closer to the bright lodge. Jed's understanding of the Indians' language was limited, but she could hear the sound of his laughter. She could not sit with Jed; the women sat on the left.

They all looked up when Katherine ducked through the tipi flap and straightened, letting the robe slide back from her shoulders. The fire was warm, and the faces reflected some surprise, but no unfriendliness. Across the way, Jed's eyes brightened, and the corners of his mouth twitched as if he suppressed a grin. He indicated the opposite side of the tipi with a pointed glance.

Did he think she didn't know that? She'd observed that much, and perhaps, it might surprise him to know, a little more. She was careful not to pass between the fire and any person as she made her way toward the women's side. Red Blanket Woman caught her eye and scooted to one side, making room. The woman's jet-black braids were slick and shiny, and the rich, welcoming luster in her dark eyes beckoned Katherine. She wasn't standing at Jed's side this time. She was on her own. And the beauty of Red Blanket Woman's eyes struck her as though she were seeing her for the first time. Katherine took the place that was offered, tucking her legs to one side to seat herself as the other women were seated.

The storyteller of the moment was a robust man, whose hair was styled in fur-wrapped braids with the toplock feathered high at the crown, like the tail of a courting grouse.

"Too-hool-hool-zote," Red Blanket Woman whispered behind her hand, and Katherine understood that to be the man's name. Red Blanket Woman raised her eyebrows, with a gesture indicating that this man commanded respect. He was too young to be a leader, but his listeners were enthralled.

Something poked Katherine in the back, and she leaned to the side to peek over her shoulder. There was Cry Of The Blue Jay, grinning up at her. The child opened her hand and offered Katherine a stick of jerked meat.

"Thank you," Katherine whispered. She glanced at Red Blanket Woman, wishing for the right words. The girl's mother nodded.

By the end of the evening, Katherine had learned a host of Nez Percé words. She knew she'd have to practice them or she would forget, but she thought she had the words for baby, pregnant, tired, long-winded, earrings and dress. Those had been spoken often with accompanying gestures. She had discovered that some of the people, mostly the men, knew some English, although they were as hesitant to use it as she was to try her Nez Percé words. When she and Jed returned to their lodge, she asked him about it.

"They've had some dealings with the missionary, Henry Spaulding. His mission is northwest of here on Lapwai Creek. Many of Half Hand's cousins from the northern bands have converted to Christianity and taken up farming."

"How wonderful!" Katherine's face brightened. "Why, Jed, I'm sure with just a little effort, these people, too—"

"They're a little worried about all the settlers they see moving in, Katherine. They've always been friendly to the whites, but they're noticing some changes." As he talked, Jed added a few pieces of wood to the fire pit, and the embers rekindled. "The settlers aren't as friendly as the mapmakers or the trappers, or even the missionaries like Whitman and Spaulding. All the settlers want is land. More and more land."

"But all I want is to teach them about God."

"They know about God, Katherine. Believe it. They know, and they honor Him in their own way." He stood and took the heavy buffalo robe from Katherine's shoulders. It fell to their sleeping pallet, and his hands rested on her shoulders. "Even as you teach, there is much that you can learn from them, too. I was proud of you tonight."

"You were?"

He nodded, his smile dancing in his eyes. "And I do know it's Christmas."

"It's past Christmas, actually, it's—"

"Epiphany. There is a good deal of French blood in my veins, Katherine, and I know when the time has come *pour un cadeau*—for bestowing a gift. I have been waiting anxiously—"

"But, Jed, I—"

He laid his forefingers on her lips to silence her. "I have been waiting like the child who has made a surprise and is about to burst with it. Turn around, Kate. Close your eyes."

She did, and he slipped his gift over her shoulders. It was much lighter than the buffalo robe, and the silky, plush fur felt wonderful on the inside, next to her body.

She gasped and wrapped her arms around herself and the cloak. It was talc-white buckskin, lined with winter gray wolf.

"Oh, Jed, it's beautiful." She whirled to give him her smile. His eyes beamed with the gift giver's pleasure. "Did you make this?"

"I made it, yes, but Red Blanket Woman tanned the doeskin for me. That's a woman's job." He lifted the fur-lined hood from Katherine's shoulders and settled it over her own lush hair.

"I must thank her. And I must—"

She looked so beautiful she made his heart swell. *"Joyeux Nóel, ma petite."*

"Why didn't you tell me, Jed?"

"Then it wouldn't have been a surprise, and I would have missed that wonderful female delight in your eyes when you—"

"But I want to give you a gift, and I didn't...I didn't think you would—"

"Good. Then I would name my gift." He put his arms around her and pulled her hips against his. "Fair?"

"I don't..." She caught the glint in his eye, and her eyes reflected it back to him. "Fair. Tell me what you want, then."

"I want you to wear this cloak."

"Of course."

"And I want to take it off you myself, slowly peeling it back."

"You are a gentleman."

"And I want to discover nothing under it but your lovely bare skin."

"Oh, Jed!" She feigned shock before lowering alluring lashes. "You should have let me surprise you."

Chapter Eight

Among the Nez Percé Katherine learned that winter was a quiet time when the Earth Mother slept beneath white blankets and the people took care not to disturb her. Winter talks and crafts and lovemaking helped to pass the time. Katherine became more skilled at tanning hides and preparing fur pelts for trade. She learned to stitch leather clothing with an awl and to apply decorative shells, the ornament that was a favorite with these people. Many of them pierced their noses with shell jewelry, a look Katherine had found distasteful at first, but she no longer noticed it. At some point she had stopped marking the differences between herself and the people who had given her refuge. Once she had passed that point, communication happened naturally.

Jed helped her learn to sign. When he saw that she was truly interested, he began signing whenever he talked to her. She was expected to follow along, but sometimes she was so fascinated by the sure, graceful movements of his hands that she forgot to move her own. He would stop, and she would look up and see the smile in his eyes and smile back sheepishly. Then he would position her hands and repeat his last words for her to practice.

"But I like to watch you."

"I like to watch you, too."

And so it went. By late winter food was less plentiful, but Jed and Katherine had become part of the band, and everyone shared so that none would go hungry. When the snow lay deep outside the lodge, there were long hours for fire dreaming.

"Do you ever think of going back to your home in the east, Kate?"

"Sometimes," she confessed. She could see the faces of her family in the flames. There were times when she even missed Abigail. "But I know I shall never see them again."

"Would you be happy there now?"

"Would you be there with me?" The lack of reply was his answer. "I would just like to know that my father is well," she said. "And you? Do you ever think of going home?"

"My people move their camps, much the way these people do, but they move together as one. I've wandered on my own for so long that I sometimes wonder whether I could even be part of them again." He tossed a green twig into the flames just to hear it crack. "But, yes, I think of going home. Not a day goes by that I don't wonder how it is with my mother, whether my grandmother still lives." He looked up at Katherine, as though she might be able to tell him some of the answers. "I wonder whether they think of me. I wonder whether they mention my name."

On the need to reassure him, she laid her head in his lap. "I'm sure they miss you, Jed. How could they not? Is it quite impossible for you to go back?"

"Would you go with me?"

She turned her lips to his thigh and kissed him there, but she had no answer for him.

"I've heard that there is talk among the Métis of taking a stand against the Hudson's Bay Company's way of doing things." The thought made him smile at the flames. "I might like to be there to see how that turns out."

Alarmed, Katherine sat up again. "What kind of a stand?"

"Whatever kind it takes to make them listen. They depend on us, and we know it as well as they do. They have a place for us in their pockets, but we don't fit in their social plan." He ticked off the complaints on one hand. "We are not white. We are not Indian. They want us to live here, but not there. They want us to do certain jobs. They want us to trade only with them. When I went back home, there was a missionary—" He chuckled. "Always there is a missionary."

"Perhaps God is trying to tell you something."

"Listen to this story, Kate, and tell me what God's message is. I was approached by a priest who said he wanted to see more 'half castes,' as he called us, in the clergy. He didn't like the term *country born*, as we are also called. He said that was an insult, and we should prefer his term. We were half castes. We made good translators, and he thought we could be the 'leaven' for the Christian mission."

The memory brought a sardonic smile to Jed's face as he gazed into the fire and recounted it. "He was impressed with my education. He suggested that I might be interested. In being a priest? I asked. No, he said I shouldn't think of becoming a priest, but I might be a deacon—even an archdeacon. And he suggested that if I would marry a woman of European ancestry and 'thin the native blood even more,' I might produce a son who would be intelligent enough to become some kind of a leader."

Katherine scowled as she thought this over. "I was thinking if I married you, I might get a daughter who could speak several languages and swim."

They looked at each other and laughed.

"No message from God in that story?" Jed asked, his eyes twinkling.

"Perhaps a warning about missionaries."

"That's what I thought, too."

"A warning you've neglected to heed."

"So it seems."

"But God had to look out for me somehow, too."

Through me? Jed wondered. But why not? The Trickster stories had always been his favorites. The wily spirit with a sense of mischief, who loved to lead men to foolishness, would set his bait with a string tied to it. *Give the man a woman to love, but let her be a white missionary. Let him have a taste of happiness, then watch him chase his tail over it the way he's done in the past.* The wise old woman who was his grandmother would remind Jed that a taste was a brief thing and warn him that the time was short.

"It will be spring soon," Katherine said. She did not add that the snow would be gone from the mountain passes and the trails would be open.

"But, for now, it's winter."

When spring came, Katherine and Jed filled each day so that there was no time for discussion of tomorrow. There was fresh meat again, and now that the Earth Mother had awakened, there was celebration.

Red Blanket Woman and the children would accompany Half Hand to Fort Boise to trade the winter's catch, and Jed helped him prepare for the journey. Fort Boise was Hudson's Bay, but it was close. There was no talk of why Jed wanted the trip made quickly. No talk of what he would do, where he would go when he left the Nez Percé.

For now, there was trading to be done, and for his part, there were few trade articles that Jed would want this year. Half Hand would be interested in a new rifle, blankets, an English trade knife, tobacco, powder and shot, flour and sugar, calico and flannel. Jed wanted ammunition, some fabric for Katherine and the rest in cash—Made Beaver, the coin of the realm. That much he could carry.

Once Half Hand returned, Jed knew there would be no more reason to delay his departure. Then he would discuss his plans with Katherine. She still had a mind to head west, and he knew she hoped he'd go with her. But Jed had other ideas. Not ideas, really. More like yearnings. He knew them well. He'd lived with them since the day his father had put him on a horse and gone south with him. It was the same old pull, the one he was always trying to ignore, or beat down when it got bad, until he thought, maybe he wouldn't go back, but maybe he'd get a little closer. Close enough to smell the river and hear the wind in the cottonwood trees. Close enough to let the Trickster tease him.

He dreamed of going home, and he dreamed of taking Katherine with him.

Katherine knew only that Jed had grown moody. He slipped away often just to be alone, and she wondered whether he missed his life in seclusion. One day, after they had shared their noon meal beside a mountain lake, she waited in silence, hoping he would tell her what was on his mind. Each time she caught his eyes, he glanced away. Suddenly he stripped off his clothes and headed for the water. Powerful strokes propelled him toward the center of the lake.

Obviously, he had no patience for her inept splashing this day. She watched him slip below the water's surface, and she wondered how deep it was. How far was it to the murky bottom and the handful of mud that eluded him? It didn't surprise her when he stayed down so long. He was Earthdiver. He could hold his breath—

Good Lord, she was thinking in heathen terms. Earthdiver, indeed. He broke the surface with a splash and tossed a water spray from his hair. Jed West. That was who he was. He had to come up for air, just like everybody else. She wouldn't watch him. The sky was clouding up, and she thought it would be fitting if a rumble from heaven drove him from the water. A patch of spring dandelions caught her eye, and she decided to do something useful. There would be greens in tonight's soup.

At the edge of the clearing stood a huge boulder, and Katherine sensed movement behind it. She approached it cautiously and peered around it. Sticking close to the pinewoods, two black bear cubs played a game of tag, one pouncing, the other darting away, then coming back for more. She was so close! They were like a pair of big, furry pups. She wished she could get Jed's attention without scaring them away.

Water rolled down Jed's limbs as he emerged from the lake, shook himself and reached for the blanket he had spread on the ground. He put on his buckskin pants and rubbed the blanket over his hair. A cracking of tree limbs alerted him first, then a flash of black in the trees. The sow bounded out of the shadows into the sunlit clearing. She was not after him. His rifle lay only a few feet away, but he turned, saw Katherine and the cubs and broke into a dead run.

"Get away from those cubs!"

Katherine whirled, then froze.

Without breaking his stride, Jed scooped up a rock and hurled it at the bear. "Back away, Katherine! Get the rifle!"

Katherine kept her eyes on the bear and let her feet find their own direction. Jed had distracted the animal. The bear stood on her hind legs and turned on him. Jed was of an equal height, but the bear was quick to display the finger-length claws and the long canine teeth that gave her one of several advantages over the unarmed man.

"The rifle," Jed said quietly.

The bear snarled and raised a paw. Instinctively Jed put up his hands to protect his face as crescent claws slammed into the base of his neck and plowed furrows along his left side to his hip. He staggered back and sank to his knees. A shot rang out. For a moment the image of the towering bear diffused like black powder in the wind, and Jed wondered which of them had been blasted away. Then his vision cleared again, and he realized the shot had missed them both. The bear came down on all fours, dismissed the man with an angry snort and lumbered away, herding her cubs into the trees.

Katherine dropped the rifle, hiked up her skirts and ran, calling Jed's name.

He was afraid that if he lay down, he would never get up, but his head was already spinning. He tipped it back and watched a gathering of gray swirl above his head. At his back he heard her calling him, heard the pounding of her feet. He didn't want her to see him. He felt the warm blood streaming down his belly and into the front of his pants. He knelt there, his hand hovering over his chest, shielding himself but afraid to touch himself or to be touched, even by Katherine. He knew the claws had laid him open.

"Oh, God."

He couldn't see her clearly, but he heard the horror in those two whispered words.

"Bind me." Even as he said it, he heard her tearing at her skirt.

The initial mitigating shock gave way to searing pain when she touched him with the first of the bandaging.

"So much blood. Oh, Jed..."

"Which kind?" he muttered. "Does it run red or..." There was no use fighting the blackness. His head fell against her shoulder. "...white?"

They were close to camp, but not within shouting range. Katherine was loath to leave him, but knew she had to get help. She couldn't move him herself. The bandage she'd made of her petticoat was already soaked with Jed's blood. *Which kind?* Lord, what a strange thing to say at a time like this. It was Jed's blood, and it was all red.

A drop of water struck her nose. It was no tear.

She laid him in the grass and whispered close to his ear, "I have to get help, Jed."

"Two Black Horses."

"I'll bring him. Please don't..." She squeezed her eyes shut and kissed him hard. "I'll hurry, love."

She raced to the village to find Two Black Horses, Half Hand's brother, and tried to drag him away from his meal. He thought her babbling did not justify the rudeness of her intrusion until she managed to make the signs for "bear" and "hurt" as she choked out Jed's name.

A fine spring rain pelted their shoulders. Two Black Horse's wife lashed a travois to the spotted rump of his war-horse, which was kept handy near the lodge. Instant mobility, fortunately, was a way of life here. Katherine led Two Black Horses to the place by the lake. She called to Jed, and to her relief, he answered.

They loaded him on the travois, covered him with a blanket and Katherine walked beside him. With every bump, Jed gripped the travois poles more tightly, but he made no sound. Two Black Horses helped get him into the lodge, and Jed asked him to send Red Moon, the medicine man.

Katherine removed the bandage and cleaned Jed's wounds. Blood oozed from the ragged furrows clawed into his flesh. The middle tracks were deeply driven. She made no comment. He knew how bad it looked without her telling him, and she knew how it felt. She could see the pain in his eyes.

"Bring the trade whiskey from my saddlebag and one of your steel needles," he told her.

She glanced at his torn flesh and drew a long, slow breath. It had to be done. Jed would not hesitate to do it for her. "What shall I use for thread?"

"Sinew. Soak it. Tie each stitch."

"Don't you think Red Moon—"

"Do this for me, Kate. Red Moon will bring medicine." He bit off a groan, and his body trembled from raw exposure. "But you are good with a needle, *ma petite*. And you must get out of those wet clothes. It's . . . cold."

"I'm all right." She covered him to the waist with a dry blanket. "I must build a fire."

"First the whiskey."

She handed him the bottle they both hoped would bring him some relief from his pain, and she made a fire. By the time Red Moon arrived, Jed's dark eyes were glazed— whether from pain or whiskey, Katherine wasn't sure. Red Moon burned sweet grass and chanted while Katherine prepared to sew Jed's flesh back together.

He handed her the bottle. "Pour this on first."

"On the wounds?"

He nodded. "Deadens it some."

Was she as pale as he was, she wondered? "I'm afraid it'll—"

"Don't pull back from it, Katherine. No matter what. It's going to hurt, you can't help it. Just do what has to be done."

With a nod, she poured the whiskey over his wounds, setting her jaw against the shudders that racked him, and the sound of air sucked through clenched teeth. The gashes gaped and bled anew. Katherine imagined pressing herself against him to stanch the flow of his blood. At least for that, she wouldn't need steady hands.

"Jed, that chanting. I don't think I can do this while he's doing all that—"

"Have you been praying, Katherine?"

She stared in surprise. "I . . . I've been too—"

"Let Red Moon do the praying, then. You do your best needlework." He touched her cheek with unsteady fingers. "Little crosses, hmm?"

When she was ready, Red Moon placed a smooth hardwood stick between Jed's teeth. He turned his head, closed his eyes, and she started working at the base of his neck. After the first few stitches, she was able to steel herself against the knowledge that she pricked Jed's flesh. She managed by telling herself over and over again simply to move from one stitch to the next on her way to having this task, like any other, well done.

Jed did his best to suppress any sound of complaint, but halfway through the process, he turned his face into the woolly pallet. The stick rolled out of his mouth, and he loosed a strangled curse, then gasped for breath. His head was spinning crazily.

"More whiskey, Kate. Please."

The sound of his pain shook her to the quick. Avoiding his eyes, she handed him the bottle and watched him guzzle the whiskey desperately, as though it had life to give. When he gave the bottle back to her, she eyed it, then took a drink herself before setting it aside. His mirthless chuckle unnerved her.

"We would both do better if you would just give over and pass out, Jed." She rethreaded her needle and made ready to start in again.

"When I drink, it is my custom to get wild first. Then— sst! damn, that—then I pass out."

She held the stick to his lips, and he gave her a plaintive look as he took it between his teeth. "Just hold on," she said gently, wishing she could stop stabbing him with the blasted needle and hold on to him herself. "I'll try to work quickly."

She wasn't sure at what point he'd made a liar of himself, but by the time she was finished, the stick had slipped to the pallet, and Jed had lost consciousness. Red Moon prepared a foul-smelling poultice, which they applied before they bandaged Jed and let him rest. Satisfied that his part was done, Red Moon left, and Katherine took off her damp cotton dress, washed the blood from herself and her patient, and lay close to him to keep him warm.

The thunder seemed like part of a dream, but the lightning that knifed him in the chest was real enough. It caught Jed unprepared to stifle his groan. He seemed to be in some murky place. The river, perhaps. There was such heaviness in his chest, he thought surely he had sunk to the bottom like a stone, and there he lay. The distant rumble bade him *rise, come up now, or you'll die down there*. He struggled to push himself up, but, *Dieu*, the pain was too much.

"Shh. Lie still now."

He saw her shadow. He saw the aura about her head. She was the bright-haired river spirit. She loomed so close, he could smell rainwater on her skin. His efforts to reach for her brought a fireball of pain, but he caught her cool, cool hand. "Help me—"

"I will."

"Stay afloat."

"Yes. Just as you helped me. Drink this."

She lifted him, cradled him against her breast, and he tasted something sweet. Then her cool water soothed his hot face.

Katherine withdrew her arm and laid him down carefully. Jed had fever, and that frightened her. She rekindled the fire and made a fresh poultice of the sorrel, chickweed and wild onion that Red Moon had left. The puckered tracks of stitches across Jed's chest were holding. Her accomplishment surprised her. A year ago, if anyone had suggested to her that she would one day stitch up a man's flesh, she would have laughed and called the suggestion a gruesome jest.

She wasn't laughing now. She bandaged the wounds again and lay close beside Jed, finally drifting off to sleep on a prayer.

Water dripping near the bed woke her just before daybreak. The wind's direction had shifted, and raindrops hissed on the hot coals. Katherine slipped into a buckskin dress that Red Blanket Woman had given her and hurried outside to adjust the flaps at the top of the tipi. When she ducked back inside, she found Jed awake, flushed and coughing.

She fell to her knees beside him. "Shall I fetch Red Moon?" He shook his head as another spasm seized him.

"What shall I do, Jed? Tell me of your grandmother's medicine. Some tea, some tincture..."

"Do you know what woodbine looks like?" She nodded. "I saw some climbing..." He coughed again and lifted his hand toward the east. "Stand of aspens."

"Yes, I know the spot." She was already on her way.

"Get the roots."

The new day was dawning within a wet, gray shell. Katherine hurried to the place where she, too, had noticed the early yellow blooms of the climbing wild woodbine. She found a sturdy stick and dug the tough, splintery roots of several plants from the moist ground. She remembered how Jed's teas had helped her, and she did not doubt that he could heal himself.

She had not been gone long, but in that time, his cough had worsened. He instructed her to make a tincture from the bark of the roots combined with whiskey, which was the best they could do for alcohol. The racking cough was the only goad Katherine needed to move the process along. By the time the concoction was ready, Jed was clutching his side, his eyes glistening like those of a trapped animal.

"Are the stitches—"

"Ten drops in a little water," he ordered, but she set down the mixture and tried to pull his hands away from his body. "Don't!"

"I think you're bleeding again."

"Ten drops!" The cough twisted Jed's breath into a heaving parody of itself. It was several moments before he could swallow the medicine she'd prepared for him. Even then, he refused to allow her to move his hands and expose what he did not want either of them to see.

"It's ripping me apart."

"Let me see. Let me help you."

"You cannot help this. You must not..." He looked at her, and in his eyes was a plea for mercy. "The bandage is all that's holding me together."

She laid a gentling hand on his brow and tried to move his hand again. "Then I shall—"

"No! Just leave me the hell alone." He closed his eyes and turned away. "Let me be, Kate."

A voice from outside interrupted them. "They say that my partner has been injured. I've come to see for myself."

"Half Hand is back!" Katherine knew she would have an ally now, and she sprang to pull back the tipi door and invite him in. "He was clawed by a bear, and it started to rain before we could get him back here." The coughing started again, and she followed Half Hand, explaining needlessly, "He took a chill."

Still clutching his side, Jed struggled to sit up. Half Hand squatted beside the buffalo robe pallet and lent a hand to the effort, supporting his friend's shoulder.

Katherine darted forward, but she stopped short of pushing Half Hand away. "Don't let him...please make him lie down. He mustn't—"

But Half Hand dismissed her with a glance. "He needs to sit up, woman. He knows what he needs."

"He needs fresh bandages and probably more stitching." She nodded at Jed, her eyes pleading. "He knows that, too."

Half Hand eased Jed's hand away from the bandaging. "There is fresh blood, my friend."

"I know. I have just used my grandmother's medicine." He pointed to the gourd that held the woodbine tincture.

"Cree medicine? That's good." Half Hand turned to Katherine. "Give the medicine its due first. West knows his own needs."

Katherine sank to her knees, her face hot, tears of frustration burning behind her eyes. Her stitches hadn't held. Jed looked sallow and exhausted, and he wouldn't let her touch him. She felt panicky. She could see him bleeding to death before her eyes.

Jed closed his eyes and worked to stem the spasms and bring his breathing under control. When he opened them, he saw her hands clenched between her thighs, then the fear in her eyes. "I don't know if I can stand any more of that needle," he confessed. "I think it may unman me this time."

"I know the kind of man you are, Jed." She touched his arm. "There's nothing you have to prove to me."

The tincture of woodbine had taken effect, quieting the spasms and relaxing Jed's agonizing muscles. Katherine applied whiskey to the wounds once more and repaired the broken stitches. He could not restrain himself this time, but Half Hand was there to keep him from twisting out of the brutal needle's reach. When the task was done, tears ran their course on all three faces.

Jed slept fitfully, his breath rattling in his chest. He called out to Katherine, then murmured half-intelligible promises and pleas. He cursed the pain in two languages, but as the fever worsened and he slipped deeper into the core of himself—the heart of his being and the stem of his brain—he muttered in his grandmother's tongue.

When night fell, Half Hand got up to leave.

"No!" Wearily Katherine scrambled to her feet and went after the man. "We have to do something for him. He's getting weaker."

"I must prepare a sweat for him."

"A sweat? But he cannot be moved. He's too—"

"The night air will take him unless we do this."

Katherine was not permitted inside the hide-covered hut where the sweat bath ritual was to be performed. Half Hand suggested that she make some sacrifice for her man, in whatever her way might be, and he assured her that prayers would be offered up all night on Jed's behalf. She doubted the power of the god to whom Half Hand and the others might pray, but she hoped the steam would at least help Jed breathe more easily.

Half Hand and Two Black Horses bore Jed to the sweat lodge on a litter. Katherine found a place in a stand of birches, and she wrapped herself in the white cloak Jed had made for her and huddled there, within sight of the dome-shaped hut and the bonfire a few yards away. Burning pine pitch scented the air. She saw Red Blanket Woman pull a rock from the fire with two sticks, maneuver it along the ground and slip it under the skin of the small lodge. Katherine's head throbbed, and her eyes burned.

New spring leaves fluttered overhead in the night breeze. Male voices rose in unison from within the lodge. Sacrifice, she thought. Make some sacrifice. What was left? She had sacrificed everything that was comfortable and familiar in her life. She had given up everything for one man—for Thomas—and he had died. Her sacrifices had been paltry. She had never loved Thomas the way she loved Jed. She knew that now. Perhaps she had been unworthy of the sacrifice Thomas had made for her. For the sake of her health, he had forgone his rights as her husband. Now she had trouble recalling his face. She wanted to ask his forgiveness, but she was beyond his forgiveness now. What was done was done. She had shared her child-

hood with Thomas. She shared her womanhood with Jed.
It sounded wrong, but it felt right.

Lord, she prayed, don't take him, too.

His chest was heavy, but he had the sense that he had
managed to stay afloat. He had drifted into a dark cave,
and there, in murky water, he bobbed with the rhythm of
his own heartbeat. He smelled sage and heard the voices
of his ancestors singing. It was a soothing sound, but it
was not like the French tune from long ago, the one that
had always put him to sleep. He remembered another
French song—the one he had once hoped to live and die
singing, the way his grandfather had done. This was the
same kind of song, the kind that made a man feel the
blood still pumping in his veins.

Lo, the poor voyageur! Sing the song, *mon fils.* Sing it
out, loud and hearty. It will carry you along the rivers,
over the portages, through miles of damp mist and cold
fog. Days without sunshine, nights infested with mosquitoes. Sing out! You still have work to do.

What work? He couldn't reach the bottom of the river.
He had tried, but his chest burned, and he had to turn
back. No mud. Not one grain of sand had he retrieved.

*Your people need a place. Dive deeper. Bring us some-
thing, Girard.*

I can't. I'm tired. I've lost too much blood.

*It will replenish itself in equal parts, and you will still
be the same man. You will still be Métis.*

Not if I change my name.

Names are easily changed.

Not if I stay away.

You cannot stay away.

Not if I take a wife.

You have taken two. One red, one white. Who are you, Girard? Who will your children be?

They'll kill me if I go back.

Look at yourself now.

Am I dead?

Not quite.

Will I live?

If you want to.

Give me my life and my woman, and let me live in peace.

Your people need a place, Girard. Dive deeper. Come up. Bring us something.

They were together in the night's fog, Katherine huddling in the trees and Jed in the warm, damp cave. Prayers came hard when images born of fear and pain filled the mind. But through it all, three men chanted and poured water over hot rocks, filling the lodge with the healing breath of the spirit. Jed's chest rose and fell, rose and fell, and the mist bathed his lungs.

They brought him back at daybreak, as they'd promised they would. Katherine was waiting with a steaming kettle of tea. She wrapped him in blankets, gave him more of the woodbine tincture, then held his head while he sipped tea made from his own herbal recipe. Beads of sweat covered his face and dampened his hair. The fever had broken.

It was more than a week before Jed could do much besides sleep and eat. Katherine kept the steam rolling in the tipi, either from a kettle of broth or tea, and she foraged near the camp for strength-building food. Spring nettles, it was said, would build the blood. Curly dock, lamb's-quarters, wild onions and plants she was directed to harvest but for which she had no names, all went into her kettle with the fresh meat that Half Hand brought regularly. On one of her excursions in the woods, she recognized a witch hazel shrub. This, she decided, would bring Jed's bed-weary body another kind of relief.

Jed was restless. He had removed his bandages. The stitches itched like hell, and he figured air was the best healer. He lay there, propped up on a willow backrest, and watched her come in, hoping she'd scold him. He was in just the right mood for barking back. He was as weak as a newborn creature and as surly as an old man. What man could tolerate lying abed this long? His backside ached worse than it would have if he'd jammed it in a saddle for a solid week.

"I'm going to rub you down with witch hazel, Jed, just as soon as I can get the bark and the leaves made into an infusion. How does that sound?"

So much for barking. "I wouldn't mind," he muttered.

"I see you've discarded the bandages. Do you think we'll be able to take those stitches out in a few days?"

"I'm ready to take them out today. They itch."

"Good. You're healing, thank God." She busied herself with preparations as she talked. "I think we should wait a day or two to make sure. I don't know when I've ever made a prettier pattern of stitches."

"Pity we have to rip them out."

"I'm afraid you'll always have a reminder here." She paused in passing to touch his chest. "It will make quite a scar."

Just that touch made him quiver inside, and he had to consciously take hold and flatten his response. "It's not the first. Won't be the last."

"It'll be the grandest, though."

Her smile melted him.

After they'd eaten and the witch hazel brew had cooled, she bade him shuck his pants and turn on his side. The water's cooling astringency made her hands tingle as she massaged his warm back, kneading tight muscles into relaxation. He groaned, releasing his tension in a way that he'd refused to release pain. She moved her soothing hands over his buttocks, calling his deadened nerves back into service. He groaned again, this time with unabashed pleasure. She shifted her ministrations to the backs of his thighs before he rolled to his back.

She had slept with him, held his body close to hers and thrilled to the touch of his skin, but the sight of his nudity, his arousal, his lean, hard body and his injured chest made her want to take him inside herself and love him until there could be no more pain for either of them. His dark eyes told her he wanted the same.

Her hands were wet with witch hazel. She reached for his hands and passed the tingling sensation from her palms to his. Then she dribbled water over him and smoothed it over his shoulders, his chest, his corded arms and his abdomen. His breath came in quick pants. He caught her wrist, and she was drawn into the glowing heat of his eyes.

"Touch me, Kate."

She swallowed convulsively as he dragged her hand along his body to his engorged shaft. He pulled her head down for a mouth-bruising kiss, leaving her as short of breath as he was when she touched her forehead to his and, with his guidance, moved her hand over him.

"Oh, Jed, I only meant to give you—"

"Shh. Just touch me. Just like this."

"To give you ease. I meant to take away the stiffness."

"You have. You will."

"But I might hurt you."

"Only if you stop." He unbuttoned her bodice and slipped his hand inside to tease her nipple. Her heartbeat fluttered under his hand. "Ride me, Kate. Give me the ease I find only when I'm deep inside you."

She moved over him carefully. He helped her find their fit and the rhythm that would bring them both pleasure. He exhorted her to hold on tight, and she did. He lifted her higher, higher, and she thought her injured mount must have sprouted wings for the way he took her soaring.

The sun rose and set twice more on Jed's time of healing. The Nez Percé had delayed moving camp until he was on his feet. Jed knew that, come morning, the announcement would be made. It was time for the small band to join up with others for the summer. It was time Katherine knew his plans.

She was removing his stitches by the light of the fire. Each snip felt like the bite of a north woods mosquito. "This is a damn sight better than cauterizing," he mused as he sat with his chin tucked, trying to watch her. "Once I had to cauterize a gash in my leg. Hated the smell of my own flesh burning."

"This is healing nicely."

He drew a deep breath. "We'll have to be leaving tomorrow."

She looked up from her work, surprised. "Where are we going?"

"To the Place of the Rye Grass. Isn't that where you wanted to go?"

Her eyes widened. "We're going to the Whitman Mission?"

He nodded. "Unless you've changed your mind about going back where you came from. In that case, I'll—"

"I haven't changed my mind. I have no wish to turn back. So much has happened since I set out on this journey." She straightened, puzzling over the turns her life had taken; and now another one was imminent. "That happened a lifetime ago, didn't it? But the mission . . . the mission lives, and I want to live up to the promise I made." She brightened more with each prospect. "I believe I can teach. They say there's wonderful farm land there, Jed. Perhaps we might farm."

"I've dreamed of trying many things, Kate, but farming was never one of them."

"But you could teach as well as I. Better." The very fact that he was agreeing to take her to this mystical place seemed promising to her. "You've said yourself that this area is almost trapped out, and the future of fur trading is—"

"I'll take you to the mission, Katherine." He would take her there for want of a better place to take her. He knew she was no woman to follow a man over the next hill for the rest of her life. It would be foolish to ask her.

Foolish, but necessary. "It's what you want, isn't it?"

"Yes." He would not leave her there, any more than he had truly left her at Fort Hall. "It's what I want."

Chapter Nine

Katherine was on the move again. For one who had once gratefully marked off each day in the wagon as one less she had to face, moving felt remarkably good. She remembered missing the comfort of upholstered seats and the conveniences of a house with a kitchen. She recalled pining for the use of a bathtub and the taste of roast lamb in the early months of her journey with Thomas. Those things seemed trivial now. She had survived the winter, and life was worth living for adventure almost as much as it was for mission.

The buckskin leggings Jed had made her pleased her as much as the pretty blue and yellow calico Red Blanket Woman had selected at Fort Boise for her at Jed's request. Katherine had made a blue skirt that was several inches shorter than she was accustomed to wearing, and considerably more colorful. The moccasins, leggings and a high-necked white blouse made a practical traveling outfit. And Katherine truly felt the urge to travel.

Everyone did. Excitement ran high as lodges were struck and hide covers folded in precisely the same manner they had been since a time beyond memory. Winter was past, and it was time to seek new grounds, new grass and new game under ever-changing skies. There was as much constancy in the passage as there was in the destination. Katherine's dream of the Place of the Rye Grass waxed full, but once the little band of travelers set out, she found herself anticipating each notch along the trail for the valley or the waterfall or the soaring peak that was sure to lie just beyond it.

After three days on the trail, Jed and Katherine split from the group as Half Hand's people headed east, toward the Bitterroot Mountains and beyond, to hunt for buffalo. The two were sent on their way with gifts. Half Hand gave Jed a red roan Appaloosa stallion and told him to find good mares. The Nez Percé had long bred the spotted horses for color and stamina. Half Hand guaranteed that the stud would throw his spotted blanket on the majority of his colts and warned Jed to beware of the thieving Blackfeet, who would do anything for a good Nez Percé mount.

Red Blanket Woman's gift to Katherine was an infant's cradle board, lined with fur and decorated with beads and melon shells. Red Blanket Woman smiled, in the way of one woman sharing baby secrets with another, as she showed Katherine how to use disposable cattail fluff inside the cradle board and how to adjust the hood to shield the baby's eyes from the sun.

"But I have no baby," Katherine said wistfully as she fingered the rows of blue and white beads and petted the plush fur.

"You will," her friend assured her.

Katherine dug a small satin purse out of her single reticule and took out her mother's cameo brooch, one of the few mementos she still possessed. She pinned the brooch to Red Blanket Woman's dress.

Later, when they stopped at a stream to water their horses, Jed untied Katherine's white prairie bonnet and replaced it with a brown, floppy-brimmed hat. Contemplating the look, he made the brim dip over her right eye. He nodded, satisfied, as he lifted her single blond braid from her shoulder and let it slide through his hand. "You're not an emigrant anymore, Kate. You belong here. You need a real hat."

She adjusted the brim to her own liking and noted that the hat was new. It must have been on his trading list. Then she tugged it back down over one eye as he had done and gave a coy smile. "Don't you think women should wear bonnets?"

"You need more protection from the sun." He turned from her and dropped to one knee beside the stream. The rocks that lay beneath the rushing water had been cleaned and polished until the bits of mica and quartz winked in the sunlight. Jed plunged his hands in and splashed cold water over his face, then dragged his hands through his hair. "I'm thinking of cutting my hair," he said as he sat back on the grassy bank. "Would that please you?"

"I like your hair. If it's comfortable for you—"

"I can't decide whether it'll be safer for you if I don't look so much like an Indian, or if I . . ."

"Safer for me?" Katherine sat down beside him. "I feel safer with you than I've ever felt with anyone—even a whole wagon train full of men and guns. Who would harm us, Jed?"

"You're a white woman traveling in the company of an Indian man. That's pretty unusual in these parts."

"A Métis," she corrected. "And I had no idea what that was until you told me."

"Not many people do, but they know 'half-breed.' If we meet up with anybody along the way, they might not give us a chance to explain anything."

"There's nothing to explain."

"Isn't there?" He tried to resist asking the question that taunted him, making him feel both scared and foolish. But finally he turned to her with it. "Katherine, did Red Blanket Woman know something I don't know?"

"Like what?"

He paused, then launched, "Are you carrying my child?"

Silence, then a quiet "No."

"Are you sure?"

"I . . ." She glanced away. They had shared so much in their short time together, and she had wondered why he hadn't noticed the problem that had begun to worry her. So many times she'd wanted to talk with him about it, but he was a man. It was the kind of thing a woman did not discuss with a man—ever. She had a woman friend, but with Red Blanket Woman, Katherine's vocabulary had been limited, and who else was there? Feeling shy, she plucked a blade of grass.

"Since I was ill, I've not had...there's been no..." Her voice got higher and thinner, and she looked to him now for some kind of help. "I had such a terrible fever, and I grew so thin. I'm afraid . . . I mean, there've been no—" He kept staring at her, not making it any easier. She rushed through to the end. "No monthlies at all since I was sick. I thought you knew."

He should have suspected it, but it was not a man's way to keep track of such things. "Then you're not sure."

"I'm not sure I'll ever have children," she said quietly. "If there were a child now, I would know."

"How would you know?" he tested.

"I would feel it, wouldn't I? I would be sick."

"You might not be sick. It isn't so with all women." He didn't remember White Earth Woman showing any sign of illness, but who was he to say? He was just a man.

Katherine was frightened, too, and he wanted to help her. That stepmother of hers had apparently taught her nothing. Jed touched her shoulder tentatively, then ran two fingers along the center of her thick yellow braid. "There would be other changes in your body. You would know them, and I think I would sense them." He cupped her breasts carefully in his hands. "Do these feel sore?"

"No. Not unless you . . ."

"Unless I what?"

Beneath the brim of the hat her eyes looked big and soft and very blue. "Unless you love them long and kiss them hard. Then sometimes . . ."

His throat tingled when he swallowed. "You must tell me if I hurt you."

"It doesn't hurt when you do it. It makes me feel wonderful."

"Then you must tell me if it hurts later." His eyes glistened with apologies as he took off her hat and set it aside on the grassy bank. He drew her into his arms, and she laid her head against his chest. He wanted to make her feel wonderful right now. "I know how to make it stop hurting."

"You have medicine for that?"

"Yes. Medicine and other things."

"Do you have anything for a woman who might be barren?"

He closed his eyes and tried to push the notion away. "If I did, you'd be a fool to take it now."

She sat up, wide-eyed and injured. "Jed!"

"I lost a woman to childbirth. It scares the hell out of me, Katherine."

"It's a chance we take," she reminded him quietly.

"I've loved you as I have because I know no other way. And it's all I have to give you now. I'm not like your sainted Thomas. I'm...I'm a selfish man.'' Suddenly wistful, he lifted his hand to her temple and caught a wisp of hair between his first two fingers. "When I watched you with that cradle board, I felt soft inside. I imagined you with a round belly and my child making it so." He captured his full lower lip between his teeth and let it slide away, moistened. "I could do that to you, Kate. So easily, so willingly, I could do that to you."

Lord, forgive me. "Then why haven't you?"

"I hoped to God I had. But that was for myself. For your sake, I prayed to God I hadn't. I prayed the way the missionaries taught me because, for *your* sake, I thought He would—"

"But I'm your woman, Jed. That's what you said."

"I know." His woman. Her cheek felt fragile against his roughened palm. "I know, I know. This isn't the time. I don't believe you're barren. This just isn't the right time for you, *ma petite*." Nor was he the right man.

"Do you think this...this interruption is God's way of telling us that?"

"Maybe."

"And the time will come later?"

"When it's right for you." *For you, sweet Kate. Not for me.*

He drew back suddenly. "You're right. You lost a lot of weight, ran a high fever for days. You nearly died. Your body is taking this time for itself."

"I hope so." She felt bereft as she watched him stand, the motion like that of a mountain cat. He turned his attention to the horses, and she followed his lead. "Jed." He turned to her again. "I've never wished you to be like anyone else. Not in any way."

"But you didn't wish to love me, did you?"

"Not at first."

"We are a pretty pair, you and I." Half-smiling, he shook his head. "I don't know what this God of yours could be thinking."

The Blue Mountains were as rugged as they were beautiful. Katherine was glad they had no wagons to contend with, for they would have had to cut timber to clear the way. She remembered reading Narcissa Whitman's account of casting aside her trunk of clothes and saying goodbye to her black bombazine wedding dress. Marcus, her husband, had been determined to make the trip with a wagon to prove that it could be done. He had started with a heavy freight wagon, abandoned that for a lighter Dearborn and finally ended up with an improvised two-wheeled cart. That, too, had been abandoned before they tackled the Blue Mountains. A few years later, the Oregon Trail was traversed by wagons all the way to the coast.

But Katherine didn't miss hers. The clothing, the few pieces of furniture, the linens and the books were all behind her; they could be replaced someday. She was learning to get what she needed from the land and from the man who showed her the way. They built a lean-to shelter each night and took their food from the woods and streams. Jed taught Katherine to load and fire his rifle, hit her target and gut her kill. He told her over the noon meal one day that she was as good an overland voyager as he'd ever partnered up with. That night, as on other nights, he did not lie with her until he thought she'd gone to sleep.

She knew he'd gone into his saddlebag again for a bottle of trade whiskey. She had said nothing to him about it, but it gave her a lonely feeling whenever he did it. She told herself not to ask him what was wrong. He might tell her he didn't want to go to Waiilatpu, the Place of the Rye Grass, that he was thinking about turning back, and she didn't want to hear that. Getting him there was half the battle. After that, she would deal with his reluctance to stay.

Watching him tip that bottle to his mouth made her shiver. His silhouette was backlit by the camp fire, which was burning low. The breeze threaded through the needles of the pine boughs that served as a roof over her head. She slid from the buffalo robes and crawled over their bed to the tree trunk that served as support for the lean-to and backrest for Jed.

He heard her, but he tipped the bottle again and ignored her coming.

She put her hand on his thigh. "I miss you tonight."

This was not the time to tell him that. He watched the flames dance.

Her hand stirred to entreat. "Won't you come to bed?"

"When I'm ready."

"May I sit up with you until you're ready?"

"Please yourself," he told her as he raised the bottle to his lips again. He'd nursed his "medicinal" stash along, but this night he would require a generous dose.

"Are you angry with me?"

He pressed his lips together. The stuff was like fire. Even after several sips, the first inclination was to spew it out. "No."

"Tired of me?"

He glanced at her now to see whether she could possibly be serious. Her face was burnished by firelight, and her eyes held such sensual promise. "I wish I were."

"Why?"

"Because then I wouldn't need this stuff to temper the flame in my gut." He studied the bottle. "Fire is supposed to fight fire."

"There's no need to keep yourself from me, Jed."

"Yes, there is." She was ready to object. "There is, Kate. We'll reach your mission within a couple of days. I can't stay there with you. I've told you that before."

"Give it just a bit of time, Jed. If it doesn't work—"

"It can't work. I'm a half-breed fugitive. The Whitman Mission is within a stone's throw of Fort Walla Walla, which is Hudson's Bay Company."

She laid a hand on his arm, and he permitted her to stall off another drink. "Tell me what happened, Jed. Why do you hide from them?"

"Better me than Jean-Paul."

"Did Jean-Paul kill this Hudson's Bay man, this Simpson?"

"Simpson killed himself."

"Then why—"

"Katherine, do you know the name of the Hudson's Bay Company's governor?" She shook her head. Now he took another pull on his bottle before enlightening her. "It's Simpson. George Simpson. Thomas Simpson was his close relation, and Thomas Simpson was a son of a bitch. He 'explored' all over hell, claiming new territory for the Company, but he always had Métis guides and interpreters along to help him find his way. He had a way of smiling while he explained why our breeding rendered us naturally inferior. He hated us, and he hated the fact that he needed us. He especially hated me." Jed chuckled and shook his head at the irony that he should be hated for the very assets his father had required him to cultivate. "I was an impudent bastard for being damn near as smart as Simpson was."

"Smarter, no doubt."

"Well, I'd been around, and I could read and write. When I signed on with Hudson's Bay, they said I wasn't agent or clerk material, not yet, but if I served as translator for a few expeditions, I might work myself into a better job. Then they stuck me with Simpson, the governor's wonder boy."

He sighed as he gazed into the fire, remembering. "After a couple of months with the man, I was ready to kill him. At first I had my hands full trying to keep Jean-Paul under control, but I swear to God, if Simpson had made one more remark about my mother, I would have done more than crack his jaw."

"Which you did?"

"Which I did." Jed's eyes narrowed, as though he might bring the incident into better focus. "He was a strange man. He could be decent, even amiable for days on end, but then his mood became as black as his heart."

"How did he die?"

"He picked a fight with Jean-Paul. I pulled them apart, but his parting comment about our mother—" He heard the voice in his head, and he set his jaw. It was a moment before he explained, "I beat Jean-Paul to the punch. Simpson pulled his pistol, pointed it at me first, then at Jean-Paul. Then he got this wild look in his eye, put the barrel to his head and pulled the trigger."

Katherine's quick breath reminded him that it was over and done. He rushed through the rest, as though it were nothing more than an old story. "There were no witnesses. The rest of the party was back at camp. When we reported the incident, no one believed us. The governor wanted blood. They arrested both of us, questioned us separately and decided to charge me. I escaped. I knew the trial would be a sham." He looked at Katherine. "So that makes me guilty."

"And spares Jean-Paul."

Jed tipped his head back and rested it against the furrowed bark of the tree. The darkness was infinite, but there were points of light that made sense. "He's my brother."

They shared a period of silence.

"What shall we do, Jed?"

He drew a breath deep enough to make his chest hurt, then let it go. "You have another life to go to. Whether it's your husband's dream or your own, you've gone to a lot of trouble to carry it through."

"I don't deny that things have changed since I . . . since you found me and took me in."

"Neither do I. It seems I'm on the move again, and I have less to offer a woman than I had when I found you."

"Give me what you can." It was an invitation, not a plea.

"It only makes it harder, Kate." He gripped the bottle, which rested against his thigh. "I'm doing my damnedest to be just as good to you as your sainted husband was, but I seem to need a lot of fortification before I go to your bed if I'm to behave myself once I get there."

"Oh, Jed. There must be a place for us." She took hold of the bottle, just above Jed's hand, suggesting with a look that he release it to her. "There must be a way, Jed." His fingers went slack, and she set his fortification aside.

She moved closer and slipped her hand inside the deep V in his buckskin shirt. She felt the nubby tracks of his fresh scars. His skin was smooth and warm. His nipple was hard.

"Kate, don't."

"Does it hurt?"

"No," he groaned. The healing wounds were still tender, but so was the touch of her hand. "Ah, *Dieu, ma petite,* let me be noble just this once."

"I think you're noble to a fault, my love." She nuzzled him and whispered against his neck, "Just this once, let me be seductive."

"Another jug of Taos Lightning and I could handle this just fine."

"You would be wild?"

"I would pass out. I would—ah, Kate—I would spare you from my..."

"You don't need any more Taos Lightning." She reached under his shirt and caressed his flat belly. When he grabbed her wrist, she dug in with tenacious fingers. "No, I want to touch you. I want you to touch me."

"What else?"

"Take me to bed, and kiss me many—" she teased his neck with a pointed tongue "—many times."

He took her in his arms, slipping his hand beneath the flannel shirt of his that she wore in place of the nightgowns she had left behind. He found her small, soft bottom. She was still his, he told himself, and she would be until he found a safe place for her. She rained kisses over his face until he thought his heart would burst with the knowledge that she wanted him. He took her to their bed, touched her soft petals with his hands and his lips until she, like a spring flower, opened up for him. Her openness claimed his heart. After this, he thought, there might be no more spring.

And so he dived deep and searched for fertile ground.

Waiilatpu, the Place of the Rye Grass, was not the mountain haven Katherine had imagined. It was a grassy plain, dotted with scraggly cottonwoods and sage. The settlement was not civilization as she remembered it, but it was a large adobe brick house along with several smaller buildings, a stretch of split-rail fence, an orchard and a gristmill. A tipi encampment stood near some trees about a quarter mile from the fence. The Walla Walla River ran to the south. A small stream made a hairpin curve through the orchard and brought water to the millpond.

"Not what you expected?"

Katherine turned to Jed and squinted into the sun, which was on the rise above his left shoulder. "I've had time to imagine it so many ways."

"Are you disappointed?"

"Oh, no," she said quickly. And then she brightened. "They probably think I'm dead. Won't they be surprised when they see that I'm not?"

It was early in the season for the emigrants to start arriving, but Marcus Whitman was never surprised by the approach of visitors. His mission had become a way station on the Oregon Trail. Black frock coat and mutton-chop whiskers proclaimed the dignity of his post, but his smile was friendly. He ducked back in the doorway of the adobe house and was joined by a woman just as Katherine and Jed rode within easy hailing distance.

"I know you," Whitman announced jovially. "You're Jed West. I made your acquaintance at a rendezvous on the Green River some years back. Do you remember?"

Jed dismounted and offered a handshake. "I remember. Looks like your work out here has grayed you some, Marcus."

"Not the work, but the passing years." He turned to the small blond woman at his side. "Mother, this is Jed West. He's a friend of Jim Bridger's."

"I brought you a straggler from the last season's pilgrimage," Jed explained. He had thought this all out carefully. He would protect her good name. "This is Katherine Fairfield."

"Mrs. Thomas—"

Narcissa cut Katherine off with a gasp. "Fairfield? We were told the Fairfields were dead."

"My husband—"

"They both took sick," Jed said. "Their wagon was left behind, and a party of Shoshone brought me word. The minister died, but Mrs. Fairfield finally recovered. We wintered with a band of Nez Percé."

"Nez Percé Indians?" Narcissa reached for Katherine's hand in a gesture of sympathy. "Oh, my dear."

"They were very kind to me. I was many times blessed. If Jed hadn't come along, I surely would have died." Katherine thought she detected a glint of judgment in Marcus's eyes, perhaps a hint of shock in Narcissa's. She glanced down at her calico skirt and wished it were a few inches longer. There was no way to make her addendum sound in her own ears like anything but an afterthought, and her face was hot with shame. "But we've lost Thomas."

"They didn't tell us you'd been abandoned," Marcus said quietly. The thought was almost too horrible to utter. "They spoke of your death and were quick to say that you and your husband had put others above yourselves until the fever took you also."

"It would not be easy to report that sick people had been left behind, but . . ." Katherine bit back the residue of bitterness. "They did what they thought they had to do. They had put us at the end of the train, but still we slowed them down." She and the child, Nancy. Not Thomas. She had not abandoned him, but she had wronged him. She longed to do penance, to build him some kind of monument on the spot. She was no less a liar by omission than those who had reported her death. But she let the lie stand even as she offered them a true martyr. "Thomas would have stayed behind had it been one of them."

Jed glanced at her, then looked away.

"I know," Marcus said. "The hardships along the trail are many, but when the fever strikes, our faith is sorely tested." He paused, unsure how much she would want to hear. "Your party lost several children in the Columbia rapids."

"I'm sorry for their trouble," Katherine said quietly.

"And we rejoice in your good fortune." Marcus clapped a hand on Jed's shoulder. "You've brought us a man who could serve our cause well if we could tempt him to stay. If memory serves me, you are a superb interpreter, Jed. Your command of languages and sign would be a valuable asset to us."

"I speak Cree, not Cayuse." He reached for Katherine's bridle reins, and she relinquished them to him. "Mrs. Fairfield has learned to sign pretty well over the winter. She's the missionary, not me." He swung back up into his saddle. "I've done my job, Marcus. Mrs. Fairfield hired me to see her safely here, and here she is." To Katherine he added, "You can settle up with me after I've unloaded the packs and seen to the horses."

"Surely you'll lay over for a few days," Marcus urged.

Jed shook his head. "I don't think so."

Katherine was stunned. She cast about for something to say, and came up with nothing more than a feeble protest. "But Jed, it's been such a long trip."

"I've got a longer one still ahead of me."

"You can't go without a meal, Mr. West. I won't hear of it." A single hand on her hip gave Narcissa a look of authority.

"Thank you, ma'am. I'll see to the horses and stay for a home cooked meal." He wrapped Katherine's mare's reins around his hand and issued orders to Katherine as though she might somehow be attached. "You go on in the house with Mrs. Whitman and sit yourself in a real chair, like you've been wishing for. We'll get things sorted out—your property and my pay—after dinner."

She had said nothing of chairs, and he had said nothing about a fee for his services. Katherine had little money, but it was his if he wanted it. He had surely earned all that she could pay. She followed Narcissa into the house, only half-hearing her suggestion of tea, and she did sit. Her body was tired. Her mind raced with the prospect of "sorting things out."

After the noon meal, Jed asked Katherine to accompany him outside. On their way out, he snatched her hat off the peg where she'd left it, and pointedly handed it to her. She jammed it on her head. They were several yards from the house before he said, "You watch yourself in the sun. You need a hat."

"I can take care of myself," she snapped, but her tone softened in the next breath. "Jed, you don't have to leave—"

"I'm leaving you two horses, and taking the Appaloosa and a packhorse. The Appaloosa bred the bay mare, so come spring, you'll have a spotted colt."

They came to the shady spot between the orchard and the stream where he had picketed his horses and left his gear. Her heart fluttered as she watched him load the packhorse. The man who had saved her life and cared for her all these months, the man who had taught her to survive and to laugh and to love, that man was about to ride away.

"I don't have much money, but you've certainly earned—"

"I don't want your money. In fact—" Jed flipped open a saddlebag and presented her with a small leather pouch. He shook it, and it jingled. "It's Made Beaver. It's good at the trading posts around here, Hudson's Bay or anybody who does business with them."

"Jed, you don't owe me—"

"It has nothing to do with what anybody owes. It's what I can give you. It should take care of your needs, at least for a while." He took her hand in his and folded her fingers around the pouch. "You don't think I was going to leave you here with nothing, do you?"

"I don't see why you have to leave me here at all."

"Because this is where you were headed all along. This is where you wanted to be." She was giving him that wide-eyed look. "You're safe here. You belong here. Damn it, woman, *this* is your blessed mission!"

"You could stay, Jed. Just a few days. In a few days you might—"

"A few days won't change anything. I don't belong here. Even if…even if things were different with me, I still wouldn't belong here."

A sudden pool of tears welled in her eyes. "I don't want you to go."

"I can't stay. And I've got no place to take you, Kate, even if you'd be willing to go."

"I—"

He took hold of her shoulders, tempted to try to shake some sense into her. "It doesn't matter. I'm not asking. I've got no kind of life to offer you now."

He couldn't shake her. She was trying hard not to cry. He caressed her arms, squeezing them gently, hoping she knew how much he wanted things to be different. "You stay here, and you do your teaching. And you remember what you learned this winter. These are people, Kate. They're not savages, or subjects, or souls or whatever else your mission board might be calling them." His voice was soft and low, almost reverent. "They're *people*."

"Just stay the night." The words and the tears burned in her throat.

"One more night?" He shook his head sadly. "We can't have any more nights, Kate. These people think I picked up Thomas, too. They don't know when he died. They don't know we've lived together the way we have, a man and his woman." In her eyes he saw the same bittersweet ache he felt in his chest. "Bridger comes through here now and again. He left his daughter here for Narcissa to raise. He'll let me know how you're doing."

"Where will you go?"

"I don't know." That was the truth of it, but he knew he had to tell her something so she wouldn't worry. "The American Fur Company's got a few posts, and they're not too friendly with Hudson's Bay. Lately they've been courting the Métis for business."

"Then you'll find a place with them, and you'll be safe, and you could—"

No, he couldn't. By the time all that happened, she'd be married again to some emigrant minister and raising a brood of blue-eyed—God, he got a twist in his gut just thinking about it.

"If you're ever in trouble, I'll know," he said solemnly, "and I'll come to you."

"How will you know?" She managed to squeeze a little anger through her tears. "How could you know? You're going off God knows where."

"That's right." He touched her lips with his forefinger. "He'll know. And that's how I'll know."

"Oh, Jed, you are such a puzzle. You are such a—"

Everything he was went into their parting kiss.

Chapter Ten

The symptoms were obvious, just as Jed had said they would be. Katherine took pains to conceal the nausea because she wanted to be kept busy. She could well imagine Narcissa discovering her condition and ordering her to bed in the same maternal tone she might have used with any of the dozen children she had taken under her wing. Narcissa would delight in the prospect of a new baby at the mission. Anyone's baby. Her only child, a daughter, had drowned several years past, and Narcissa had since taken in orphaned emigrants and abandoned mixed-blood children, including the daughters of mountain men Jim Bridger and Joe Meek.

Katherine decided that Narcissa would know about her pregnancy soon enough. In the meantime, she took care to wear her floppy-brimmed hat when she worked in the vast vegetable gardens or made lye soap or milked cows. When either Marcus or Narcissa admonished her not to overburden herself, she insisted that she had come to the mission to work. She only hoped they would give her more to do. She wanted to teach. After the harvest, they promised, when the weather was cooler, the people would be more receptive.

If she could have convinced herself of the importance of her work, she thought she would have found peace of mind. She became friendly with Esther, the Indian woman who helped with the housework, and Leah, who lived in the encampment with the few Indians who worked the mission's truck farm. The Cayuse were hunters and fishermen, and Marcus's attempts to turn them into Christian farmers had thus far met with limited success. The missionaries were determined to teach the Indians to speak English without themselves learning the native tongue. The Cayuse resisted. Marcus evangelized the people who lived in the camp. Beyond that, the mission had become a hostelry for emigrants on their way to the Willamette Valley. Marcus offered medical services to anyone who needed him, but the emigrants had become the focus of his work.

Katherine made the encampment her mission. When her Bible stories in sign and English were surprisingly well received, she asked her new friends to help her with the Cayuse language and petitioned Marcus for permission to visit the main Indian village. He refused.

"These are the receptive ones," Marcus told her. "They have come to us. When they are willing to put their hands on a plow, I know there's hope."

"I thought our job was to take the Word to them."

"We've brought civilization." His broad gesture indicated the gristmill and the orchard beyond it. "Permanent homes and crops in the ground. The Cayuse are a stubborn people. They like to catch a few fish, then sit around and smoke their pipes all day. But what we have here, little by little it piques their curiosity. They come for food and medicine, and a few have stayed to work."

He clasped his hands behind his back as they walked along the fence together. His ministerial tone reminded her of Thomas's. "Are we not 'fishers of men,' Katherine? The nets are out, and soon we'll have a catch far greater than we can handle."

"Isn't it possible for the Cayuse to get their living their own way and still come to know God? I simply thought to teach—"

"Teach them to work, Katherine. Just the way you do. You're a fine example, and one these savage women would do well to follow."

She cringed to hear the word Jed had despised. "They've set examples for me. They speak English quite well, while I muddle along in their language."

"We all promise ourselves we'll learn the languages, but we find so little time for it. Perhaps it's best. They'll need English soon enough. Our population doubles every year." They passed the house the doctor had built to be a way station for emigrant families, and he smiled proudly. They were coming, just as he'd said they would years ago, after he made his first crossing. "Just wait until September. Now that we're officially under American jurisdiction, they're coming in droves."

As the summer wore on, privacy was more difficult to come by. The number of residents at the mission fluctuated daily, and Katherine often found herself sharing her little upstairs room with a child or two. There were times when she craved nothing so much as a few moments alone, just to dress without being watched. She wanted to keep her secret to herself a little longer.

The emigrants' quarters, a structure nearly as large as the main house, was busy by August. Laundry and cooking chores became more and more demanding. Frustration mounted for Katherine, and she spent more time at the Cayuse encampment, where she felt she could do the work she had come to do. She realized, even if no one else admitted it, that the Whitman Mission primarily served emigrants.

Leah was the first to mention Katherine's pregnancy one afternoon when they were cutting corn to be sun dried.

"Is it so obvious?" Katherine ran her hand over the thick gathers in the skirt she had managed to let out behind closed doors only a few days ago. She thought she'd hidden her little melon of a belly quite well.

Without interrupting her work, Leah acknowledged Katherine's gesture with a quick jerk of her chin. "You do that often with your hand. That is the way of a woman who tests her body for change and thinks of the little one inside."

Katherine looked down at her hand, then quickly reached for another ear of corn. "I've wanted to tell someone, but of course it seemed a little soon." She peeled the shucks and let the soft corn silk lie in her palm. "Do you think Narcissa knows?"

"Narcissa is busy here, busy there. She does not always see what lies closest."

"I've told you that . . . my husband died on the journey."

"Yes." Leah looked at her earnestly. "When these wagons stop here, you search much among them for a man." Laughter bubbled in Katherine's throat, but Leah tapped her on the knee and waggled a finger. "There will be many to choose from, Katherine. These wagons are full of men whose women have died, just as your husband did. You must choose wisely. Some of these white men are—" she rolled her eyes and touched her head "—strange. You must not settle for a strange one."

They looked at each other and laughed, but when the laughter died, Katherine glanced away. Before she knew it, her secret was out. "My husband was not the child's father."

Leah made no comment, and Katherine saw only concern in her friend's dark eyes.

"Thomas died last summer. The man who brought me here fathered this child."

"The half-breed?"

"His name is Jed West."

"I was at the house that time, cleaning. I saw him." Leah shook her head slowly. "Those half-breeds, they're no good. Did he force you?"

"No. Oh, no. He cared for me, Leah. He took care of me when I was sick, and he taught me so many things. He brought me here because I asked him to. I thought he would stay but—" Katherine sighed and added corn shucks to a basket already half-filled of them. "He said he didn't belong here."

"Half-breeds have no people," Leah said.

"He does have people. Far to the east, where the Cree and the Sioux live. They call themselves Métis."

Leah grunted. "Some of those kind live west of here with the fur traders. But where do they belong? Not here. Now he gives you a mixed-blood baby, and he runs off on you." She made a sound that clinched her disapproval. "Eeee, that man is no good for you, Katherine."

"He doesn't know about the baby." Katherine saw the surprise in Leah's face. "*I* didn't know. When he left here, I didn't know I was breeding. There had been no...no woman's blood since before I got sick, and I almost believed I could never conceive. I'm not even sure when to expect the birthing, and now I don't know where my baby's father is."

Leah had to reconsider for a moment. Finally, she said, "A man should be told." With a shrug, she added, "Even a half-breed."

That evening, Katherine told Narcissa about the baby. They spoke of neither Thomas nor Jed, but Narcissa echoed Leah's observation that many widowers would pass through before winter set in. The thought of shopping for a husband chilled Katherine's blood. Her heart was filled with memories of Jed, memories made more profound by the filling of her womb. No bereaved emigrant would take Jed's place.

By late September the demands the emigrants made on the mission were almost overwhelming, but no one was turned away. Shelter was provided for a steady flow of transients bound for the fertile valleys west of the Cascade Mountains. They arrived bone-weary, hungry, often sick, and the missionaries welcomed them with food, medicine and a place to rest before tackling that last wall of mountains.

Among the visitors, Jim Bridger's was a familiar face. He had come to visit his daughter, Mary Ann. Katherine sought a private moment with him, and she asked about Jed. He'd headed south, to California, Jim had heard. "But he'll be back," Jim predicted. "Too damn many people in California. One of these days, Jed's gonna be headed home."

Home? Katherine wondered what the word meant, for herself as well as for Jed.

The Delancy children brought measles with them when they arrived early in October. They were listless and pale, and their mother attributed their condition to the hardships they'd faced in the Blue Mountains. The rash appeared within a couple of days, and the missionaries braced themselves for a house full of sick children.

Katherine recalled suffering with the measles at Christmas time when she was eight years old. She'd had to miss most of the seasonal festivities, but she had gotten over it. It was one of the hazards of childhood. Marcus worried about the spread of the disease, but it seemed to Katherine that a greater concern was the lack of space. They were boarding people in the blacksmith shop now that the emigrant house and the mission house were both full.

Marcus tried to dissuade Katherine from paying a visit to the Cayuse encampment, but after a week of nursing sick children in crowded buildings, she ignored his protest and discovered the real cause for Marcus's concern. The Cayuse children had the measles, too. But for them, this was not just one of childhood's little adversities; they were dying.

Katherine collected the herbal remedies Jed had taught her to use for fever and sore throat and took up nursing in the Cayuse encampment. The epidemic spread to the surrounding Cayuse villages. Marcus gave Katherine sole responsibility for the camp while he made calls on the villages. Some of the adults contracted the disease, but it seemed that no child was left untouched. Katherine had some luck keeping healthy family members apart from the sick ones when she warned that the disease would spread. She explained that she would not contract it because she'd had it as a child, and she grieved with the families of three children who died. Leah's toddler was one of them. Old Esther, who had worked in the kitchen, was dead within two days of her first symptoms. Others, including Leah's eight-year-old Thomas, were holding their own under Katherine's vigilant care.

"I don't understand it," Katherine complained to Narcissa over tea one evening. "For the white children, it's usually just a matter of a few days in bed. Why are the Cayuse dying?"

"I don't know. Ten years ago, the Mandan, Hidatsa and Arikara tribes were decimated by smallpox. They say that after the epidemic was over, hardly a soul was left alive."

"Smallpox is bad for us, too, but measles is to be expected among children, almost like skinned knees."

"I think when they come to accept our Lord—"

"Leah is a Christian," Katherine quickly reminded Narcissa. "But her little Thomas is terribly sick, and her baby is dead. I don't think this is God's doing."

"The road to salvation is full of suffering."

"We brought this on them, Narcissa. This mission is a hostel for emigrants, and the emigrants brought the measles." Katherine felt her anger rising, even though Narcissa was not saying anything she hadn't heard, even recited herself a time or two. But the rhetoric no longer made sense. These people were *dying* of measles. "I'm beginning to think they would have been better off if we'd left them alone."

"Oh, no, Katherine. God will change their lives. If not in this generation, surely in the next one."

"If there's to be a next one." She thought about all the good she had thought to do here, and she thought about her child. Another generation. "The work here is not what I thought it would be. It's not what Thomas said it would be."

Narcissa's back stiffened. "We know what work we do here, Katherine. Marcus dreamed of bringing the Word of God to these people, but our progress has been small. We serve the poor, tired emigrants—the people who will turn these lush valleys into farmland and build homes and churches and schools."

Narcissa sipped from her cup, and her tone became more sympathetic. "We do what we can for the Indians. Some of them love us, you see, and they stay close to us and try to follow our teachings. And we love them, too. Marcus comes home after three or four days in the villages, and his heart breaks when he tells me how many have died. But his faith is unshakable."

Katherine nodded. Marcus did the work of a dozen men, and no one dared fault him. More tea was sipped. Then softly, deftly, Narcissa changed the subject. "This child of yours will bear your husband's name." Katherine glanced at her quizzically. "Your husband was a man of faith. A man like Marcus."

"Thomas was a good man."

"But he did not father this child," Narcissa said gently. "No."

"The child will be a mixed-blood, then."

"Yes."

A quiet moment passed between them.

Narcissa leaned closer. Her breast rested on the rim of her cup. "Let me have the baby, Katherine. My little Alice drowned in the river here eight years ago, and there've been no babies since. I would—"

Katherine lifted her chin. "No. I love this baby as I love its father."

"I could see that when he was here." Narcissa sat back, staring into her cup. She ran her thumb over the curve of the handle, then glanced up pointedly. "I also saw that he left you."

"He didn't know about the baby." Katherine felt a sudden chill. "Neither did I."

"It won't be easy for you if the child favors his father's darker side. Of course, the Indian blood will have been diluted by yours. Perhaps—"

"Stop it! Jed is Métis. He's a proud man, and if it were not for—" Katherine caught herself. How many secrets did she intend to disclose? She rose from her chair on the need to distance herself from Narcissa. "I will not be looking for a husband among the emigrants, and if I cannot teach here at the mission, I shall take my child and find another place."

"You're welcome here, Katherine. I'm making no judgment. The good Lord knows, you've suffered enough." Narcissa reached for Katherine's hand. "Perhaps Mr. West will come back for you."

"I believe he will." She looked Narcissa straight in the eye. "My faith, too, is steadfast."

October was a rainy month, dark and dreary, inviting death. Katherine tended the sick, but she fastened her thoughts, like tenacious barnacles, on the prospect of new life. She had been given a tiny room of her own adjacent to the kitchen. At night she lay in her bed and held her swelling stomach in her hands, smiling in the dark when a tiny hand or foot pushed her own distended flesh against her palm.

She thought of her conversations with Leah and Narcissa. She had anticipated disapproval, even condemnation, when she confessed that Jed, not Thomas, was the father of her child. They were not legally married. But that was not the issue. She had stopped thinking of Jed as a mixed-blood, and it was unsettling to hear the term applied to her baby. She remembered how often Jed had claimed his heritage. He was Métis. If her child was not to know his father, how could she teach him what that meant?

Her faith was steadfast. A strong sense of power had filled her as she'd said the words. Not Thomas's faith. Not Marcus's, not even Jed's, but her own. It seemed a remarkable claim, but she realized, for the first time, that it was true. She believed, despite the suffering around her, that God was good. And she had important work to do, not in Thomas's stead or Marcus's or Jed's, but her own work.

And, yes, Jed would come back to claim his woman and his child.

By mid-November, half the Cayuse population in the area—175 people—had succumbed to measles. Leah's son, Thomas, had recovered. Katherine thanked God for sparing *this* Thomas, but Leah gave Katherine credit for her good medicine. Marcus, too, praised Katherine's work, but Katherine realized that few Indians who became ill were able to survive. Why was God so stingy with His miracles? All she and Marcus could do was treat the fever and try to keep patients warm and dry. November's cold rain and heavy fog made the task difficult.

Marcus had lost track of the days as the month dragged to a close. It was late at night when he returned from the village, and still there were children at the mission who needed his attention. It was too late to sleep, too early to wake Narcissa. He decided to get himself a meal, then check on the workers' camp.

Katherine heard the clatter of skillet and kettle, and she knew Marcus was back. She dreaded his report, yet she got out of bed and followed the noise, hoping. Always hoping. Marcus smiled when she joined him in the kitchen, but the dark hollows under his eyes turned his expression into something ghastly.

"Have you slept at all?" Katherine asked.

"Not since . . . what's today? Monday? Not since Saturday, I think. Fortunately, I seem to function quite adequately without sleep." He tossed a cut of meat into the skillet, and it sizzled. "I'm frying steak. You'll join me?"

"None for me, thanks. It's too early."

"One for the baby, then." Another small steak hissed when it hit the pan.

"I'll get the tea," Katherine said as she took cups from a shelf. "Things are no better, are they, Marcus?"

"No. No better." He poked idly at the meat with a fork. "The Cayuse are saying my medicine is bad. They see that the white children live, while theirs die. Yesterday, when I brought one father the news that his daughter was dead, he spat upon me and walked away. I fear they blame me for the disease itself, and I . . . I am beginning to wonder."

"It's the grief, Marcus. Some families have lost all their children. And the old people." She shook her head as she poured from the kettle, watching the steam roll off the boiling water. "There are so few of the old ones and the young ones left. The rest have only to grieve."

"I've done the best I could." He stabbed the steak, flipped it over and turned to her with a desolate look in his eyes. "I'm short of supplies, short of ideas and short-tempered. I've even been cutting short my prayers."

"Do you hear the drums, Marcus?" She paused, and the slow cadence sounded in the distance. "The people are praying."

"Back to their heathen—"

"No, Marcus, they're praying. And He hears. I know it. I've seen—" Katherine stopped her tongue and pressed her lips together. Because he could not have valued what she had seen, she decided not to tell him. But she insisted, "They're not a godless people, Marcus. Not the way we thought."

"A few were coming 'round before this plague struck." He offered a quick glance, a gentle smile. "You need rest, Katherine. The weather is miserable, and I'll not have you traipsing through the mud today." He transferred the smaller steak to a plate and handed it to her. "Eat now, and go back to bed."

"I'm fortunate to have a bed," she said as she took a seat at the table. "As of today we have seventy-four people here, what with all these emigrants, and no place to put any more."

"We cannot turn anyone away." He set his plate on the table. "Perhaps next spring we should put up another building. For now, we'll just have to squeeze them in somewhere." He attempted another smile. "But we accommodate women and children first, and you are one of each."

Katherine took Marcus's advice and went back to bed after she ate. She slept longer than she intended to, for when next she went to the kitchen, she found Narcissa preparing the noon meal. She was groggy, and she mumbled an apology for sleeping late. She splashed water on her face and set about preparing an infusion from black cohosh root, which she administered to the eleven sick children in the house. That done, she decided Narcissa would need help serving the noon meal, but she heard men's voices in the kitchen as she descended the stairs.

Marcus threw his cloak over his shoulders and tucked his Bible under his arm. A tall Indian man stood by the door, waiting. "You've seen to the children upstairs, Katherine?" Marcus asked.

"Yes. They're doing well."

"I shouldn't be long," he said as he followed the man out the door.

"Chief Tiloukaikt's son died this morning," Narcissa explained as the door clicked shut. "It's the third child the chief has lost. The man who came for Marcus said there were two other deaths last night." Narcissa's sigh was long and hollow, as though drawn through a tunnel. "My poor Marcus is exhausted."

There was a knock at the door, and Katherine answered. Leah stood outside, holding up a blanket to shield her head from the drizzle. "Come with me, Katherine."

"I was just about to help Narcissa—"

"Come *now*."

"Who is it?" Katherine asked gently. "Thomas? Is Thomas sick again? I'll get my cloak."

She filled a jar with the medicinal tea she had made earlier and slipped into the fur-lined cape that Jed had given her. Leah hurried her along. The drizzle had become a thick, gray mist that shrouded the valley. Katherine's foot slipped in the mud, but Leah caught her arm and wordlessly towed her toward her tipi.

Curiously, there were no emergencies in the camp. Tall John, the blacksmith's apprentice, had been ill for two days. The big man lay helpless as a baby. Leah had taken her sister's child into her own lodge, and the child seemed to be holding her own. Together, Leah and Katherine administered tea and bathed their patients. When they had done all they could, Katherine reached for her cloak.

"Tiloukaikt's son died this morning," Leah said.

"I know. Poor man. He must be heartbroken." Katherine started toward the tipi door, but Leah stood in her way. The Indian woman glanced over her shoulder anxiously. "Is something wrong?" Katherine asked. Leah said nothing, but kept still and listened. Katherine followed suit. There was a distant clatter, then the report of gunfire.

The two women stared at each other. One knew. The other was incredulous. Another crack sounded, and another. Leah glanced down at the little girl, the innocent child who lay in Leah's own sleeping robes, trusting her aunt to care for her and keep her from harm.

"What's happened?" Katherine whispered. "Who's shooting?" Again she started for the door.

Leah grabbed her arms. "You will be safe here, Katherine."

"Are we being attacked? What are they doing?"

They heard more gunshots.

Katherine gasped. "The children!" She grabbed the arms that held hers. "Leah, there are so many children in the house. Please! Help me get them—"

"They will not harm the children. They say Whitman's medicine is bad. He poisons our people."

"No, no, it's the disease. We must stop them. We must try to make them listen to—"

"We can do nothing." Leah squeezed Katherine's arms, hoping her friend would understand how important it was that she stay where she was and not think too much about what the men did. "It will be over soon."

"Over?" Katherine jerked free of Leah's grasp and stumbled from the tipi, trying to make sense of the word. "Over?"

The fog lent an eerie, gray-white pallor to the darkening afternoon. The mission buildings were barely visible. Katherine tried to run, but her skirt tangled around her legs, and her belly weighed her down. Her pumping legs gained her little ground. Shrieks, shouts, gunshots and children's wails pierced the heavy air as Katherine ran, skirts flapping and arms flailing. The mist swirled about her as in a scary dream. She could see the yard now. Narcissa was carted from the house on a settee, her chest red with blood. More shots rang out, and Narcissa's body jerked as each bullet struck. One of the men who carried the settee dropped his end and shoved the body into the mud.

Katherine sank to her knees beside the rail fence as she watched the corpse tumble to the ground. Narcissa's claim rang in her ears. *They love us, and we love them, too.* Katherine made herself into a ball, with her baby as the core. She buried her face between her knees and rocked on the balls of her feet as she whispered a prayer.

Suddenly she was torn from her shell and jerked to her feet. The face of the Cayuse who held her was unfamiliar and terrifying. His black hair was wet and plastered to his head, his mouth turned down and his dark eyes were emotionless. He dragged her toward a small huddle of hostages and shoved her into their midst. She recognized Mary Ann, Jim Bridger's daughter, and she pulled the sobbing child against her side.

"They've killed Father," the child wailed. Katherine put a hand over Mary Anne's eyes, even though she knew it was too late. The girl must have seen Marcus die, for he was the man Mary Ann called "Father."

Four men prodded the group of women and children toward the tipi encampment. An occasional gunshot rang out behind them, but they dared not turn around or try to run. In terror, they moved as they were told to do. Orders were issued in Cayuse, and the camp was struck as the cluster of stunned emigrants waited, shivering, bunching together for some kind of security.

Leah appeared. She searched among the captives for Katherine and seemed relieved when she spotted her. The man who had dragged Katherine away from the fence approached, and Leah spoke with him, then went to her tipi and brought Katherine her white cloak.

"Tomahas is my brother," Leah explained as she slipped the cloak over Katherine's shoulders. "A woman's brother is responsible for her sons. He knows your medicine was good for Thomas."

It was the same Leah she had been with moments ago. The same friend who had been frightened, just as Katherine was. The same woman who had stood fast, trying not to let fear get the better of her, as Katherine was.

"What are they going to do with us?" Katherine's voice was thin and weak.

"You will not be harmed. You have helped my son." Leah glanced at Katherine's protruding belly. "I will help yours."

Chapter Eleven

There wasn't much in San Francisco. The United States had recently claimed the territory from Mexico, but there weren't many people there who spoke any of Jed's languages. There were plenty of mixed-bloods, but they were mestizos, not Métis. He'd tried to explain who he was to a dark-eyed whore, who'd laughed and told him a mixed-blood was a mixed-blood, and no fancy name was going to change that. He'd decided they didn't have much in common, and that he could do without what little she did have. He got drunk instead. Taos Lightning was Taos Lightning. He couldn't argue with that.

The days and nights blended into one miserable hangover. Jed's head throbbed with voices, a condition that seemed to be part of any sickness with him. He vowed to stop getting sick. When his mind was murky anyway, he didn't need to hear those exhortations to "dive deep and bring us something." Nor did he enjoy hearing Katherine's voice, even though it was soft and sweet and full of sunlight. After a few weeks, he headed back to Oregon Country, telling himself he'd hook up with Half Hand again and make his living the only way he knew how. Plenty of mountains out that way. No emigrant was ever going to make a farm out of those mountains.

By late November, Jed decided his mind was surely going. That damn woman wouldn't leave him alone. Her face appeared in his tin mug, when all he wanted was a sip of tea to warm his insides. Her soft features appeared in the stock of his rifle as he oiled the wood with methodically slow, caressing strokes. When he stretched his cold hands toward the camp fire, he saw her in the flames.

"Ho, there! Jed West!"

Jed's rifle was already in his hands, but the voice was familiar. "That you, Bridger?"

"It's me." Jim Bridger appeared on the ledge thirty feet above Jed's head. "Been cuttin' your sign for two days now. Is that beaver tail you're blisterin' down there?"

Jed glanced at the meat he'd impaled on sticks and noted that the tail's scaly hide was ready to be peeled. "Come on ahead, Jim. Plenty for two."

"Don't shoot me, now," Jim jested as he skittered down the embankment on his heels. "Didn't think you'd be quite as skittish as the rest of us, you bein' part Indian."

"Makes me *more* skittish. What are you doing up this way this time of year?"

"Lookin' for you. Thought we'd team up."

Jed came to his feet and extended his hand. Bridger's was stiff from the cold. "I've got a partner, Jim."

Jim's brow furrowed as, puzzled, he asked, "Ain't you headed up to the Whitman Mission?"

"What for?"

"You got a woman up there, that's what for. I seen her when I was up that way, two or three months back. Same one you took to Fort Hall, then picked her up and hauled her up to the mission." Jim shook his head and squatted near the fire to warm his hands as he rambled on. "Damn women. Soon as a man finds a good one, she gets herself

in a family way, and you try to put her up somewhere safe
so you can get on with your—"

"What the hell are you babbling about? I took Katherine to the Whitman Mission because the woman's a
missionary, and that's where she wanted to go."

Jim screwed his head around and looked up, surprised. "It ain't yours?"

"What ain't mine?"

"Hell, it's gotta be yours. That's a one-man woman if
I ever seen one." Jim scrambled to his feet, figuring face-
to-face was the only way to tell a man this kind of news.
"You didn't know? You got a papoose on the way, West."

Jed grabbed Jim by the lapels of his woolen coat. "You
saw her?"

"Said I did."

"And she's..."

"Big as a spring heifer." Jed allowed his hands to be
pushed away. Jim straightened his coat. "Damn it, man,
I figured you was headed up there to try to get her back."

"She'd have to be..." Jed turned away. He calculated
eight months, maybe more. He remembered the cradle
board, and he imagined her, the way he'd pictured her in
dreams so many times, with his child growing inside her.
His child! "But you're right, she's in a safe place, and I
might just be the last person she wants to see right now."

"Safe place? If she's alive, I reckon she's thinkin' your
ugly face would be a sweet sight about now." Jim spun
Jed around by the shoulder. "You ain't heard about the
trouble up there."

"What trouble?"

"Cayuse murdered the Whitmans, couple weeks back.
They say about fifteen dead and maybe fifty captives.
Nobody's been able to get near the mission to rescue them
people."

Dead. The word clattered in his head like a clapper inside a bell. "They don't know..."

"I'm figurin' chances are good my Mary Ann's one of the captives." Jim clamped his hand on Jed's shoulder. "Your woman, too. It's like that, ain't it?"

"Yeah." Jed shook his head to clear it. "It's like that. How fast can you travel on that ol' plug of yours?"

"I reckon I can keep up with that Appaloosy." Jed was already tossing his saddle on the horse's back. "Hey, what about them beaver tails?"

"Bring 'em along." He shoved his rifle in its scabbard and looked to Jim for assurance. "You don't think they'd hurt her, do you? Not heavy with child like that."

"No tellin'. You just keep your head on straight, Jed."

They reached Fort Walla Walla within a week. Jed ducked under the low doorframe and followed Jim into the quarters occupied by the post's chief factor, John McLoughlin. The air inside was acrid with the smoke from a poorly vented fire, and the four men were cast in shadows.

Introductions were superficial. Everyone knew Jim Bridger, and he claimed the floor. McLoughlin—wizened, grizzled and frontier wise—listened with one ear while he tried to figure out where he'd seen Jed West before. Jed and the fourth man, Pierre Sayer, recognized each other as Métis, and Sayer doubted that Jed's name had always been West. Bridger missed all the unspoken connections and demanded to know what the Hudson's Bay Company representatives intended to do about the captives.

McLoughlin retrieved a pipe recently gone cold from a pottery bowl, lit it and puffed it back into play. "They're Americans, Bridger. What makes you think there's anything we can do?"

"You deal with them Cayuse all the time."

"So did Whitman."

"The Whitmans never did them people no harm, John. You know that as well as I do."

McLoughlin's brow fell into a deeper row of furrows. "Whitman took in emigrants. For the past seven, eight years now there's been a steady stream. Farmers don't do the fur business any good, you know."

"No, but you've been known to lend them a hand once in a while, too."

"Yes, and Simpson censured me for it back in '43. I don't know what I was supposed to do. They get this far on a shoestring, and they've got nothing left. Wagons come straggling in, women and children half-starved." McLoughlin's unruly eyebrows flew up as he demanded, "What's a man supposed to do?"

"You do what you can," Jed suggested quietly. "If the Cayuse have held captives this long, they must want something. What do you think they want?"

"Half the Cayuse population died of measles this fall, man. What do you think they'd want? Probably food. Probably blankets."

"Preferably clean blankets that haven't been anywhere near an emigrant with measles," Sayer put in.

"They blamed Whitman for the measles?" Jed asked.

"His medicine was bad," Sayer said. "They figured there was no other way to stop him."

Jed decided Sayer was the man to talk to. "Is there a pregnant woman among the captives?"

"Most of the captives are women and children." Sayer took in every aspect of Jed's appearance, from his hair, short by mountain standards—cut, Sayer guessed by the neat look of it, not long ago—to his height, which was considerable by any standard. "Your woman?"

Jed nodded once.

"The Whitmans are dead," Sayer said without apparent regret. "I know that much. They killed most of the ones they knew. The missionaries. The teacher, the blacksmith, the miller—'course they were all men."

Jed's gut tightened, but his face remained expressionless. "She would have been one of the missionaries."

"We can offer to ransom them," McLoughlin said. "The Cayuse haven't been able to do much hunting this fall. They must be desperate for food."

Jed directed his question to Sayer. "How soon can you make the contact?"

"I'll know by tomorrow." Sayer started for the door as soon as he got the nod from McLoughlin. Before he left, he turned to Jed. "Want me to ask for her by name?"

"No. Don't single her out. It might go harder for her then."

"The Cayuse are tired and hungry," Sayer said. "If you could have seen the way the dead were piling up..."

"I know. I've seen it. Tell them...just tell them we'll bring food for their children."

Sayer nodded and left.

"Back in Brandon District on the Red River?" McLoughlin asked. "Is that where I've seen you, West?" His eyes narrowed. "How about Pembina?"

"Listen, McLoughlin, if you think you've got something to settle with me, we'll see to it after we get those people back." Jed took two steps and stood toe to toe with the man. "It doesn't matter whose side they're on anymore, does it? They're in trouble."

McLoughlin laughed. "You're right. It doesn't matter anymore." He folded his arms across his chest and smiled, his eyes glittering with the satisfaction he assumed Jed would share with him. "George Simpson lost his gamble.

British business interests versus the American dream. The question was settled by a bunch of farmers. All of a sudden they outnumbered us.''

Neither the question nor its resolution interested Jed. ''Jim and I will drive the wagons if you'll provide the supplies.''

''Good. My next problem was going to be finding volunteers to go into that hornet's nest.''

''And beyond that?'' Jed challenged. ''You got any more problems?''

''There's no love lost between George Simpson and me. If memory serves me right, your problem is with him, Mr—'' the wild eyebrows rose and fell again ''—West?''

When Jed only looked through him, McLoughlin continued. ''I was in Pembina back in '39 at the time of young Thomas's demise.'' McLoughlin's dramatic eyebrow gesture was habitual. Jed's expression remained unchanged. ''Thomas Simpson was a genius, and George thought the sun rose and set in him.'' McLoughlin sat at the edge of the table and made his point with his pipe stem. ''Thomas was also a madman, and everybody knew it. But George would never have accepted the truth. You were set up. I don't know how for sure, but I know you were.''

The fire crackled in the big stone fireplace.

Jed's voice was low and even. ''We'd save time if we anticipated the Cayuse's needs and got the wagons ready.''

Shod hooves clicked on the frozen ground, and three sets of harness jangled with the teams' rhythm. Two freight wagons loaded with blankets and supplies had made a sizable dent in the trading post's store. For want of other volunteers, Pierre Sayer had enlisted his wife, Clarise, and son, Richard, to help. Clarise drove the third wagon, a huge railed flatbed that would carry the captives back to the fort. Pierre and Richard drove the small herd of horses Tiloukaikt had demanded. The Cayuse had never been a horse-rich nation. Clearly they anticipated being on the run once the hostage issue was settled.

The Place of the Rye Grass became visible across the stream. A lone Indian man emerged from a grove of trees. The wagons halted. Jed held his hands up, palms out, to show that he carried no weapons. Jim did the same. The mission buildings stood as mute witnesses to the carnage that had taken place there in their midst. At the Cayuse's signal, the wagons rolled again, following the scout toward the grove. The drivers were not afforded a close look at the mission grounds.

Jed remembered what a busy place it had once been, and he could almost hear the clanging of hammer and anvil, the splash of water at the gristmill, the racket the children made as they chased one another through the yard. Where was Katherine? Was she waiting for him within the grove, or had they buried her near the knoll where he'd left her standing? Ah, *Dieu*, if they had killed her, what would they have done with her body? If he did not find her among the captives, no power on earth would keep him from seeking her out, wherever she lay.

Within the grove a ragtag cluster of people huddled together. The bare bones of autumn trees drew deep purple afternoon shadows across their faces. They were a collection of defeated people waiting for someone to decide where they would go next. The Cayuse brave was joined by four more on foot, and the leader signaled for the wagons to stop at the edge of the grove. The drivers were motioned down from their seats. Two of the Cayuse began examining the contents of the wagons, while the mounted brave took control of the band of horses, driving them upstream. Back in the trees, a whimpering child was hushed. Jed started for the group, but one of the Cayuse stepped in his path.

"We give you this many of your people, safe and unharmed. Take them from here, and let no more come among us."

Jed shouldered his way past the man and took two hesitant steps as he scanned the crowd, his heart thudding so loudly he could hear nothing else. Then he saw a small white-robed figure sitting on a log with a child on her lap. Her head was hooded, and she shared the warmth of her cloak with the child. An Indian woman was standing close by.

Suddenly, for Jed, there was no one in the grove but the one wearing the white cape. He was unaware that he was running or that he'd called out her name. His mind had played too many tricks on him, and he dared not look back or blink or weep. Experience had taught him that she might vanish still. She lifted her chin. The fur-lined hood nearly swallowed her face, but, by God, it was her. It was Katherine.

He knelt beside her, pushed back the hood and took her face in his hands. "Are you all right?"

Her eyes glistened like the winter sky. "I have not been harmed."

The child was lifted from Katherine's lap, and Jed spared a glance over his shoulder when he heard Jim declare, "Mary Ann! Lordy, honey, I've been— Is she sick, ma'am?"

"No," Katherine said. "She's tired, but she's fine." She smiled at Jed, but inside she was trembling so hard it made her chest hurt. She didn't want him to know that. She just wanted him to know what a blessed sight he was. She clutched her cape to her breast with one hand while she reached with the other to touch his wind-chapped cheek. "I knew you would come."

"I said I would, if you needed me."

"I do." She closed her eyes. "Oh, Jed, I do."

He slipped his hand beneath the cape and found the hard, swollen mound that housed his child. "It's true, then."

He was sure there was sand in his throat.

"I didn't know it when you left."

She could hardly breathe for the joy of just taking in the sight of him.

His teeth flashed in a quick grin. "I feel it moving! Kate!" He glanced left and right, then lowered his voice. "Did you feel that?"

She gave a little laugh. "Yes, I did."

"*Mon Dieu*, you're so big!" He held her belly in both hands now. Possessive, he was, at once proud and humble. He was all expectant father, and his eyes shone with it. "How soon?"

"You must leave her with me," the Indian woman said.

Jed's first acknowledgment of the woman's presence was a piercing stare, even as Katherine was quick to protest. "You cannot stay here, Leah. It would be too dangerous for you." She looked at Jed. "But I'm not going anywhere just now."

"Now?"

Katherine gave a curt nod. She closed her eyes again, and her face turned pink.

"You mean...*now*?"

"Tiloukaikt says she must go with the others, but it is her time," Leah said.

"Is it—" Belatedly, Jed had the presence of mind to realize he was asking the wrong person. "Katherine, is it bad yet?"

"At first I thought it was just another backache, but—"

Jim's voice interrupted. "Jed, let's get these people loaded up. We'll be travelin' half the night as it is. Thought we'd hand out a ration of—" His moccasined feet skidded to a halt in the grass behind Jed. "You're not fixin' to have that baby now, are you, ma'am?"

"We'll make them wait, Kate."

"No," Katherine said quickly. "They've waited long enough. It might be hours."

"Tiloukaikt says you must go now. Already Tomahas and the others..."

Leah's warning trailed off as the smell of burning grass and timber turned heads. Suddenly the mission house went up in flames.

"Looks like you'd better get those people out of here," Jed allowed. "Leave me your horse, Jim. I'll get him back to you."

The Cayuse leader, Tiloukaikt, spoke to Leah, and she translated. "He says you must all leave this place."

"Explain to him that Katherine can't go, and that I am her husband. I will stay with her." Quietly, he added, "Katherine is right. I don't know how soon, but there will be reprisals. You can't stay."

"This is a time for women. When it's done, I will follow my people."

"But, Leah," Katherine pleaded, "you have Thomas to worry about, and little—"

"They are with my sister-in-law, and I will be with them soon. By the time your people can return with their guns, I shall be gone." Eyes glittering with defiance, Leah sat beside Katherine on the log. "And my friend will have her firstborn child."

On all sides, people prepared to take their leave. The emigrants clambered aboard the flatbed wagon as the two freight wagons with their Indian drivers lumbered off through the trees. Flames whooshed over the mission house roof, and the boardinghouse was put to the torch. Jim held a brief conference with the Sayers, and Clarise hurried to Jed's side.

"Our cabin is about ten miles from here. My husband will let me off there, and I'll bring the cart for her."

"I'm not going any—" Katherine's labor had not reached the hard stages, but the pains, as bad as any she'd ever experienced, took her breath away. "Anywhere."

Nearby, mounted braves shouted to one another and raced among the mission buildings as yet another one caught fire. The freight wagons pulled away without an offer of help for Katherine from any of the women on board. This was not an unusual occurrence. Indian and pioneer women alike dropped to the side of the trail to give birth. Some births were easy, some were hard, and many simply were not to be, but rarely did they interrupt the journey.

But this was Jed West's woman. Right there, in the midst of a terrible clash of cultures, she would bear him a child. And he would find a way to hold back the cold and the darkness and the din for her, because as she had said, it was clear that she wasn't going anywhere until it was over.

Jed made a lean-to over a thick bed of autumn leaves, and he built a fire in front of the open side. Leah had more words with Tiloukaikt, who apparently admonished her before leaving her a horse and exclaiming what amounted to "Women!" in a tone of universal male frustration. Jed assembled the gear Jim had left behind—blankets, food, saddles for both horses, along with

Jed's rifle, bedroll and saddlebags. He kept an eye on Katherine as he hauled water and prepared a bed for her.

He remembered his first experience with childbirth, and the onset of Katherine's labor seemed gradual by comparison. Each time her breathing became labored with pain, he ignored the crackling of the conflagration across the stream and Leah's soft-spoken encouragement, and he homed in on those panting breaths, those small groans, trying to gauge the intensity of the pain by the depth of his sympathy. He had to put White Earth Woman from his mind. If he allowed himself to dwell on the way he'd lost his first wife, he would shame himself now. What he wanted to do was run, hide in the woods and wait it out. Best he perform a lackey's duties and stay out of the way. Leah asked for a man's flannel shirt, and he fairly leaped to his saddlebag to provide that. It was something he could offer. He tended the fire while Leah dressed Katherine in his shirt.

Soon there was nothing for him to do but wait. The intervals of soft, childlike whimpering that pierced the stillness within the grove were making him crazy. When finally she voiced a complaint—her back hurt terribly—he went to her, planted the heels of his hands in the small valley of her lower back and kneaded her quivering muscles.

"Does this help?" It was a shy, hopeful question.

"Yes. Oh, yes." She glanced at Leah. "How much longer?"

"No one can say. The pains are not hard enough yet."

"Not hard—" The color seemed to drain from her lips, and her eyes grew wide as the full moon. "This can't get much worse."

Jed managed a wan smile, his eyes full of sympathy as he blotted the sweat from her forehead. *Oh,* ma petite *, it can get so very much worse.*

"Talk to me, Jed. Tell me what to name our baby. Leah says I carry it low, and that means a b-bo—"

He waited out the pain while it rode her hard. *Talk to her. Talk to her.* He was afraid to talk to her—afraid his thin, masculine crust would crack and his fear would show. He rubbed faster, harder, determined to drive back the pain. He rubbed her until she went limp in his hands.

"If...it's a boy—" She was nearly out of breath, but she talked anyway. She had to. There were so many things she'd been unable to share with him. "I thought...I thought perhaps...perhaps your grandfather's name." She glanced over her shoulder. "Which you've never told me."

"Claude."

"And the last name?"

"Azure." It rolled off his tongue with French vowels and a throaty *r.*

"You were Girard Azure?"

He nodded. Hearing his name on her tongue gave him a quick, dizzying rush, and he felt a contraction of his own when next she experienced one.

"And...your mother's name?" she gasped on the downside of her pain.

"Annette."

"Tell me about—" A contraction seized her again too soon, and she grabbed his arm. "I can't take any more, Jed. It's too much."

"It will be over soon. I promise." And then he crooned, "Soon, *ma petite fleur. Bientôt. Ma promesse. Que je t'aime, ma femme.*"

She collapsed against him, and when she caught her breath, she asked, "Will you sing to our baby like that?"

"If it doesn't scare him."

"What does it mean? *Que je...*"

"How I love you." He pressed his lips against her cheek and tasted the salt of her labor. "My wife, my woman. I would take the pain if I could."

"You can't because—ah! it hurts—because I am punished with it."

"Punished?"

"Since the first woman . . . seduced her husband into— oh, dear God. Oh, oh, oh . . ."

"Punished, nonsense! You endure the pain because God knows you're the stronger one, Kate. Look at me." She had retreated into herself with the pain and was in no position to look at him. But he looked; the leaves of a quaking aspen were steadier than his hands. "God knows . . . He knows I could never— Leah, you've got to do something for her!"

Leah produced a honeycomb. "I have hoarded this for such a purpose. A little at a time," she said as she squatted beside Katherine and held the sweet to her lips.

Katherine shook her head, but Jed took her chin in his hand and held it still. "It's honey, Kate. Remember?" She moaned, but she took some on her tongue. "You remember when I brought you the honey, and you let me lick it from your finger."

"It was . . . ohh . . ."

"It will make you strong," Leah promised. She loosed a harsher tone on Jed. "Now walk her. She must break her water."

"She can't. The pain is too—"

"I know her pain. She can walk with it. She is a woman, isn't she?"

Jed wrapped Katherine in a blanket, lifted her from the bed and set her on her feet. "Walk with me now, *ma petite*."

"I can't." She hung from Jed's neck like a flour sack, and he did all the walking.

"Kate..."

"Make her *walk*," Leah commanded.

Grimly, Jed made Katherine carry most of her own weight and forced her to walk through a paralyzing contraction. "Jed, I hurt," she ground out angrily.

Guilt washed over him. This was his doing. He glanced at Leah, and he knew why this was women's business. She scowled back at him. "Your pity will kill her. Make her walk."

His stupidity would kill her, he told himself. His love. Damn his eyes, his *lust*. He'd never do it again. She gripped his neck, held her breath, and he stood steadfast when he really wanted to run like hell. He swore to himself that he would never put her through this again.

Between pains, Leah gave Katherine more honey to keep her going. She offered small sips of water and applied grease to her lips to keep them from cracking. Sparks flew from the camp fire, and across the river the mission fire burned lower. Katherine labored on, while Leah and Jed attended to every sign of change. They ignored the sound of an approaching wagon, and when it arrived and Clarise joined them, they all but ignored her, too.

"The first one always seems to come so hard," Clarise said. "I brought willow bark tea. It will comfort her later."

Jed wondered why he hadn't thought of that. Clarise took Leah aside, and he heard snatches of talk about bleeding and poultices. Where was his head? "There's a medicine bag in my gear," he told them. "Nettles for the poultice and—"

Warm water suddenly gushed between her legs, followed by a compelling contraction.

"Bring her to the pallet," Leah directed.

Katherine was inclined to lie down, but Leah motioned for her to squat. She couldn't. She *had* to lie down. She had no more strength, and she couldn't stand anymore— "Jed, pleeeease!"

"I'm here." He got behind her and squatted himself, lining up his back with one of the trees that supported the lean-to as he took her down with him. "I'll help you. Lean on me. Put your hands here." He positioned them on his thighs.

She braced herself, her arms stiffening into two sturdy pillars, as the need to bear down overcame her. Leah pushed the long shirt up over Katherine's distended belly. "The head is coming," she announced.

The news made Jed's pulse race. Katherine's arms quaked as she gasped for breath. "Oh no. Oh no." She groaned pathetically. "The pain is back. Too soon. T-too—ooo"

Jed steadied her shoulders. "Get on top of this one," he whispered. She arched her back. "Push down hard, Kate. Good. That's good. You're so good, Kate."

"I have the head. Once more, Katherine."

"Oh...oh...oh..."

If he hadn't been backed up against a tree, she would have knocked him over. "You're wonderful, Kate! Almost there. Almost there. You're gonna do it, love. You're—"

"Ohhhhhhh!"

Leah was ready when the little fry slid into her hands, mewling as he came. Clarise stood close by, and when the child was separated from the mother, she took him while Leah tended Katherine. Chest heaving, Jed blinked, trying to focus, trying to get his bearings. Here at hand were three women—one Indian, one white, one mixed-blood—and new life.

Clarise held the bawling baby up for Jed's inspection. "Your woman has given you a son."

The baby was glazed, puckered and pinch-faced, but his lusty squall proclaimed his health. Jed pressed his face into Katherine's damp hair and whispered, "Thank you," even though he doubted anything he said made sense to her just then. Leah was manually forcing another contraction.

"I can do it," Katherine mumbled, sensing her triumph as she dug her fingers into Jed's thighs. "I can do it. I know I can...do...it."

When at last Jed laid her on the pallet and took time to look at her, admire her, he was awed by her the way her eyes and her skin glowed with the flush of her achievement. Her hair was wet and matted, her lips trembled, and he thought he had never seen a more breathtaking sight. Unless, of course, it was the sight of his woman taking his whimpering son into her arms. Jed needed to take part, to stay close. He loosened her top three buttons, opened the shirt, then lay beside her while she introduced his son to her breast.

Poultice and cattail down helped to stanch the flow of blood. Katherine was given cowslip tea, which eased her body and permitted her to enjoy the euphoria that had come with the child. She laughed when he rooted around her breast like a sightless puppy, and she winced when the sucking began to sting.

"My, but he has a powerful little mouth," Katherine said. Jed chuckled near her ear, and she tipped her head back to rub the corner of her forehead against his. "Just like his father."

"He looks so small." He kissed her cheek, then reached over her shoulder to discover whether such tiny fingers could be real. The baby grasped his finger and went right on sucking. Jed laughed. He felt like a child himself, full of wonder and easy delight. "Who would believe ears could be that size?"

"So much hair," Katherine marveled, making a baby cap of her hand. "Thick and black. Just like his father's."

"I was never that small."

"Oh, Jed, I'm sure you were just this small once. And just this hungry. Look!" The little cheeks stopped their sucking and let her nipple slide away. "And just this sleepy, too," she whispered. "Getting born is hard work."

Leah appeared as if on cue and reached for the baby. "He must be cleaned properly and bundled. Your cradle board was found and brought to me for safekeeping."

Jed was grateful to Leah for not mentioning where it had been found or by whom. Katherine would tell him of her ordeal, and the tragedy she had witnessed, but not now. Death had no meaning on a night when God—her God and his—truly held them in the palm of his hand.

"I wish I could fix my hair for you," she mused as she gazed into her husband's eyes.

He smiled down at her. Matted corn silk. He touched it and found it to be still damp. "Tomorrow."

"I wanted to be beautiful when you came back, with my hair all curled and a pretty new dress. Instead..." She gave a little laugh and rolled her eyes.

"Instead you nearly scared the life out of me."

"That bad?"

"Oh, Kate." He smoothed her hair back from her forehead. "You cannot imagine how beautiful and terrifying you were tonight."

She reached to touch the hair at his temple. "You've cut your hair."

"I went to town. San Francisco. Thought I'd see what I could see."

"And what was that?"

"All kinds of things. All kinds of people."

"Practical women?" There was no trace of accusation in her languid question.

"Some." He grinned slowly. "They were no use to me, though. Even if I'd wanted one, I would've been too damn drunk to get my money's worth."

"Jed." She rolled her head from side to side, but couldn't bring herself to chide him.

"No point in trying to live without you, Kate. I don't want another woman, and they won't let me be a priest."

There was satisfaction in her smile. "And now you have a son."

"Now I have a son." He hesitated, then asked shyly, "Claude?" She nodded, and he grinned his wonderful, teasing grin. "Can you say it properly?"

"Claude," she said, smiling.

"Not like a damned Englishman. Like a Frenchman. *Claude.*" She did better the second time, and he kissed her for her efforts and offered a solemn, "Thank you for the name. He was a good man, my grandfather. You would have liked him, Katherine. He loved life. He loved my grandmother, my mother and me."

"Don't ever leave me again," she said suddenly, grabbing his hand. "Promise."

"Oh, Kate." It embarrassed him to remember the way he'd rode away. "I never left you. Not really. You know that."

"I knew you would come back, but even now I think . . . he might find that we're a burden. He might—"

"No. Never a burden. I only want you to be safe, you and Claude."

"Wherever you go, we want to be with you."

He squeezed her hand. "I left, thinking you were in a safe place. Bridger found me, and he told me . . . but he didn't know who. At Fort Walla Walla, they couldn't tell me." Still holding her hand, he rolled to his back and stared at the low, slanted roof. "They didn't know. I made up my mind, Kate. Whether you were alive or dead, I was going to be with you."

"Oh, Jed—"

"And then tonight, Kate, when that pain tore at you the way it did . . ."

"It's gone now. The minute he was born, it was gone."

His throat went dry as he remembered. "White Earth Woman died that way."

"I know, Jed."

"The baby wouldn't come. The women told me to stay away, but I knew what was happening." In the quiet night, his voice was low and haunted. "I wanted to help her. There was so much blood, and her life just leaked away." He closed his eyes and saw only red.

"Was the baby—"

"Dead. I could save neither one." He turned and saw her profile. A tear trickled from the corner of her eye, and he was afraid he'd said too much. "I can't save people. I'm just a man. I can't even save myself." He braced himself on his elbow so she would have to look at him and know how close he had come to failing her. "Tonight, when it got so bad...when you called my name and begged me to make it stop, I wanted to run.''

"It's all right, Jed." She smiled as she wiped her tears on the back of her hand. "So did I."

"I ran after I brought you to this place, Kate."

"But you came back."

"I've been running so damn long, I don't know how to stop. And I don't want you running with me."

"Then you'll have me following you." She put her arms around him and laid her cheek against his chest. "Take slow steps for a while, Jed. At least until I get my strength back."

Late that day, they took their leave of the Place of the Rye Grass. Leah had done her job well. It would not be long before she would find refuge in the mountains with her people. Clarise tended Katherine and little Claude in the back of the buckboard while Jed drove to the Sayers' cabin in the hills. There they would all spend the winter. Young Richard Sayer gave up his bed in the loft, and Jed agreed to "partner up" with Pierre, who had already gotten a good start on the winter's fur catch.

They heard talk of settlers hunting down the Cayuse. They heard about the settlers' militia and their demands for United States territorial status. The Hudson's Bay Company would soon have more competition than it could contend with in Oregon Country. Pierre assured Jed that John McLoughlin was not interested in who Jed was or in helping Governor Simpson catch up with him. He had vied for Simpson's position and lost, and Simpson wielded his power with relish. Business was gradually shifting to the north of the forty-ninth parallel.

As was his custom, Jed was the outside man, while Pierre dealt with the trading post. He was gone for days at a time, but he came home to a warm bed and a loving woman. During the day the small cabin afforded little privacy, but late at night the loft became a love nest. When Claude stopped demanding to be fed in the middle of the night, Jed usurped that deliciously quiet time on those cold, late-winter nights and made it snuggling, whispering, touching, loving time.

He loved watching Katherine embrace her new life. Claude never wanted for attention, and Katherine worried aloud that all the holding he got might spoil him. But she came to understand that the Métis pampered their babies. Sharing the baby multiplied the joy of having him. Clarise had lost three children since twelve-year-old Richard was born, and she was delighted to have a baby to hold. Richard fashioned a rawhide ball as a toy and carved a horse head from an antler. Claude's favorite of Richard's creations seemed to be a gourd rattle. Whenever Richard shook it for him, Claude's arms and legs would churn like four little whirligigs.

When spring came, Jed and Pierre recalled the season on the prairie—the rolling green carpet splashed with purple and yellow wildflowers, the expansive blue sky and the wind that carried the scents of Pierre's lake or Jed's river, the rich sod and the buffalo. They spoke of the prairie sometimes, for Pierre's people had lived north and east of Jed's, and there were comparisons and contrasts to be made. Sometimes they didn't speak at all. They simply sat side by side on a sawhorse and watched the sun rise out of the eastern sky. Their Métis blood stirred for the hunt.

The women saw the longing in their men's eyes. Clarise waited to be told, but Katherine had not yet mastered that kind of patience. One morning she walked across the yard, carrying Claude on her hip. Jed looked up and smiled. He secured the half hitch on the drying rack he'd just repaired and took the baby from her as soon as they reached him.

"What did you call your grandmother?" Katherine asked. Jed greeted his son with a kiss on the cheek, the way he always did, but he raised a quizzical eyebrow in Katherine's direction. "All children call their grand-mothers by some special name. What name did you use?"

He shrugged and tucked the baby against his chest. *"Grand-maman."*

"Claude must meet his *grand-maman.* Maybe even his great *grand-maman.*"

Jed's hand covered Claude's whole head as he smoothed the baby's thick, soft hair. "They may be gone, Katherine."

"You need to know." He glanced up, his eyes filled with gratitude for her insight. She nodded. "You need to take him to them, if they're still there."

"I want them to know you."

"And so they shall."

"But I don't want to answer for a murder I did not do. I could never live behind bars, Kate, and now that I have you and Claude..."

"You cannot go on this way. You committed no crime." She touched his shoulder. "Perhaps it's all been forgotten."

"I can't ask you to follow me all over the damn—"

"I still want to teach, Jed." She laughed a little. "Mostly, I want to learn, but I taught a little in the Nez Percé camp and at the mission. Are there children in your Red River Valley?"

"Yes."

"And can they all read and write?"

"No. There are few teachers."

"There, you see? A calling for me at last. 'Thy people will be my people.'"

"And my God?"

"God is God. Neither your rituals nor mine will ever change that."

He put his arm around her shoulders, bringing mother and child into his embrace. "We Métis simply have twice as many."

Chapter Twelve

Unlike the westward wagon crossing, the journey from mountains to plains was not rushed or harried. Jed knew the mountains. His party traveled on horseback and carried no extraneous baggage. He traded with friendly Indians and detoured around the hunting grounds of those, like the Blackfeet, who were not likely to welcome trespassers. Pierre was an experienced hunter, but he had not plied the Rockies to the extent that Jed had done, so he deferred to Jed's leadership.

During the first weeks of their journey, Katherine had a sense that the group was wandering. She wanted plans, maps, daily destinations and a sense of how much ground had been covered by nightfall. Some days, they didn't travel at all. They would camp beside a mountain lake, pull out all the fish they could eat, swap stories and enjoy the weather. When it rained, they would find shelter or make some, and they would wait it out. There was no slogging through mud, no calculating how much time must be made up by the first of the month.

"But we'll get there before it snows, won't we?"

Jed laughed, and pulled Katherine into his arms, hoping she would settle back with him and just watch the rain. They had taken shelter in two shallow caves, while the horses, oblivious to rain, grazed in a mountain meadow close by. Jed figured they had everything they needed—food, bedding, a private shelter and a sleeping baby.

"It's been eight years since I've been this close to snatching a glimpse of home, Katherine. Eight years without a word of my family. I know where I'm going, and we'll get there." He leaned back against the rock wall, tucked her shawl around her shoulders and held her close. "In our own good time."

She laid her head against his chest and sighed. She *was* comfortable. The lack of urgency about their pace left time for enjoying the journey, but for that niggling need to make everything a task and every task a thing that must be done and marked off. "It just seems to me, when you've got a purpose in mind, you ought to be about it without so much dawdling."

"We're moving along more efficiently than any wagon train." He kissed the top of her head. "More pleasantly, too. Would you rather be huddled in a wagon right now?"

"No."

"Or trying to pull one out of a slough?"

"No." She snuggled into his soft buckskin shirtfront. "This *is* a nice way to spend a rainy day." She had a nice view of his smooth chest through the front V slit in his shirt. She liked that.

"No man can change the weather for his convenience, and fighting with the elements when you know you'll lose just doesn't make any sense. Best to wait it out."

"But when will we be safely out of the reach of those Blackfeet?" She'd never seen a Blackfoot Indian, but the very fact that Jed had planned a route around their territory made her nervous.

"We'll get to Fort Union before the end of summer. This is all Indian territory, Katherine. Blackfeet, Crow,

Cheyenne, Sioux. We're liable to meet up with some of those people along the way."

"It's the Blackfeet you seem concerned about." She tipped her chin and glanced up at him. "So I must be concerned as well."

"We're taking pains to avoid them if we can. They don't welcome many guests." She had bad memories. He knew that, and he wanted to help her with them. If she stayed with him, there would be more Indians in her life. With a gentle finger he drew a line along her cheek. "You don't have to worry about that, *ma petite*. I won't let anyone hurt you."

Her voice became small, as if she spoke of a guarded secret. "I dream about Narcissa sometimes. I watched them kill her, Jed. Sometimes in my sleep, I see it all happening again."

Just as softly as she had spoken, he coaxed her. "Tell me what you saw."

"It was drizzling like this, but it was colder. More gray."

"A November rain."

"Yes. Bone-chilling." Safe in Jed's arms, Katherine allowed her mind to drift back. "I was in Leah's tipi when I heard the trouble. Shooting and screaming. Children, I thought. We had so many sick children.

"Leah tried to stop me, but I ran. It was like a dream even when it happened. I saw them bring her out of the house on a settee. She was already bleeding, and I thought, they're helping her. They've put her on the settee, and they're getting her out of there. Then they shot her. She jumped when the bullets hit her. And hit her, and hit her. One man shoved her into the mud, and then he held her up—" her eyes were glazed with the memory as she recited it tonelessly "—and whipped her face with a crop."

Jed hung his head and whispered, *"Mon Dieu."*

"I wanted to do something, but I couldn't move." She looked at him fearfully. "I couldn't even call on God, as you just did. My throat was paralyzed. I had no voice, no feelings. I could not even say God's name."

"Then I thank God for keeping you still just then." He pressed her head against her chest and held her protectively. "But I cannot thank Him for permitting you to see that."

"For permitting it to *happen*, Jed." Katherine sat up quickly. "Why did He let it happen?"

"Why were those people dying, Kate? The Cayuse people. You watched them die, too."

"That's true." She closed her eyes and nodded. "I did little more than watch the disease take them. Those little children, one by one, sick...then dead."

"A less violent way, but it works just as well."

Her eyes widened, and she whispered, "No one meant to—"

"If Claude had been one of those children—" She tried to turn away from the suggestion, but Jed grabbed her shoulders. "If one of them had been Claude, would it have mattered to you that no one meant to?"

She returned his challenge with a hot stare. "And if I had been one of those who was bludgeoned or shot to death, would it have mattered to you that my killer's children had died of measles?" She saw that the horror had crossed his mind before. "Narcissa didn't bring the illness. And Marcus...poor Marcus tried to help them. He tended them night and day, doing all he knew how to do for them. They smashed his skull with a tomahawk,

Jed. Jim Bridger's little girl, Mary Ann, was there. She saw it all.''

"If they had murdered you—" He shook his head. He could not think of her dying and leaving him empty. "I don't know, Katherine. The battle has only begun, and I am born of both sides. My blood wars with itself. What kind of a life can I expect to give you? And Claude..."

"A life with you." He was distancing himself from her now. She could feel it. She laid her hand on his chest. "That's what we want. When Claude is old enough, he'll tell you the same."

"I said I wouldn't let anyone hurt you. Not while I draw breath." He covered her hand with his and pressed it hard, letting her feel his heart beat. "But I cannot stop the conflict. It's bound to get worse. And we may be caught in the middle."

"You've always been caught in the middle."

"Not when I lived in the mountains." Her slight shoulders filled his hands. "We could go back there, Kate. We don't see red and white when we look at each other, do we?" She shook her head and smiled bravely. "But the minute we walk into a trading post or a camp or a town..."

He leaned back against the rock wall, letting her slide away. "But you wouldn't be happy stuck up on the top of a mountain. You're a woman—a lady. You need your women friends and yard goods and church on Sunday."

"I need the man I love. I wanted to return to the cabin when you decided we should winter with the Nez Percé." She thought of the way she'd behaved then, and she didn't like the woman she remembered. "At first it felt strange. Everything was so different, and I couldn't speak with Half Hand's people, couldn't understand them." She glanced at him guiltily. "At first I didn't even try. I thought it would be too hard. But when I stopped thinking that way, I learned some things." She smiled. "I learned quite well, actually."

"Yes, you did."

"I can learn more. I can say Azure the way you say it. And Claude. And Girard." The way she rolled the *r*'s brought a smile from him. She was very close to him now. She was warmth and tenderness. She stirred him simply by saying his name.

"And *je t'aime*," she said softly. In the corner of the cave, their son made little sucking sounds in his sleep, and they shared their joy with their eyes.

"I love you, too." He tucked her hair behind her ear.

"I can be content wherever you take us. But you, Jed—" She scooted closer. "I see the longing in you. I see the restlessness and the need to clear up this Simpson matter." He started to protest, but she added. "You're going home to stay, aren't you?"

"It's a risk, I'm afraid. For Jean-Paul. For me. But I just want to see them, Kate. Just for a day." Katherine rested her hand on his cheek and nodded. "I just want to know that they're still there."

They could hear the shots fired at Fort Union to announce incoming traders long before they glimpsed the massive palisade. Pierre let Richard fire the answering volley. The boy sat up straight in his saddle and did his job, speaking, as it were, for his father's party. In a few years he would be old enough to be one of the partners.

Katherine's heart pounded, and she beamed at Jed, who rode beside her with the cradle board strapped to his back. Claude would be given back to his mother before anyone at the fort saw Jed playing the woman's role, but the baby was getting heavy, and the truth was that Jed often demanded his turn at carrying the child. He smiled back at Katherine now, puffed up with the thought that she would be introduced as his wife. She was beautiful. Her yellow hair glistened in the sun, and her eyes danced with anticipation.

Katherine felt like a child herself. She had spent most of her life in a city, where there were inns, theaters, carriages in the streets and tinkling bells over shop doors, but never had she been more excited at the prospect of seeing the sights. She glanced back at Clarise, whose bright-eyed smile reflected Katherine's own feminine expectancy.

The fort stood on a flat above the bluffs overlooking the river. Fort Union's flagpole resembled a ship's mast. At the top of the pole, outdistancing the peak of the corner block tower by twenty feet, a carved white fish spun in the wind over a flapping American flag. Imposing as it was, the fort was no military outpost, nor was it Hudson's Bay. It was owned by the American Fur Company, which John Jacob Astor had built into a thriving enterprise and later sold after he'd made his fortune in the fur business. Fort Union's location near the confluence of the Yellowstone and the Missouri rivers was ideal for convening hunters and traders.

Clusters of tipis stood outside the walls, and Jed knew he would meet Crow, Chippewa, Assiniboine, perhaps even his cousins, the Plains Cree. He led his party through the gate as the August sun beat down on his bare shoulders. He and Pierre had brought a respectable catch of furs, bundled in standard ninety-pound packs of about two hundred mixed-skins—beaver, bear, mink, fox, lynx, marten, otter and muskrats, or "rats." But what amazed him as he crossed the square were the piles of buffalo hides—hundreds of them stacked beneath the ramparts along the palisade. Apparently the storehouse was full.

They were met by Norman Kittson, the agent, who had of late declared his intention to take a bite out of Hudson's Bay Company's fur-trading monopoly. The sight of well-made packs brought in by hunters he'd never dealt with before delighted the fur trader. Kittson had put the word out. His aim was to lure the Métis and the Indians in the border region to abandon Hudson's Bay and trade with him. The two families were invited to supper at the agent's house.

The clerk, his apprentice, the post's trader and several other lesser officials roomed and took meals in the agent's house. Kittson had asked two of the men to move to the men's quarters temporarily so that the two families might be made comfortable. Katherine was simply grateful for the bed and the privacy, but Jed didn't miss the pointed stares they had received from the men who had adjourned to the guardroom after supper to have a smoke. He bristled and stared back. Yes, the golden-haired beauty was his woman. Her son was also *his* son. Neck bowed like a stallion's, Jed stood his ground, and no man voiced the challenge that Jed saw in each face.

"I hope you'll find our rude accommodations adequate for your needs," Kittson was telling Katherine when Jed turned around. It was the host's cue to the women that it was time for them to retire.

Jed took the baby from Katherine's arms and handed him over to Richard, who was always pleased to tend the child. "We won't be long," Jed promised the boy. Clarise mumbled something to Pierre, then followed the children upstairs, while Jed took pleasure from the disapproving look he got from Kittson. Damned if he was going to let Katherine out of his sight until those wolves had smoked their fill and gone back to their dens.

"I don't often ask the men to vacate their rooms for guests." With a gesture Kittson offered chairs near the fireplace. No one moved toward them. Unruffled, he took a cigar box from the mantel and continued. "But you are no doubt aware that you are . . . an unusual group of visitors."

"In what way?" Jed challenged as he accepted a cheroot from the box Kittson offered.

"First of all, you have brought in a handsome catch. Fine-quality furs, compressed and packed by men who have obviously had a good deal of packing experience."

"We carried them a good distance. They had to be packed well."

"One has to wonder why you carried them this far. I hope it's because you're tired of dealing with Hudson's Bay, and you've heard that I pay top American dollar for good furs. We'll have an offer for you tomorrow, and I think you'll be pleasantly surprised."

"We trade as we please," Pierre said. He puffed on his cigar, plucked it from his mouth and grinned. "Hudson's Bay does not own us."

"You are Métis," Kittson surmised. Pierre squared his shoulder and nodded. Kittson turned to Jed. "I could swear I've seen you before, but the name is not familiar to me."

"We haven't met." It was true. Jed knew the American agent only by name, and he wondered what familiar chord he had struck with Kittson.

"If you say so. But you are Métis."

"Yes. I am Métis."

"From Pembina?"

"That area. Originally. I have not been back in some years. I've been hunting Snake River country close to eight years now." He decided not to mention the time he had spent with the Sioux. That information might have been another piece to whatever puzzle Kittson was toying with as he eyed Jed.

"Ah, that explains why we haven't met. That was before my time. Still, you seem so familiar to me." He smiled. "Perhaps I'm thinking of some relative. I have friends among the Métis in Pembina."

Kittson turned to Katherine and tried to smooth over the awkwardness a woman's presence during the men's evening social posed for him. He was a negotiator, after all, and he could adapt to any man's eccentricities for the sake of striking a bargain. The way to West's good side seemed to be through his wife.

"Mrs. West, you have adapted remarkably well to this country. Missionaries and settlers, male and female, are carved of hardy stock."

"Jed has taught me well."

"And you're young. Adaptability is the province of the young." He raised his brow, adding frankly, "However, I do feel that it may take some of the men a little time to adjust to the unusual nature of your, uh—"

Jed interrupted. "My father was an Englishman, Mr. Kittson. I was educated in St. Louis. Does that ease your sense of propriety any?"

"No need to take offense, West. You have a lovely wife, who would turn heads on the streets of New York. Out here, she could well cause a riot." He offered another congenial smile. "But you look like a man who could settle any question merely with a stern look."

Kittson decided to get to the point. He tossed his cigar into the fire and propped one foot on a hearth-side bench. "I want you and Mr. Sayer to let me outfit you for the next season. I'll give you fair prices for your furs. Trade in goods and supplies or cash, however you want it. In addition to furs, I'll buy all the pemmican you can get, all the buffalo hides, whatever you want to deal in. You know the Indians. You know the mixed-bloods. If you can get more of them to deal with me, I'll make it well worth your while." He turned to Pierre and saw the spark in his eyes. "Interested?"

"I'm interested, yes. I have always been interested in trading as I pleased." He glanced at Jed and grinned. "I think that's why they sent me to Oregon Country. They thought I was a troublemaker in my lake country. I have too many friends. Too many relations. They didn't want me stirring them up."

"Maybe they need to be stirred up," Kittson said. "Why shouldn't a man trade with whoever offers him the best deal?"

"Because of the charter, they say. Hudson's Bay has a charter from the mother country. But I say times have changed. I say charters can be changed, too, or the hell with them."

Kittson laughed. He liked Sayer's spunk, and he knew he had a convert. "What about you, Mr. West? You know, with your skills, you could go far with this company."

"I've heard promises like that before, but I found them to be empty."

"I'm with the American Fur Company, Mr. West. Not Hudson's Bay."

"I'll keep that in mind, Kittson, and I'll think about your offer. I've been away for a while, and I need some time to get my bearings."

"Certainly. Take your time. You can afford to. You'll do well on the furs you brought in. You aren't working for Hudson's Bay?"

"I've been a free trader for a long time," Jed said.

"And I've been with Hudson's Bay for a long time," Pierre added. "But they tell me where to live, what to hunt, what to eat, what to wear. Everything comes from their store. I pay their price, but they do not pay mine."

"Then you'll enjoy dealing with me. If we can't come to an agreement, you're free to go elsewhere." Kittson laughed amiably. "Unlike Hudson's Bay, we recognize that there is another choice. We intend to compete with them favorably and open up the fur trade a little more."

"Suits me," Pierre said. "After we do business tomorrow, I shall think about choices. Right now—" he punched Jed's arm "—my choice is bed."

Jed turned to Katherine. "I have another matter to discuss here. Would you go up with Pierre and get Claude settled?" Relief was evident in Katherine's assent. She was exhausted. "I'll be there in a moment," he promised as Pierre and Katherine left the dining hall.

"It's a delicate matter," Jed confided after they were gone. "Is there a Black Robe on the post? Some kind of a preacher?"

"Father LaPointe is out at the camp." Kittson nodded toward the door, but Jed knew he meant the Indian encampment beyond the palisade.

"I want to ask him . . . to do us a service. And I want it done quietly." Jed glanced at Kittson, who showed no sign of surprise. Jed knew the Black Robes were doing their damnedest to get people on the frontier married and baptized and listed in their rolls. They were at it all the time, stalking rendezvous, Indian camps and trading posts with a holy doggedness. Jed had left school and never thought to become part of any of that again. Not until now. "I guess it would mean a lot to my wife if we had the words said over us. We haven't had much of a chance to get it done her way."

"Did it your way, did you?"

Jed thought about driving the man's smile down his throat, but there was some truth to the comment. "She's my wife. Make no mistake, Kittson."

"I can see that she is." The smile faded, leaving a glimmer of understanding in Kittson's eyes. "And you are surely her husband. But LaPointe will want to make it legal and baptize the child. That's why he came out here."

Jed sighed, nodding. "Katherine came for the same purpose."

"Our purposes change. The hand of Providence was working in your favor, Mr. West." Kittson reached inside his coat and drew out a flask. "I want to propose a toast," he said as he uncapped the bottle and offered it to Jed. "To a very lucky man."

The following morning Kittson proved his generosity with a handsome offer for the furs. Jed knew the man was blatantly courting them, but Pierre was impressed. He extolled the advantages of free trade long after Jed had stopped listening. Jed's mind was on other things. Like making his marriage legal. Like presenting Katherine, staunch Protestant missionary, with a proposal that was not apt to set quite right with her. He had seen the Protestant Scots haggling with the Catholic Frenchmen over Cree souls, and he knew that even the Hudson's Bay's claim to its monopoly paled in comparison with the claims the rival sects made on their converts.

Jed knew he was no negotiator. His best approach was to make a direct offer.

"I have spoken with the priest," he told her in the privacy of their room. She was putting the baby to her breast, and the curious look she paused to give Jed did not stop Claude from finding the source of his meal. Jed smiled at the sound of the baby's noisy suckling, then looked at Katherine, who waited for an explanation. "He will bless our marriage if we will let him baptize Claude."

"A priest?"

"I know it isn't...quite the way you might want it, Kate, but it's the best I can do."

"A priest," she repeated, as if she were testing the word.

"He's the only Black Robe around."

"Black Robe?"

"Minister, priest, Black Robe. It's all the same to me." He sat next to her on the bed, slipped her blouse down her arm and kissed her shoulder while he watched Claude. The baby's fat little hand rested possessively on the breast that fed him. "I want us to be married," Jed said. He brushed his lips back and forth against her shoulder.

Her heart fluttered, but her voice was deceptively even. "You have said that I'm your wife."

"I want it in writing." The white ribbon that held her chemise was untied, and the ends, crimped where the bow had been, hung limp. With a forefinger he pulled the cotton garment away from her other breast and found blue-white milk dripping from the pink, puckered nipple. "If anyone doubts..."

The air felt cool on the skin he'd exposed. The baby tugged on her breast persistently, rhythmically, drawing nourishment through her. She felt rich and fertile, a lovely dampness that made things grow. Jed's warm breath made her flow freely. She wanted more. She wanted him to tell her more about what he wanted and why. She felt feminine, powerful, loving, and she wanted him to affirm her.

"If anyone questions..." He'd nearly lost track of his thoughts. She had used the rose water he'd made that morning, and she smelled of milk and roses. Her breast was plump and soft, and it had a center bud that was so lovely. So ripe. He closed his eyes and caught warm drops on his tongue. Sweet, warm milk.

"Ah, Kate, how beautiful you are." One more taste, he thought, and when his tongue flickered over her again, gathering some of the drops and losing others, he heard her sigh and knew she felt as full as he did. Bursting. Needing to be milked. She plunged her fingers into his hair and kept him close. His son would need the milk. A good father would not take it. But he loved putting his lips close to her nipple, now skimming, now letting his tongue come away with just a taste. And he loved making her sigh.

He wanted a charter. He wanted a monopoly.

When Claude took to the other breast, Jed settled back on the bed just to watch. Katherine had pinned up her hair, and she was his to admire. Her cheeks were rosy, and the same pretty blush washed down to brighten her neck and chest.

"I see other men look at you, and I know what they're thinking," he told her quietly. "They're thinking you don't belong with me."

"It doesn't matter what they think." She looked down at the baby, then up at Jed, and she knew she was as beautiful as he'd said she was, and that she was important to him. "I do."

"Will you say that when the Black Robe asks if you take this man for your husband?"

"Of course. I have taken him already. It's just that—" She glanced at the high window. The shutters were open, and she could see blue sky. Jed was her husband. That fact was as clear as the sky. She wanted a wedding, and it pleased her that Jed wanted one, too, but a priest? "I certainly never thought to say my vows before a *priest*."

"Before God, Katherine. The priest is only there—" Jed waved a hand as he sought to explain "—to make it all legal. So that no one can question my right to live with you...to have you as my woman. To claim you as my wife and your children as my children. I want the law on my side, at least in this."

All the stock pastured under guard outside the walls of the post by day was returned to the massive stable at night. Jed stood in the doorway and looked the compound over. Here and there a small fire burned sagebrush to chase mosquitoes away from small groups of men, who spoke quietly, occasionally laughed a little louder. Jed's horses were fed, and across the way, in a small room, his son slept and his wife worried about what she would wear tomorrow for their wedding. And he had a business offer from a man who seemed decent enough, although Jed wasn't sure he liked the idea of all those buffalo hides piling up. He wondered who could be using that many buffalo. But at least Kittson wasn't Hudson's Bay. He wasn't demanding exclusive trade. There was plenty of good hunting in this country. He could find a good spot where there would be water, wood and game, build Katherine a little cabin, hole up for the winter, and come spring...

Come spring he wanted to give his family a place among the people who shared his blood. He was so damn close that he could hear their voices on the prairie wind, and he could feel the soft-spoken river slipping by in the night. Fort Union overlooked the Missouri, but the river that seemed to be flowing close enough to touch was not the Missouri. It was the Red River. *Winnipeg.*

Jed's thoughts were broken when he noticed that a man had moved away from one of the camp fires and was approaching the stable. Jed pushed his shoulder away from the doorpost and stood waiting. The man was tall and lean, and his jaunty walk seemed familiar, but dark as it was, Jed couldn't see the man's face. He came within several yards, then stopped.

"Are you the man they call Jed West?"

Jed's ears could have been playing tricks on him. Or the wind. The prairie wind could fill the ears with voices that made a man feel a little crazy sometimes.

"I'm looking for someone," the man said hesitantly. His tone betrayed the fact that his search had been long and discouraging. "I thought you might know him."

Jed's heart thudded against his ribs, and his mouth went dry.

"The man is my brother. He's been gone for—"

"Too long." Jed's throat was full of sand. "Come closer, Jean-Paul, and I will tell you of your brother."

"Gi—Girard?"

"It's Jed." He stepped forward, offering his hand. "Jed West."

"I...I am Jean-Paul—"

Jed used the handshake to pull his brother into the shadows of the stable. He gripped Jean-Paul's shoulders as the younger man whispered, "Azure."

"*Mon frère*, you've become a man. I might have walked right—" They embraced, slapping each other on the back and laughing. "Right past you in a crowd. You've become a man!" Jed marveled again as he lapsed into the Michif language, the mixture of French and Cree he had spoken as a boy.

"Of course. After almost nine years—" With their hands on each other's shoulders, they circled each other in a kind of reunion dance. "Girard, we never heard from you. *Maman* has been—"

"Maman?" Jed gripped Jean-Paul's shoulders more tightly. "Is she well?"

"She is old. She misses you, Girard. It seems she's spent her whole life missing you."

The joy of simply talking within the family again prevented Jed from detecting the shadow of resentment in his younger brother's voice. "I must see her. I know I've caused her too much worry. And *Grand-maman?*"

Jean-Paul hesitated. "She cannot live out the winter. She is . . . No one understands how she's lived this long. She hardly recognizes anyone." He let his hands drop to his sides. "But she would probably know *you.*"

"I'll bet she would." Jed slapped Jean-Paul's back enthusiastically. "I'll just bet she would. We couldn't stay, of course. I don't want to cause any trouble. But just to see them—" He took hold of Jean-Paul's arm and pulled him along. "Hell, I haven't even seen you. Come over here by this window. Last time I saw you, you were skinny and . . ."

The moonlight revealed the face of a man, but Jed first saw the resemblance to the boy he remembered, then the changes.

"Ah, Jean-Paul. So many times I've wanted to send a message with someone who might have headed north, but I knew such a message would have to change hands two or three times before it might reach you, and I couldn't trust anyone. After I escaped, they never bothered you about Simpson anymore, did they?"

"They questioned me about you."

"Asked you if you knew where I was," Jed surmised.

"Yes."

"But they never came after you for Simpson again."

"No."

"I figured they would say I wouldn't have escaped unless I was guilty, but there was no other way."

"That's what they said."

"I was ready to break you out, too, Jean-Paul, but then they let you go. I guess they were satisfied that I was the one."

"They hung Wanted posters everywhere."

Jed chuckled. "I saw one. Damn good likeness, too. Maybe that's what Kittson remembered."

"Kittson won't turn you in. He's got no use for Hudson's Bay. And nobody was sorry to hear about Simpson being dead. Not our people, anyway."

"Still, it was a bad time for us, *mon frère.*" Jed laid his arm across his brother's shoulders. "No matter what we said, they were never going to believe that madman turned his pistol on himself."

"No. They wouldn't believe that."

"I told my woman I wasn't going to sit behind bars for something I didn't do, but it wasn't a question of sitting behind bars. They were set for a hanging before the judge even had his wig powdered."

"Are you ever going back, Girard?"

"Just to see them. *Maman et Grand-maman.* I want them to meet Katherine." His hand went to Jean-Paul's shoulder again. "And I have a son, Jean-Paul. A wife and son! Come, you must meet them." He raised a cautioning finger as he propelled Jean-Paul toward the door. "But no more Girard. It's Jed. It seems strange to hear someone use my old name again."

"Wait." Jean-Paul stepped out of Jed's grasp. "Girard, I must tell you something, and after I tell you...you may not want your family to know me at all."

"Nonsense." Jed tapped Jean-Paul's arm with his fist. "You're my brother."

"A poor excuse for one, but by now you must know that. I was afraid, Girard." Even now his remembered fear reverberated in the dark. "Some brave man, eh? Your brother? Always ready for a fight, remember? Always ready to prove how tough I was. Until they mentioned the gallows. They had me all trussed up and ready for the spit, and they kept asking the same questions over and over again."

"After we were arrested?"

Jean-Paul grunted his assent. "Suddenly I wasn't so brave anymore. They kept saying that our mother and grandmother would need someone to care for them, and if both of us were convicted, there would be no one. Our women would die, too. And they said you were a trouble-maker, that you had been away and you weren't like us anymore."

"Did you believe that?"

"No. I told them you hadn't killed anybody. I *told* them that."

A moment ago Jed had smelled and tasted only joy. Now he found himself in a dark, close place, and he smelled manure and tasted fine dust. He felt trapped, forced to stand still for something he knew he didn't want to hear. "They accused both of us," he recalled.

"Yes." There was a rustle of straw and Jean-Paul shifted his feet. "At first."

"What do you mean, *at first*?"

Jean-Paul swallowed audibly. "At first they asked if we'd ever fought with Simpson, and I told them I had. Later they stopped asking about us. They started asking about you. 'Did your brother ever argue with Mr. Simpson? Did they ever come to blows? It happened often, didn't it? Your brother is quite a strong man, isn't he? Did your brother lay hands on Mr. Simpson on the day of the murder? Did—'''

"Murder." Jed shook his head. "The crazy man shot himself."

"They said he didn't. They said—"

Jed grabbed Jean-Paul. "You saw him!"

"I know." He dropped his chin to his chest, and his voice became raspy. "I know. Not a night passes that I don't see him again, pointing the gun to his head. And then I see you. And then I see myself...pointing the gun...at my brother's head."

You were set up. But not by Jean-Paul.

The confession pinched Jed's heart. "No, Jean-Paul," he said quietly.

"Yes! I signed a paper. I signed my name, just the way you taught me."

"What did the paper say?"

"I don't know." A ragged sob clawed at the stillness. "You never got around to teaching me to read, Girard. They promised nobody would hang if I signed."

"Shh. It's all right. You were seventeen years old, for God's sake."

"I am not seventeen anymore, and I shame myself. Not only have I betrayed my brother, but I—" he wiped his face on his sleeve "—weep like a child. I keep asking anyone who comes along if they've seen you, heard of you. 'Course, I didn't know you'd changed your name." There was a moment of pain-filled silence. "I'm sorry, Girard."

"They used you."

"I know. But I let them. I saved myself."

"Governor Simpson wanted a murderer, so they gave him one. Or the name of one. I got away."

"Ah, *Dieu*, I was afraid you were dead."

"And now you see that I'm not."

As if on cue, Katherine's soft call drifted through the high window. "Jed? Are you in there?"

"I'm here, Kate." To Jean-Paul he confided, "I told her to stay in the room until I got back, but she hasn't learned to mind yet. Probably never will. She's from the east."

Jean-Paul slipped back into the shadows. "Give me a moment before you—"

Jed squeezed his brother's shoulder and headed for the door just as Katherine rounded the corner. "You should not be out here alone, Katherine," Jed scolded, reaching for her hands. "It's not safe."

"But you're out here, and I wanted to tell you something."

"What?" *Poor Jean-Paul. About to meet his sister-in-law with a face full of humiliating tears. A moment, Katherine.*

"I don't mind the priest."

Jed laughed. "He doesn't mind you, either."

"I mean, the fact that he isn't—"

"That he wasn't sent by the right mission board?" He was only talking. He didn't give a damn about any mission board. He had a wonderful surprise for her.

"It doesn't matter," she said, as though she had nearly convinced herself. "There, you see? I can bend. As long as we're—" She heard a rustling in the stall behind Jed. "I thought I'd heard you talking in here."

"And so I was."

She tried to get a peek behind his back. "There's someone here with you, then?"

"There is."

"A . . . a man?" She hoped it was a man.

Jed was bursting with the news. "That surprised me, too. To see him as a man." He called over his shoulder. "Jean-Paul?"

"Jean-Paul? Oh, Jed, truly?"

A man of slighter build and smaller stature stepped out beside Jed.

"Katherine, this is my brother."

Chapter Thirteen

Nearly two years after they had begun a life together, Jed and Katherine exchanged marriage vows in the Christian tradition. There was no gold ring to be had, and so he carved a wedding band from a deer antler. He wore his floral beaded buckskin shirt, and she wore a calico dress in a shade of blue that matched her eyes. She and Clarise had stayed up the night before stitching tucks in the bodice. Clarise tied a length of her own blue ribbon in Katherine's hair, and Richard found a fistful of purple coneflowers and lacy white yarrow for the bride's bouquet. Before witnesses, Jed and Katherine were joined.

He was handsome. With her heart bumping within her breast like a bee trapped inside a glass jar, she raised her chin, then lifted her gaze and thrilled to the lively luster in his dark eyes.

She was lovely. His heart thudded like hooves hitting drought-hard clay as he waited, watched, hardly dared breathe until she lifted her lashes and looked at him with eyes that glistened like cool, clear, drought-quenching blue water.

And they made promises.

The wedding was a compromise, as the rest of their lives would be. He had claimed her as his woman, and she had borne him a son. But they would live in a margin where two worlds overlapped, and one of those worlds demanded that a marriage be recorded. And so it was done. His priest, her ritual. His name, her law. Legally she became Katherine Azure.

It was a long trek east and then north to the river valley Jed had always called his home. Jean-Paul, who had been trading only as far west as Fort Union, made the trip with them, along with the Sayers. Day after day they rode through hock-high grass. Rolling hills gave way to nearly flat prairie. Cottonwood, willow and ash trees lined the river bottoms, offering shady respite for plentiful herds of deer, pronghorn, buffalo, and for human migrants, as well.

The men took what game they needed for food, but there was much camp fire discussion concerning the piles of buffalo hides they had seen at Fort Union and the increasing demand by both trading companies for meat and pemmican. Pierre welcomed the opportunity for more trade. Jean-Paul noted that the Métis had begun to sell meat and pemmican to the growing population of settlers in Minnesota, which lay east of their river. The great northern buffalo herds were becoming scarce, and the hunters, particularly the Métis, were looking southward, toward Sioux country. Hunting there could be risky, but rewarding.

Jed, who had lived among the Sioux, wondered aloud about the risk of depleting the supply of food and hides needed by whole nations of people. The herds had always been plentiful, and it was hard to imagine that the northern herd was almost gone. Furbearing animals, too, were becoming harder to find. He knew this from experience. There had always been hunters here, but now they hunted differently. They hunted to take more than they needed. Who would use all those hides?

Jed had seen the Hudson's Bay Company limit hunting in the north, which was their stronghold, while in Snake River country, where Americans threatened to displace the British businessmen, the company encouraged unlimited fur trapping. Huge areas were trapped out. The trappers were retreating higher into the mountains. On the west coast, settlers, who sought land, not furs, were crowding the trappers and the Indians. The face of the land was changing. If these things happened here, what would become of the Plains people?

Speculation and debate continued until, as each camp fire turned to embers, they all agreed that some things would never change. There would always be hunters camped on this hard ground, and the stars would always be there to guide them home.

By the time they reached the Red River, Claude had cut four teeth and taken his first steps, leaving his mother's hands and heading for the safe harbor between his crouching father's knees. Jed whooped and held the laughing boy high above his head in celebration. Katherine clapped her hands and wondered how far those legs would one day carry her son from her. Too soon he would choose meat over her milk. Wearing the proud father's grin, Jed retraced the baby's steps in a single stride, and the child reached for his mother. She hugged him close. Her milk had brought him this far, and he was not ready to give it up. Not quite yet.

Katherine was about to meet the woman who had nurtured her husband. It was a sobering thought. Annette Azure. The woman who had once tended Jed, just as Katherine did Claude. She had washed him, clothed him and fed him. The sound of her voice had calmed him in the dark. She had had first claim on his trust, his affection. Would she approve of the wife her son had chosen?

The aging woman and her ancient mother lived with the community of Métis Jed had known so well as a boy. The two women had always wintered in a soddy and enjoyed the mobility of the tipi in the summertime. Just as it has always been, Jed thought as he surveyed the valley from a hilltop vantage point. The riverbank was dotted with lodges, at once familiar and strange. Time had passed. A generation had grown old, another had matured, another had been born. He longed for the familiar, but he felt the effects of having distanced himself. Would they still know him? Was he, as Jean-Paul had said, not like them anymore?

Jean-Paul rode up beside him and pointed to the valley, singling out a small cottonwood grove. The tops of one tipi's lodgepoles were just visible, and there was camp smoke. Beyond the grove, the river ran deep and wide. The breeze carried Jed's hair back from his face, and he could smell the water. He filled his lungs and let the river trace the channel it had carved long ago in his soul. Without a glance or a word to anyone, he dug his heels into the Appaloosa's flanks and descended the slope.

He found his mother draping the blankets she'd just washed over stout tree limbs. She was smaller than he remembered, slightly stooped, and her graying braids reached her waist. She turned at the sound of his loping horse. The last of the blankets fell to the ground as she clapped both hands over her mouth, cutting off a girlish squeal. Jed reined in, but he swung to the ground before his mount had completely stopped, and he caught his mother in his arms.

"Oh, my son, my son..."

"I'm here, *Maman*."

"Can it be true?" She turned her beautiful face up to him, and his heart was full. "Can it be true?"

"Yes, *Maman*."

"It's been so long." Her hands fluttered over his arms and shoulders, taking a mother's inventory just as she had the day he was born. "You've been well?"

"Yes. I've brought you a daughter." He brought her out of the grove so that she could see the approaching party. Jean-Paul rode beside Katherine, who held Claude in the cradle board he was already outgrowing. "And a grandson," Jed added.

"A white woman?"

"Her name is Katherine, *Maman*. She is American. From the east."

"Ahh," she said, shading eyes that squinted into the sun. "She is beautiful. I can see that from here."

"She speaks English, but she's willing to learn. I would have her speak her husband's language, and I would give my son a home among my people." He touched her shoulder. "It's no good, wandering the way I have. I've missed you."

"We would have you stay this time." Her hand came down, and she turned to him anxiously. "Is it safe for you, Girard? They won't try to hang you, will they?"

"I won't let them hang me, *Maman*. I've done nothing wrong."

Jean-Paul led the rest of the group into the yard, but Annette had only eyes for the baby. "Let me see my grandchild!"

Katherine freed the child from the confines of the cradle board and handed him down to Jed before dismounting herself. Claude reached for his grandmother's braid, but refused to let her hold him, so she turned to Katherine. "You have given my boy a fine son."

Katherine felt awkward. "I...yes, I certainly think so. He's growing so fast."

"My boy is good to you? He does not treat you mean?"

"Yes—no!" She glanced at Jed, who only laughed and shook his head. "Jed is a fine husband."

"Jed?" Annette turned a puzzled expression on her older son.

Jean-Paul spoke up. "That's his name now, *Maman*. People call him Jed."

"Your *grand-maman* will never call you Jed. Don't confuse her with any—"

"Where is she?" Jed asked.

Annette nodded toward the tipi. Jed handed Claude back to Katherine and motioned for her to follow him. "She speaks almost no English," he reminded her. "But she'll have you speaking Michif in no time."

"You go ahead," Katherine said quickly.

"They tell me I'm a fine interpreter, too." He took her hand. "I want you both with me."

At the door, he asked for permission to enter. A sound came forth, less than a whole word, but Jed took it as an invitation. Jean-Paul had warned him that their grandmother was fragile, but he was not prepared for the withered brown face, the white hair and the rheumy eyes.

He squeezed Katherine's hand. *Are you still with me?* She squeezed his hand back. *I'm here.*

"*C'est moi, Grand-maman.* It's Girard."

"Girard?"

He knelt beside her. A willow backrest propped her bony body into a sitting position. She looked almost lost in her dark blue muslin dress and woolen shawl. The air inside the tipi was hot and stale, but the shawl was pulled tightly around her shoulders.

"I've been gone too long," he said quietly. "Maybe you don't remember me."

"Girard?" Her eyes wouldn't bring the sight of his dear face into focus for her, but she found his hand. "I remember you. You took my plum pits."

Jed laughed joyously. "I needed them. I was told to chase the crows away from the meat-drying racks."

"Rocks!" She cackled. "I told you to use rocks."

"But the plum pits were there in the basket. They were handy."

"I was saving them for a game, you troublesome pup!" She cackled until a fit of thin, dry coughing seized her. When it faded away, she continued. "Why have you stayed away so long, Girard?"

"I . . . I had to see the world, *Grand-maman*."

"See the world? Did you see the great water?"

"I saw one of the oceans, *Grand-maman*. But not the one *Grand-papa*'s father sailed."

"Ah." She nodded. "I would like to see water that big. Such a task for the earthdiver to bring mud from the bottom of water that deep. Remember how you would ponder over that story? 'How could he hold his breath that long?' you asked. 'I have tried, *Grand-maman*. I cannot do it.' But you could do it better than the other boys, couldn't you, son?"

"I worked at it until nobody else could stay down as long as I could." He grinned at Katherine, who understood only that Jed was happy to be home. "She remembers how much I enjoyed swimming as a boy," he explained in English, then took up the Michif again. "I got to be quite a swimmer, didn't I, *Grand-maman*?"

"Yes, you did. And did you hold your breath while you were out searching for the world?"

"Sometimes." It hurt him to watch his grandmother squint at him as she tried to focus nearly sightless eyes. But she saw. Through the murkiness, the old woman saw. "Sometimes you hold it when you fear losing the breath in you altogether," he reflected. "The life's breath, the spirit. If you lose it, you'll drown. So you keep to yourself."

"You would not drown," she said. "The earthdiver does not drown."

Jed laughed and patted her hand. "That's just a story, *Grand-maman*. I have a surprise for you." He turned to include Katherine. "My wife, Katherine."

Katherine knelt beside Jed, and the old woman reached for Katherine's hands and face, touching, examining, seeking without restraint in the way of the very old and the very young. She spoke, and Katherine turned to Jed for meaning.

"She can't see much," he explained. "She asks if you have golden hair. Say *oui*."

"Oui, Grand-maman."

The wrinkled hands found Claude's leg. The baby looked down at the hands, then at the old woman's face. Something kept him from shrieking in protest. *Grand-maman* spoke again.

Jed grinned proudly and coaxed Katherine along. "She asked about the child. Say—"

"C'est Claude," Katherine said quickly. She hesitated, then plunged ahead. *"Le fils de Girard."*

"Claude?" The old woman repeated the name lovingly. Jed squeezed Katherine's shoulder as his grandmother asked, "You named him for your *grand-papa*?"

"Yes," Jed said. "To honor him in the way of—"

"In the way of the Frenchmen. That's fine, Girard." She rubbed the baby's leg. "He would like that. He would be very proud. Where did you find your woman?"

"In the mountains."

"Eeee. Not one of those English, is she?"

"She is American, *Grand-maman*. She was very sick when I found her, but I used your medicine, and she recovered."

"Ah, you remembered the medicine. And she lives. And two become one, even as one divides himself between two worlds—air and water." She nodded, and her head began to loll against the backrest. "Only the earth-diver manages such a feat."

"Are you tired, *Grand-maman*?"

"He is a good boy, Claude. He listens well. He tries. Never gives up...never..."

"Is she all right?"

"I think she was slipping in and out of focus." Jed eased the sleeping old woman away from the backrest and laid her on the buffalo skin pallet. The part about Earth-diver, he told himself—*that* part was all out of focus. "She's lived a long life, and she's tired."

"But she knows you, Jed."

"Yes." He smiled wistfully as he watched over her, filling himself with his grandmother's face. "She does know me."

He had intended to leave. It would have been a short trek to United States territory, and there he might have avoided trouble with Hudson's Bay. But Jed's home was a people, not a place, and he reminded himself that he had done nothing wrong. He was tired of running. Perhaps the incident had faded from people's minds. He had a new name now. He had friends and family. Hudson's Bay needed the goodwill of the Métis, now more than ever. And there were laws to protect a man from being punished without trial. After weeks of staying one more day and then another, Jed saw that Katherine was beginning to nest. Even though his mother had begun to treat her like a daughter, his wife needed a home of her own.

He never announced that they were staying. He simply stopped intending to leave.

When a Métis family needed a winter home, as Jed and Katherine did, the people held a cabin raising. The building was framed out, logs were hewn, a stone fireplace was built and sod was cut for the roof. Many hands made the job go quickly, leaving time for Métis fiddle music to turn a work fest into a party. Katherine saw a new side of her husband—the fun-loving side, who had been taught songs and dance steps that were a happy blend of traditions. He was hesitant at first, protesting that he'd forgotten them all. But he hadn't forgotten, and he was soon tugging on his wife's hand, cajoling her to join in.

"I cannot dance a step!"

"Nonsense! You can't be any worse than I am."

"I would be, Jed. I never learned. In our house it was—" She looked around her. Men and women, women and women, children of every age dancing their feet off, flattening the grass to the lively strains of the fiddle. Oh, they were having fun! Jed took Claude from Katherine's arms and handed him to Annette. Then he stood there, toe tapping, knees flexing, eyes dancing and mouth grinning. "We never danced, you see," she continued. "It wasn't permitted."

"It is here. Required, in fact."

"But I can't do what they're doing, Jed. I don't know how."

"Yet!" With a laugh, he pulled her off the stump she'd been keeping warm all night and educated her in the art of celebrating—Métis style. The festivities lasted late into the night, until the last of the children had been carried off to their blankets, and the last of the couples had drifted away, arm in arm.

The people were generous. Katherine learned bits and pieces of language and customs as she set about making the new cabin a home. There were gifts of furs and blankets, clothing and kettles, but eventually the time came to pay a visit to the Hudson's Bay trader. Jean-Paul offered to do it for them, but Jed had decided to conduct his own business. Sooner or later, there would be questions. He would answer them if he had to, but he would not run anymore.

Claude was left with his grandmother. It was early November, and the sky was filled with the threat of first snow. After a long ride, Katherine was glad to be able to walk and stretch, then go inside the trader's quarters and warm up. Three men—the trader and two others—watched her take off her white cloak and fold it over her arm. It made her uncomfortable to be watched so intently. She thought of Frank Granger, and she glanced over her shoulder to make sure Jed was close by. He put his hand on her shoulder.

"That's a nice cape you got there, ma'am," the trader said. "I could give you a good price for that."

"It isn't for sale." Katherine glanced at Jed again. "My husband made it for me."

"Nice work."

"Thanks." Jed extended a hand. "The name's Jed West."

"Edward Williamson."

"My wife, Katherine." He ignored the judgment in the man's eyes. "We're just setting up housekeeping, and we'll be needing some things."

"That so? You got furs to trade?"

"I'll be paying in cash."

"Made Beaver?"

"You take American dollars?"

"If I can get 'em." Williamson leaned on a pile of fur packets. "You work for the Company?"

"No."

"You country born?" Williamson asked Jed.

"I'm from Connecticut," Katherine put in quickly. The tone the man used angered her. The questioning frightened her. "I met my husband in Oregon Country," she explained, hoping that would put Jed's identity into a different perspective. "Now, I wonder... where are your goods, Mr. Williamson?"

"My goods?"

"I see nothing but furs here. Where are your trade goods?"

"You give me your order, and I fill it. We don't generally take the Indians in the back room to pick through the goods. It's all good quality, according to Company regulations. You just tell me colors, amounts—"

The door opened, admitting a gust of wind and two more men. They wore buckskins and carried pistols, like the other men in the room, but one had a distinctly official air about him. He surveyed the room as though it were in his charge, then nodded at Williamson.

"Major Caldwell," Williamson acknowledged.

"I've got business with your customers, Ed." He stepped up to Jed and stretched his neck, but he couldn't match Jed's height. "I'm Major Caldwell of the Chelsea pensioners. Are you the one who calls himself Jed West?"

"I am." The time had come sooner than Jed had expected. The pensioners were Hudson's Bay Company militia.

"The chief factor has some questions to put to you, West." He turned stiffly to Katherine. "Are you here in the company of this man, madam?"

"This man is my husband."

"If you wish to accompany him, I'm sure we can—"

"*I* wish to accompany him." One of the men who had been standing in the background stepped forward, extending a hand to Jed. "James Sinclair, Mr. West. I have some experience with the court, and I believe I know what this is all about. There's been a great deal of speculation about who you are and what to do about you." The small, lean, dark-eyed man glanced at Major Caldwell. It was a glance that took control. "It's the Simpson matter. And I think we can clear it up."

James Sinclair was not a barrister, but he was the best spokesman the Métis had. The previous year he had gone to London to petition the British government on their behalf against the Hudson's Bay Company's monopoly in the fur trade. No action had been taken on the position, and tension between the Métis and the company continued to mount. The Simpson affair was an old wound, and Girard Azure had been identified at Fort Union. Company informants had carried the word. Riding into a Métis settlement would have been sticky for the pensioners, so they had waited until the man who called himself Jed West had walked into the trading post with his wife. Sinclair, too, had waited. He was a negotiator, and he didn't want this old torch getting near the trade-issue powder keg.

Jed was taken to the office of the chief factor, while Sinclair escorted Katherine to his own home and introduced her to Marie, his Métis wife.

"I've sent for Jean-Paul," Sinclair told Katherine. "Your husband's only crime was his escape from custody, and he had good reason to avoid the courtroom. The trial would have been a mockery. But things have changed a bit, and this time he has representation. He has me." He patted her hands, which were folded on the table between them. "I know what I'm doing, Mrs. West. Your husband will be free to go home with you tonight. I promise."

The waiting was terrible. Marie Sinclair spoke little. She kept offering Katherine food and glancing anxiously at the front door. Katherine remembered the look in Leah's eyes when she knew something terrible was about to happen. She, too, had glanced anxiously at the door.

"Has there been trouble here lately, Marie?"

"James insists that everything can be handled through the proper channels, that this problem with Hudson's Bay will be solved without fighting." She peered through one of the house's precious glass windows and sighed when she saw no one but the blacksmith carrying a bucket of pitch into the livery. "Your husband has been much praised for killing Thomas Simpson."

"But he didn't kill Simpson."

"There were many stories about it. Some say Simpson tried to kill him. Some say your husband was protecting his brother." She turned from the window. "The climate is the sort that turns rumor into legend, and those who take sides become at once heroes and villains. Such a man might be shot in the back for his efforts."

"Are you speaking of my husband, or yours?"

"My husband has made his stand. It's gained him powerless friends and powerful enemies."

"You speak of your own people as powerless?"

"My husband believes in the courts and the law. We are British subjects, he says. The law is on our side." Marie went to the stove and removed the second kettle of water for the second pot of tea. "If men want to fight, they'll find some excuse," she said.

"Your husband wants to promote his cause through legal channels, and mine simply wants to be left in peace."

"Is he a free trader, your husband?"

"Yes," Katherine admitted. "But for the past eight years he has been trapping and trading in American territory."

"Sooner or later, it will come to a fight. They're all spoiling for one, just like a barn full of little boys. Somebody is sure to push somebody too far." Marie shook her head sadly. "I hope the death of one or both of our husbands does not become their cause."

Afternoon became evening, and evening turned to night. Katherine realized Jed would not go home with her *this* night. Marie said no more about her concerns, and Katherine contemplated the situation Jed had walked into. He was a trapper because his grandfather had been a trapper. He had not been permitted to follow his father's profession because he was Métis. But his gift for languages was part of his heritage, too, as was his knowledge of herbal medicine, which had probably saved her life. Two worlds, he had told her. Two worlds at war within him, at odds all around him. Would he be their sacrificial lamb?

No, Katherine determined. He had sacrificed enough, and so had she. They had work to do. *Both* of them. God had brought them to this place for a purpose, and they would find it, and they would fulfill it. They would begin as soon as Jed was cleared of these old charges.

She drank cup after cup of tea and paced until she finally fell asleep in a parlor chair.

It was Jed who awakened her.

"It's over, Kate."

"Over?" She tried to blink sleep away.

He nodded. "We can go home."

She sat up, looking around and concluded that, while she had slept, Jed had been interrogated throughout the night.

"No charges." James Sinclair's voice came from somewhere in the background. Katherine saw only Jed's weary smile.

Sinclair brimmed with the tale, and it fairly spilled out into the room as he moved from chair to table to hearth and back to chair again with wiry exuberance.

"The witnesses—Jed and Jean-Paul—contend that Thomas Simpson shot himself, and there is no evidence to the contrary. The deposition Jean-Paul signed back then was easily dismissed. The Métis are demanding their rights, and they are becoming a force to be reckoned with. If the Company tried to make something of this, they'd have an army of Métis down on their necks, and they know it." He smacked a fist into his hand. "The law is on our side, Jed. We can stay within the law and get the concessions we demand. Mark my words."

Jed wasn't marking anything but the look in his wife's eyes. "No more running," he promised her quietly. "We can leave or stay, but we won't have to—"

"Oh, Jed, I was so afraid they'd keep you there." She reached for him, embraced him and shed tears of relief against his neck.

Sinclair offered them the use of a room and a bed and reminded Jed that he'd been up all night. Jed needed no reminding, but he pointed out that he'd brought an empty cart, and he intended to fill it with supplies and whatever trade goods his wife wanted for her new home. After the trading was done and they'd shared a meal with the Sinclairs, they accepted the offer of a bed. Before nightfall, they were asleep.

The early-morning air was cold and heavy. There was a predawn stillness outside the shuttered window. Katherine stirred beneath the pile of heavily batted quilts, and an arm slipped under her shoulders and drew her across the bed. His skin was warm, and she knew he'd been awake, waiting, at least a little while.

"How soon will you be wanting another baby?" he whispered.

She snuggled closer, seeking the warmth of his body, enjoying the early-morning smell of sleep. "Why do you ask?"

"When Claude was born, I swore I wouldn't put you through that again, but the memory's faded a little and—" he dipped his head to kiss her shoulder "—the desire hasn't. How many do you want?"

"Well, now that I've weaned him . . ."

"How many and how far apart?"

She giggled. "How many can you make?"

"At a time?" He growled and rolled over her. "Shall we try this time for two or three? It might take more dedication, more time and effort."

"But you're up to it."

"I'm feeling pretty strong this morning." He kissed her again and laid his head back against the feather pillow. He needed to talk first.

"Ah, that Sinclair was good," he told her. "He knew what to say, how to say it. All I had to do was tell them what happened. And Jean-Paul..." His voice became solemn with the memory of his younger brother's ordeal. "Jean-Paul admitted to signing the statement, all right, but all he knew was they promised not to hang me if he signed. And he didn't know what was in the statement. They hadn't read it to him, and he was too damn stubborn to admit..." Jed sighed. "All he could write was his name. That was all I'd taught him." He chuckled mirthlessly. "Once he got the hang of it, he was pretty proud of that signature. He was always looking for an excuse to use it."

"You're not angry with Jean-Paul."

"No. He was just a boy. They started talking about hanging, and he was scared spitless." He turned his head. The morning was beginning to lighten, and he could see her soft shadow past the puff of pillow. "We've got to teach him to read, Kate."

"I think that's a wonderful idea."

"You do? You don't think he's too old?"

"Not if he wants to learn."

"Even if he doesn't, he owes me a few years." He looked up at the beams above his head. "My grandfather made a life for himself taking furs, plying the waterways in his canoe, singing his songs. That old woman who's ready to die—she was young once. She often went with him when he hunted. Hell, she could skin out a 'rat so pretty, you wouldn't see a nick in the flesh. Now her hands quiver, and she can't see. When she goes, those old times go with her."

"She's lived a good, long life, Jed. Longer than most."

"It's not the same anymore, Kate. Sayer talks about free trade, but pretty soon, there won't be anything left to trade. It'll all be trapped out. And the buffalo. *Mon Dieu*, at the rate they're going at Fort Union... There were enough hides there to make lodges for a whole—'' he gestured expansively ''—a whole summer encampment. And if you'd ever seen one, you'd know that's a lot of hides.''

"This land is full of buffalo."

"Not for long. If they kill them all, then what? Where will the meat come from then? These people depend on the buffalo, just as the Sioux do."

She knew "these people" were the Métis. He was one of them again, but he had seen more. He had wider vision. "You could farm."

"The land belongs to the Company." The answer came automatically, but on its heels came second thoughts. "At least they say it does. They have this charter they wrote, and they set up a council with people voting on this and that. We don't have a damn thing to say about who hunts where and who trades and how much anything is worth." He tucked his hand behind his head as he considered all that he'd seen and heard the day before. "Sinclair is right. Sayer too, in his way. We've got to stand up for ourselves."

"You're not going to... fight anyone, are you?"

"I don't know. Pierre talks about fighting, but I like Sinclair's idea. Try to use their laws. Do you know, he went all the way to London?" He paused. "I'm thinking...we could do better for ourselves if more of us could read."

"The way they put up that cabin, a schoolhouse shouldn't be too much problem." He heard the cautious note of hope in her voice. This was what she'd wanted all along. "We'll need books."

"We'll get books." He turned to her, bracing himself on his elbow. "We move around a lot in the summer, Kate. That's the way we live."

All she'd heard was *we'll get books*. "You're going to help me? We're going to teach?"

"Don't know if I'll be much good at it."

"You'll be wonderful! I ought to know. I've been a pupil of yours for two years now." She laid her hand on his cheek. "I'll still get my language lessons, won't I? I'll need to speak Michif."

"Oh, you're entitled to all kinds of lessons, Madame Azure." He hovered over her, smiling. They could see each other clearly now. "We've made promises." He brushed her hair back. "This morning's lesson—" he kissed her forehead "—will be conducted in French, *ma chérie*." The last was whispered against her skin while his fingertips skated over her breast.

"Mmm. French is such . . . an expressive language."

He'd never felt so expressive. He rocked against her and grew more so. She moved her legs apart for him. "Then tell me it's good," he exhorted her.

"So . . . good." *Come inside, and it will be better.*

"Say *bon*."

"Ah . . ." *There you are.* "*Bon*."

"*Oui, ma petite,*" he whispered, stroking. "*C'est bon.*"

"I love you, Jed."

"Say it again."

"*Je t'aime.*"

Chapter Fourteen

Pierre and Jean-Paul spent the winter hunting, while Jed watched over the women and helped Katherine persuade a dozen children—some days more, some days fewer—to attend classes at their cabin. She and Jed worked effectively as a team, and as the children's interest increased, so did the families'. The Azures were repaid in gifts— food, firewood, beaded garments and lovely willow baskets. Jed did a little hunting and hired out as an interpreter, but he had bad feelings about the future of the fur trade.

It was a season for endings and beginnings, showing themselves by turns. In January, when a Chinook wind brought a warm thaw and long icicles grew on the corners of the cabins, *Grand-maman* died peacefully in her sleep. Hearts were heavy. In February, when they slept with Claude between them to keep him warm, Katherine told Jed that there would be a second child. And hearts were light again.

In March, when an early spring made the sod roof sprout yellow-green grass, Métis talk turned to buffalo hunting and the quantities of meat, hides and pemmican that would be hauled to trading centers in Red River carts. Jed's ominous feelings made him pace and grumble.

There would be an end to it all, he said. Every year the herds were harder to find in the north. Every year they ventured farther south, into Sioux Country. But he and Katherine would be with the people, and the people would do what they had always done to get their living.

Jed had made arrangements through the church to buy schoolbooks. At least he had good feelings about teaching the children. When the beaver and the marten and the buffalo were gone, there would still be Métis, who would have to be fed. Somehow. If they could read, perhaps they would find answers.

It was in May that the big trouble came. Katherine had gone to the river for a bucket of water when she heard the earth rumble. It sounded like stampeding animals—cattle, buffalo or antelope. She dropped the bucket and scrambled up the slope.

Horsemen! Hundreds of them! They churned up clouds of dust around the commotion and wild shouting. Several shots were fired, and Katherine suddenly felt cold and sick and panicky. The Place of the Rye Grass sprang to her mind—the shots, the shouting and the bloodshed. A few yards away, a horse crow-hopped, then kicked up his hind legs, and a dog yelped as it skittered out of the way. Katherine hiked up her skirt and hurried toward the house.

Jed stood in the yard with a ring of dark-haired wide-eyed children around him. Stumbling toward him, Katherine kept an eye out over her shoulder. Lord, there was an army of them! She recognized Jean-Louis Riel, whom everyone called "the Irishman," racing in circles and calling the settlement's men to arms.

"What's happened?" Katherine shouted even though she'd reached Jed's side.

He shoved the baby into her arms. "They've arrested Pierre Sayer."

"Why?"

"It's hard to hear what they're saying. Near as I can tell, they've charged him with illegal trading."

"But Jean-Paul is with him. They were both—"

Jed was already headed back into the house for his rifle. "I have to go with them, Kate."

"Jed!"

"I have to go!"

In a moment he was back, slinging his possibles bag over his shoulder as he ran. "Tell *Maman* I'll take care of Jean-Paul. I won't let them hurt him. Watch the children." He gestured toward the house. "Keep them back. The horses are spring-wild."

The horses? Katherine would have said it was the men. Pierre had given them their cause.

The Appaloosa was picketed near the house, and within moments Jed was mounted. Katherine shooed the children toward the door, but she watched her husband until the mounted mob swallowed him up and thundered out of sight, four hundred strong.

Moments later, Clarise showed up on horseback at Katherine's door.

"The Irishman says they want to put my husband on trial, Katherine. Does this mean they will hang him?"

"I don't understand this illegal trading." The children had scattered, some running after the horses and imitating the war cries they'd heard their fathers make. Claude bawled while Katherine bounced him in her arms and shook her head. "Surely they cannot hang a man for trading."

Clarise slid to the ground. "I must go to the place where they are holding him. I must see him, see that he is—"

"Jed will see, Clarise."

"I must see him. Do you think they'll let me see him?" Wild-eyed, Clarise grabbed Katherine's arm. "Come with me, Katherine. Talk to them for me."

Guns and horses and angry men. The sun was high and bright, but Katherine's head spun with visions of gray drizzle, of shouting and gunshots and angry men; a bullet tore into Narcissa's chest, a tomahawk into Marcus's brain.

Oh, Lord, Katherine prayed as she gave her son into his grandmother's care. Let there be no killing.

Katherine had been to the chief factor's office before. She knew there was a stockade for prisoners, but she didn't know where court might be held. Her first stop had been at the home of James Sinclair, but she learned that he had already been summoned to the Company's headquarters. There were armed men everywhere. At the factor's office, she found James Sinclair standing over a table and shuffling through a raft of court documents.

"What are you doing here, Katherine?"

"Have you seen Jed?"

James eyed her accusingly. "Is he with that mob?" He pushed the papers aside. "Good Lord, I thought he had more sense. There's going to be bloodshed here, and it isn't going to do our cause any good. British troops by the boatloads. That's what we'll get."

"Can we see Pierre?" Katherine laid a hand on the terrified Clarise's arm. "This is his wife, Clarise."

"Please," Clarise asked softly. "I want to see my husband."

"I'll see what I can do."

He started for the door, but the red-faced Major Caldwell came through it first, gesturing wildly. "Riel is out there, standing on the steps of the church, reading a statement claiming Hudson's Bay Company's charter is invalid. It's outrageous!"

"No more outrageous than your arresting that man, Caldwell. You don't have the manpower to keep them from coming in here and taking him, and you know it." James nodded toward Clarise. "Let this woman see her husband." Caldwell opened his mouth to protest, but James cut him off. "Pierre Sayer is her husband. You could profit by courting somebody's goodwill, Caldwell. Let her see him."

Caldwell's jaw worked furiously as the two men stood toe to toe. Caldwell was not up to the challenge. Wordlessly, he conducted Clarise out the back door.

"Katherine, see if you can find Jed. I need his help in this."

"But he's here to help Pierre." Katherine wasn't sure who was on whose side. She only knew her family was suddenly embroiled in this. "And Jean-Paul. Where's Jean-Paul?"

Sinclair seized her arm and immobilized her with a hard stare. "Katherine, there's a mob out there. I don't know where anyone is. I *do* know that Pierre Guillaume Sayer has been ordered to stand trial, and if they break him out of there, we're going to have hell to pay." Realizing that he was shaking her, he released her arm and stepped back with a sigh. He calmed his voice. "Jed knows all about running from the law. I know Pierre is his friend, but they've got to back off before this goes too far. We can make a stand here in the courtroom. I know we can."

Katherine made her way to the church, searching for familiar faces and asking for Jed as she went. The men were angry. Katherine didn't care about any of the politics, but she cared about the anger. No matter how righteous, that kind of anger was frightening.

"Katherine, what are you doing here?"

She turned at the sound of Jed's voice, and the sight of his face flooded her with relief. "I came with Clarise. Jed, you must try to stop them from doing anything—"

"They've got Pierre. If they convict him, Jean-Paul is next, and half the men here—"

He gestured around him, for he was part of *them*, but she stayed his hand. "James Sinclair is with him. He wants to plead Pierre's case."

"Plead his case? Hell, he's guilty! He worked for Hudson's Bay and traded with Kittson."

"And if you break him out and he runs, what then?" He glanced away, but she insisted, "What then, Jed?"

Jed shook his head, but he knew what would follow. He had lived what would follow. For eight long years. "What can Sinclair do?"

"I don't know. But he says if there's a riot here, we can expect British troops." There was steel strength in his forearms, but more power in the small hands that gripped them. "Jed, please. Try it his way first. Talk to them. It can't hurt. You outnumber them, at least for the moment."

He stared at her. She was his woman. She was all women. Her smooth, pale skin became brown and leathery, blond hair became white and blue eyes became brown. But the eyes—blue to brown and back to blue again—the eyes were clear and sure and feminine. Make peace, they said. Keep the children safe. Talk to them. Interpret for them. Negotiate.

And two become one, even as the one divides himself between two worlds.

Jed pushed his way through the crowd and joined Riel on the church doorstep. By the time he stepped above the crowd, he felt a dizzying sense of purpose, and he realized he had been holding his breath.

Only the earthdiver manages such a feat.

Riel spoke of rights and taking what was theirs, and the crowd cheered. One of theirs was in jail, Riel told the crowd. The man had done nothing wrong. The Métis had been pushed too far. Something had to be done.

In the middle of Riel's exhortation to the crowd to free Sayer, Jed intervened.

Dive deep. Bring us something.

"Some of you know me. You call me Jed now, but my name is Girard Azure." There was a scattering of cheers. Jed's own tribulations at the hands of the Company were well-known. Riel nodded his approval and stepped aside to share the platform.

"Pierre Sayer is my friend, and I won't see him rot in prison for a crime that is no crime." More cheers. "But neither would I wish a life in exile on him or anybody else. I lived that way too long. This is my home, and it's Pierre's home, too. We belong with our Métis people."

"They won't drive us out, Jed!" someone in the crowd shouted.

"Maybe not today. But how long before they send in the British army to back up the pensioners?" He knew Riel had an answer, and he wanted to get his in first. "Sinclair wants to plead Pierre Sayer's case before the court. I say, give Sinclair a chance."

"What the bloody hell are you talking about, Azure?" Riel demanded. "They'll crucify him."

"We're here to see that they don't. Pierre's my friend." Jed stood his ground. "Sinclair spoke up for me, and I'm a free man after eight years on the run. I'll fight for my friend if I have to. But first I want to see if their laws can work for the Métis. If they can't—'' He surveyed the crowd. "Then we'll fight for our freedom."

While the crowd discussed this among themselves, Sinclair himself appeared. He promised to bring Sayer back out after the trial—a free man. The Métis retreated to the doorsteps and the fence posts and the shade of the livery, and they waited—four hundred strong—to see how the court treated Pierre Sayer.

The trial was a quick affair. With a mob of angry Métis outside, no one wanted to drag it out. Pierre Guillaume Sayer did not deny the charge. He had, he admitted, traded with the American Fur Company. He was found guilty. And then he was set free with no punishment. When Pierre Sayer emerged with James Sinclair into the bright spring sunlight and held up his hands to show that there were no more bonds, the shouts went up from the Métis.

"Vive la liberté!"

"Le commerce est libre!"

Shots were fired in the air, and the victory celebration commenced. The charter of Hudson's Bay Company was still in place, but the Métis had successfully asserted the right to trade as they pleased. Long live freedom, they said. Trade is free!

"Grand-maman" would say that something has changed, but nothing is begun that has not begun before, and nothing ever ends that will not begin anew.''

Katherine looked up at her husband. He was tall and proud. He had touched bottom and surfaced and, for the moment, had quelled the war in his blood. "It's not truly over, is it?"

"No. The cycle will resume, sooner or later. People have to be able to feed their families. When there is nothing left, the fighting begins again."

"And where will you stand, Jed?"

"With the Métis. In the middle." He put his arm around her. "Where does my wife stand?"

"With her husband. You prevented bloodshed today."

"Perhaps."

"There would have been killing, Jed."

"It would have settled nothing, but I'm afraid it will come." He tucked an errant wisp of hair behind her ear and smiled a bittersweet smile. "But not today. Today we have a small victory. And tomorrow—" He touched the corner of her mouth with his forefinger, and she smiled for him. "Tomorrow we start teaching that brother of mine to read."

"Let's go home."

"Let's take the long way. By the river."

*   *   *   *   *

A NOTE FROM THE AUTHOR

Many people who are enrolled as Native Americans, in accordance with varying tribal and federal laws, are actually mixed-bloods. In both Canada and the United States, after nearly four hundred years of contact between the native people of this continent and the immigrants from Europe—years of intermingling through times of war and peace, years of inconsistent dealings through an assortment of treaties, laws and policies—the mixed-bloods are seen by some as the living representation of the "bridge over troubled waters" between cultures. Such an in-between state is often unenviable, for a person of mixed racial and cultural backgrounds may be told by some that he is not white and by others that he is not Indian.

The Métis of the Red River Valley in North Dakota and Manitoba were such people. Probably the most peaceful blending of European and Native American cultures came when French and some British—mostly Scots—trappers and traders settled in that area and took Cree and Ojibway wives as early as the seventeenth century. What followed was a blending of language (a mixture of French and Cree language called Michif) and tradition. The Métis were traders, interpreters, buffalo hunters and nomads. The nineteenth century saw them searching for their place, asserting their claim as a new people—not white, not Cree, but Métis. They had a tumultuous relationship with the Hudson's Bay Company, which often employed them and on occasion used them as settlers to strengthen claims in the Northwest Territories. When the fur trade declined, the Company generally cast these people adrift.

In 1869-70, when sovereignty over the Canadian Northwest was transferred to the new dominion of Canada, the Métis took up arms under the leadership of Louis Riel. They demanded to be recognized as people, and for a short time their National Committee was the governing body in the Canadian Red River Valley. The Red River uprising was eventually suppressed by British and Canadian forces, and Riel fled to Montana. He returned to Canada in 1885 to lead a second rebellion. He was captured and executed.

Though many have blended in with government-recognized tribes or with non-Indian society, the Métis are largely a displaced people today. In Canada, some mixed-bloods managed to claim Indian status when Treaty Number 9 was signed in 1905; however, the majority of the mixed-bloods were granted no treaty rights. In the United States, relations with the government and attempts to gain legal status as a mixed-blood Indian people have been frustrating. In Montana, where a group of Métis took refuge following the uprisings, some were placed on the Rocky Boy's Reservation; others in Montana are landless. The Turtle Mountain Indians of North Dakota are, for the most part, descendants of the Pembina Chippewa and the Red River Valley Métis.

HISTORICAL ENDNOTES

Three documented historical events are woven into the fabric of *Heaven and Earth*:

In 1839 Hudson's Bay Company explorer Thomas Simpson, a young cousin of the Company's Governor George Simpson, died mysteriously on a trek through Sioux Country with a group of Métis. Simpson made no secret of his hatred of the Métis, and they hated him in return. He suffered from depression, and, although Company officials suspected he was murdered, they could not disprove the Métis' claim that Simpson had committed suicide.

Until 1870, the Hudson's Bay Company claimed an exclusive right to all fur trade in the Northwest Territories. In the 1840s Norman Kittson, of the American Fur Company, threatened Hudson's Bay Company business by luring away Métis trade. The Métis declared their grievance against the Hudson's Bay monopoly in a petition to the British government in 1847. In 1849 Pierre Guillaume Sayer, a Métis, was arrested on a charge of illegal trading. Jean-Louis Riel, father of Métis rebel Louis Riel, backed by four hundred armed Métis, declared that the Company charter was invalid and free trade was legal. Sayer was tried, convicted and released without punishment. The Métis celebrated this as a victory and presumed the right to trade as independents thereafter.

On November 29, 1847, Dr. Marcus Whitman, his wife, Narcissa, and twelve others were killed by Cayuse Indians at the mission Whitman had built on the Walla Walla River in what is now the southeast corner of Washington. The killings took place after more than half of the Cayuse population had died of measles, brought to the mission by white settlers that fall. The Cayuse believed that Whitman had poisoned them with his medicine. Forty-seven white captives were taken. In December, a Hudson's Bay Company outpost ransomed the captives and escorted them to safety. In the two years that followed, the Cayuse, who had fled to the mountains, were hunted by pioneer militia. Finally, Chief Tiloukaikt, Tomahas and three others gave themselves up and were tried and executed.

Before he was hanged, Tiloukaikt was asked why he surrendered. His reply way: "Did not your missionaries teach us that Christ died to save His people? So we die to save our people."

Harlequin Historicals®

COMING NEXT MONTH

#51 GOLDEN PARADISE—Susan Johnson

Countess Lisaveta Lazaroff never expected to be rescued
by Russia's youngest general, nor could she predict that
explosive passion would bring them together. A scholarly
beauty and an arrogant soldier, their love was destined to
survive the ravages of war.

#52 THE MISS AND THE MAVERICK—
Deloras Scott

Carrie O'Brian didn't think she'd ever regret her decision
to head west, until drifter Luke Savage hired on as her
driver. Rough, crude and ill-mannered—he was not at all
the city-bred beauty's type, until they were in each other's
arms.

AVAILABLE NOW:

#49 FREEDOM FLAME
Caryn Cameron

#50 HEAVEN AND EARTH
Kathleen Eagle

HARLEQUIN American Romance®

THE LOVES OF A CENTURY

Join American Romance in a nostalgic look back at the twentieth century—at the lives and loves of American men and women from the turn-of-the-century to the dawn of the year 2000.

Journey through the decades from the dance halls of the 1900s to the discos of the seventies . . . from Glenn Miller to the Beatles . . . from Valentino to Newman . . . from corset to miniskirt . . . from beau to significant other.

Relive the moments . . . recapture the memories.

Watch for all the CENTURY OF AMERICAN ROMANCE titles in Harlequin American Romance. In one of the four American Romance books appearing each month, for the next ten months, we'll take you back to a decade of the twentieth century, where you'll relive the years and rekindle the romance of days gone by.

Don't miss a day of A CENTURY OF AMERICAN ROMANCE.

A CENTURY OF
AMERICAN ROMANCE
1910s

The women . . . the men . . . the passions . . . the memories . . .

Take 4 bestselling love stories FREE

Plus get a FREE surprise gift!

Harlequin Superromance

A powerful restaurant conglomerate that draws the best and brightest to its executive ranks. Now almost eighty years old, Vanessa Hamilton, the founder of Hamilton House, must choose a successor.
Who will it be?

Matt Logan: He's always been the company man, the quintessential team player. But tragedy in his daughter's life and a passionate love affair made him make some hard choices....

Paula Steele: Thoroughly accomplished, with a sharp mind, perfect breeding and looks to die for, Paula thrives on challenges and wants to have it all ... but is this right for her?

Grady O'Connor: Working for Hamilton House was his salvation after Vietnam. The war had messed him up but good and had killed his storybook marriage. He's been given a second chance—only he doesn't know what the hell he's supposed to do with it....

Harlequin Superromance invites you to enjoy Barbara Kaye's dramatic and emotionally resonant miniseries about mature men and women making life-changing decisions. Don't miss:

- CHOICE OF A LIFETIME—a July 1990 release.
- CHALLENGE OF A LIFETIME
  —a December 1990 release.
- CHANCE OF A LIFETIME—an April 1991 release.